ENGLISH TEA MURDER

"What happened? Why are we being kept on the plane?" asked Rachel as they gathered in a little group.

Pam was looking around. "Where's George? How come they didn't call his name?"

Lucy cast a questioning look at Sue, who delivered the bad news. "He's dead."

Pam was stunned. "What?"

"How on earth?" asked Rachel.

"I knew something was wrong. There was a fuss, but I never imagined . . ." said Pam.

Rachel was clasping her hands together. "Was it the asthma?"

"He was having trouble breathing at the airport," Lucy said.

The inspector was now standing at the front of the cabin, addressing Lucy's group. "Thank you all for your cooperation. You're free to go and I hope there will be no further unpleasantness to spoil your visit to the UK."

Pam was bouncing on the balls of her feet. "Let's get this show on the road!"

Lucy smiled, resolving not to let Temple's unexpected death ruin her vacation. After all, she hadn't really known the man. And she was finally here in England.

"Tallyho!" she exclaimed.

Books by Leslie Meier

MISTLETOE MURDER

TIPPY TOE MURDER

TRICK OR TREAT MURDER

BACK TO SCHOOL MURDER

VALENTINE MURDER

CHRISTMAS COOKIE MURDER

TURKEY DAY MURDER

WEDDING DAY MURDER

BIRTHDAY PARTY MURDER

FATHER'S DAY MURDER

STAR SPANGLED MURDER

NEW YEAR'S EVE MURDER

BAKE SALE MURDER

CANDY CANE MURDER

ST. PATRICK'S DAY MURDER

MOTHER'S DAY MURDER

WICKED WITCH MURDER

GINGERBREAD COOKIE MURDER

ENGLISH TEA MURDER

CHOCOLATE COVERED MURDER

Published by Kensington Publishing Corporation

A Lucy Stone Mystery

ENGLISH TEA MURDER

LESLIE MEIER

KENSINGTON BOOKS
www.kensingtonbooks.com

KENSINGTON BOOKS are published by

Kensington Publishing Corp.
119 West 40th Street
New York, NY 10018

All Kensington titles, imprints, and distributed lines are available at special quantity discounts for bulk purchases for sales promotion, premiums, fund-raising, educational, or institutional use.

Special book excerpts or customized printings can also be created to fit specific needs. For details, write or phone the office of the Kensington Special Sales Manager: Attn. Special Sales Department. Kensington Publishing Corp., 119 West 40th Street, New York, NY 10018. Phone: 1-800-221-2647.

Kensington and the K logo Reg. U.S. Pat. & TM Off.

ISBN-13: 978-0-7582-2932-8
ISBN-10: 0-7582-2932-1

First hardcover printing: July 2011
First mass market printing: January 2012

10 9 8 7 6 5 4 3 2

Printed in the United States of America

Chapter One

Something was wrong. Very wrong.

Lucy Stone tapped the miniature TV screen fastened to the back of the seat in front of her, but it didn't even flicker. The tiny little image of an airplane that represented British Airways Flight 214 was still hugging the coast of the United States, and more than five hours of flight time remained before they would cross the blue patch representing the Atlantic Ocean to land on the dot symbolizing London, or more accurately Heathrow Airport.

Lucy nudged her seatmate, Sue Finch, who was flipping through a copy of British *Vogue* that she'd snagged while passing through the roomy first-class cabin, which was dotted with luxurious armchairs complete with footrests and privacy screens—a far cry from the cramped economy cabin where they were sitting.

"What is it, Lucy?"

"We're going to die."

"I don't think so." Sue turned the page and pointed to a photo with her perfectly polished fingernail. "What do you think of Katie Holmes's new haircut?"

"We're six miles up in the air and the temperature

outside is MINUS one hundred and fifty degrees and all you can think about is Katie Holmes's haircut?"

Sue leaned over and peered at Lucy's screen. "Thirty-seven thousand feet, honey. That's not six miles."

"Yes, it is! Do the math! A mile is about five thousand feet."

Sue was now studying a photo of Victoria Beckham in minishorts. "Her legs are like sticks."

Lucy was busy recalling her multiplication tables. "Okay, I was wrong and you're right. SEVEN miles. That's absolutely crazy. And who even knew the thermometer goes down to one hundred and fifty degrees below zero. We live in Maine and the coldest it ever gets in Tinker's Cove is minus twenty or so." Lucy frowned. "And that's pretty darn cold."

"I don't know what you're so upset about. The temperature only goes up to ninety on a hot summer day, but the oven can go up to four hundred and fifty. I guess it's the same with cold."

"These planes are not as sturdy as you think," muttered Lucy darkly. "Remember the one that landed in the Hudson River? It was brought down by a *goose*."

"Well we're in luck, then, because it's way too cold up here for any geese." Sue indicated a photo of a top hat decorated with the Union Jack. "Look at this. There's a show of hats at the Victoria and Albert Museum. Maybe we can go."

"If we survive the flight."

"Oh, stop fussing." Sue tucked a wisp of glossy black hair behind her ear. "Flying is safer than driving. You might as well relax and enjoy the flight. That tinkling sound means the drinks trolley is coming."

Lucy might not be an experienced traveler, but she

had done her homework. "You're not supposed to drink alcohol when you fly. It causes dehydration."

"Don't be ridiculous. If we're seven miles above the earth in freezing weather, we should drink every drop they'll give us."

Lucy was struggling to reach her carry-on bag, which she'd stowed beneath the seat in front of her. "How much do drinks cost?"

"They're included. And you'll get a nice dinner and breakfast, too."

Lucy fluffed her short mop of curls, which had gotten mussed when she reached for her wallet. "I had to pay for a Coke when Bill and I flew down to Florida for his uncle's funeral."

"That's on domestic flights. They take good care of you on these transatlantic flights. So relax. Watch a movie. This is supposed to be a vacation."

Sue was right, reflected Lucy as she pumped her heels up and down to avoid blood clots in her legs. This was her first trip out of the country, except for a few vacations in Canada, and she'd been looking forward to it for months. She'd always wanted to go to Europe, and now she finally had the chance. A few rows farther down the aisle, she could see her friend Pam Stillings's elbow, recognizable from the colorful sleeve of her tie-dyed shirt. It was due to Pam's job teaching yoga at Winchester College's night school that Lucy and Sue, as well as their friend Rachel Goodman, had learned about the trip. "Only two thousand dollars, and that includes airfare and hotel, admissions, everything except lunch and dinner, for nine whole days," Pam had exclaimed at one of their regular Thursday morning breakfasts at Jake's Donut Shack. "We should all go. This professor, George Temple—he's in my yoga class—is organizing the whole thing. All we have to do is sign up."

"Our kids are grown, and our husbands can manage by themselves for a week," said Sue. "Let's do it."

"I don't know if Ted will let me go for such a long time," said Lucy, who worked as a part-time reporter for the Tinker's Cove *Pennysaver.* Ted Stillings was the owner, publisher, editor, and chief reporter. He was also Pam's husband.

"I'll take care of Ted," promised Pam.

Rachel Goodman smiled sadly, running her finger around the thick rim of her white coffee mug; her big eyes were as dark as the black coffee. "I'd love to go, but I can't leave Miss T for a whole week." Rachel provided home care for the little town's oldest resident, Julia Ward Howe Tilley, and was very fond of her.

"Molly could fill in for you," said Lucy, referring to her daughter-in-law. "Patrick's almost a year old now. I think she'd enjoy getting out of the house, and I know Miss Tilley would enjoy seeing Patrick."

"Then I guess we're agreed," crowed Pam. "We have to put down a deposit of two hundred and fifty dollars to hold our places, so give me your checks as soon as you can."

It had seemed like a great idea at the time, but Lucy had no sooner written the check than she began to feel guilty. For one thing, unlike her friends, she wasn't an empty nester. Toby, the oldest, was married and settled on nearby Prudence Path with Molly and baby Patrick, and Elizabeth, next in line, was a senior at Chamberlain College in Boston. Sara, however, a high school sophomore, and Zoe, in middle school, were still at home. Bill, her restoration carpenter husband, would have his hands full managing his work and keeping an eye on the two girls. Even worse, she realized, she'd miss Patrick's first birthday on March 17.

"Don't be silly," Bill had argued when she voiced her concerns about leaving home for more than a week. "You've always wanted to go to England, and this is your chance—and you can find a terrific present for Patrick in London."

So Lucy had studied the itinerary and read the guidebooks and packed and repacked her suitcase several times. She'd even gone to the bank and changed five hundred American dollars into three hundred and fifty British pounds, which hadn't seemed like a very good deal at all.

"On the contrary," the bank manager had informed her. "The pound was trading at two dollars just a few months ago. You would have gotten only two hundred and fifty pounds if you bought back then."

"I hadn't realized," said Lucy, tucking the bills with Queen Elizabeth's face on them into her wallet.

"Have a good trip," said the manager, giving her a big smile.

Remembering the transaction, Lucy patted the little bulge her money belt made under her jeans, where she'd stowed her foreign money, emergency credit card, and a photocopy of her passport, just as the guidebook had advised. She checked the progress of the drinks trolley, which was making its slow way down the aisle, and glanced at George Temple, seated across the aisle from her. Temple, the tour leader, had suffered an asthma attack at the airport, and she hoped he was feeling better.

In contrast to the wheezing and coughing he'd exhibited in Terminal E at Logan, Temple now seemed quiet and withdrawn. He was sitting in an odd posture, hunched forward and completely ignoring his seatmates, two Winchester students who were also along on the tour. Pam had pointed them out to Lucy while they waited at the gate. The one next to Temple—a girl with spiky black hair; numerous piercings in her nose, lips, and ears; and a tattoo of a chain around her neck—was Autumn Mackie. "A wild child, a bit of a legend on campus," Pam had said. "But I can't figure out what she's doing with Jennifer Fain. She not only looks like an angel, but she also acts like one." Jennifer, who was seated by the window, had long blond hair and was wearing a loose, pink-flowered top that looked almost like a child's dress over her skinny gray jeans. It gave her a sweet, innocent air that contrasted sharply with Autumn's black Goth outfit.

The two made an odd pair, whispering together like the best of friends, but Temple wasn't noticing. He was sitting rigidly, leaning forward with his hands on his thighs, his shoulders rising and falling with each labored breath.

Lucy reached her hand across the aisle and tapped his arm. "Are you all right?"

"Asthma," he said, producing an inhaler. "This should help."

Lucy watched as he placed the inhaler between his lips and took a puff, sucking in the aerosol medication with a short, harsh gulp. When he exhaled, it took a long time and was accompanied by a wheezing sound that caught the attention of the two girls, who giggled. Temple ignored them and took another puff of medicine, and this time it seemed to go better, with less wheezing.

Reassured that he was gaining control of the attack, Lucy pulled the in-flight magazine out of the seat pocket and turned to the entertainment menu, choosing a film she hadn't seen: *Doubt*. The drinks trolley was closer now, and Jennifer was rummaging in her backpack, eventually producing a plastic ziplock bag that appeared to contain trail mix. She ripped it open and tossed it to Autumn, who caught it and began stirring the contents with her fingers, finally producing a raisin, which she popped into her mouth.

Temple's breathing seemed to worsen, but Lucy's view was blocked by a flight attendant, who asked if she'd like something to drink.

"White wine?" Lucy inquired.

"Of course. And would you like another, for your meal?"

Lucy looked at Sue, who nodded sharply.

"Thank you," said Lucy as two little wine bottles were placed on her tray table, along with a plastic glass and a tiny packet of pretzels. Sue opted for the same, but when the trolley moved on, Lucy saw that the girls had refused the refreshments and were sharing the bag of trail mix, passing it back and forth between them. Temple had accepted a glass of water, which was sitting on his tray, and his condition seemed to have improved. He was resting quietly now, leaning back in his seat, and the wheezing had stopped. Lucy felt she could relax, too, and poured herself a glass of white wine. On the tiny screen, Meryl Streep, costumed in the black bonnet and long-skirted habit of a nun in the 1960s, was terrorizing a schoolyard full of boisterous children. Lucy took a sip of wine, then another, and was soon absorbed in the movie.

Meryl Streep wasn't much liking Philip Seymour Hoffman—that was clear from her pursed lips and disapproving expression—when Lucy felt a tap on her upper arm. She turned toward George Temple and was shocked by his appearance. His face was grayish, his lips blue, and he was trying to tell her something but couldn't get the words out.

"Stay calm," she told him, pushing the button with the graphic of a flight attendant. "I'm ringing for help."

The two girls, she saw, were completely oblivious to his condition, listening to their iPods with earbuds and bouncing along to the music.

Temple nodded slowly and again raised his inhaler to his mouth, but before he could take a puff, Autumn Mackie gave an extra big bounce and flung out her hands, knocking the inhaler into the untouched glass of water. Horrified, Lucy watched as Temple turned slowly toward her and passed out.

The flight attendant, not at all the glamorous stereotype but a sturdy, middle-aged woman with thick English legs and a blouse that billowed out of her waistband, took one look and hurried back to the compartment containing medical supplies. As she returned with a small oxygen tank and mask, an announcement came over the PA system.

"We have a medical emergency. If there is a doctor or nurse aboard, please make yourself known to a crew member."

"Gramps!" It was Jennifer, her face pale, rising up by pulling against the back of the seat in front of her. "My grandfather is a doctor!"

An older gentleman, gray-haired in a tweed jacket and bow tie, was already hurrying down the aisle, a small leather case in his hand. He quickly examined Temple, checking his pupils and his pulse. "Anaphylactic shock," he told the flight attendant.

"I'll get the EpiPen." She whirled around, ready to dash down the aisle.

"I have one," said the doctor, producing a small plastic cylinder. Opening it, he extracted a syringe and snapped the cap off, revealing a short needle that he jabbed into Temple's thigh, right through his trousers. He then massaged the site of the injection, watching for signs of recovery.

Lucy couldn't see Temple—her view was blocked by the doctor and the flight attendant—but she could hear sobbing from one of the girls. The plane was quiet, everyone aware that something serious was happening. The drinks trolley was stalled, its return to the galley blocked by the caregivers in the aisle.

"A second shot?" whispered the flight attendant.

There was movement as the doctor felt Temple's pulse, then closed his eyelids. "I'm afraid it's too late."

The attendant quickly crossed herself, then asked Autumn for her blanket.

Autumn drew her dark brows together and scowled. "Blanket? The one that was on my seat?"

"Right. I'll get you another, but I need to cover this gentleman."

"Jennifer, give her your blanket," said the doctor.

"Okay." Jennifer obediently handed over the neatly folded square of blue acrylic, wrapped in plastic, and watched as the flight attendant ripped it open and carefully spread it over Temple's body.

"What are you doing?" Autumn's face was hard, her tone challenging. "You can't leave him here!"

"I'm afraid we have no alternative." A male flight attendant had joined the little group. "The plane is full. There are no empty seats."

"So you're just going to leave him here?" Jennifer had turned paler than ever. The black mascara she was wearing stood out like two rows of exclamation points, dramatizing her huge blue eyes.

Lucy turned and looked at Sue, grabbing her hand. They clung together, stunned by the enormity of the scene they had just witnessed.

"I know this is terribly upsetting and unfortunate, but there's really nothing we can do," said the steward, rubbing his hands together briskly. "So, who'd like another drink before dinner?"

Chapter Two

"**A**re you crazy?" Autumn Mackie's face had gained some color; red blotches were appearing on her pallid cheeks and tattooed neck. "You can't expect me to sit next to a stinking corpse all the way to London!"

The steward's expression was quite stern. "Miss, please lower your voice."

"I will not lower my voice. This is outrageous! It's probably illegal! There's a health issue here!"

"Once again, I must ask you to lower your voice. I do not wish to have to restrain you, but I am empowered to do so."

The little hoops in Autumn's eyebrows trembled. "Restrain me? For what? What am I doing?"

The steward's expression was impassive. "You are disturbing the other passengers and interfering with the crew's performance of its duty." The scent of cooked food was filling the cabin, and there were sounds from the galley of trolleys being shifted and loaded. Lucy was ashamed of herself but felt quite hungry. It was almost eleven o'clock, hours later than her usual dinnertime.

"I am not the crazy one here," declared Autumn,

stabbing at her chest. "This is a dead body. It's unsanitary. I don't want to have anything to do with it. Get it?"

"I understand, miss. This is an unfortunate situation, but we must make the best of it."

"I have a solution," said the doctor before the steward could reply. "I will change seats with the young lady."

"Is that agreeable?" inquired the steward.

"Yes. Anything to get away from this . . . this corpse."

The steward turned to the doctor. "Thank you very much indeed."

"It's nothing, really. I would actually prefer to sit with my granddaughter." He smiled at Jennifer. "I will go and fetch my things."

"All right, miss. If you will just climb over . . ." The steward was holding out his hand to Autumn, offering support so she could clamber over Temple's body.

"Well, move him!" ordered Autumn. "I don't wanna touch him!"

"I'm afraid we must leave him in place for the coroner," said the steward.

At this the two girls exchanged glances; then Autumn quickly scrambled over Temple's still corpse, averting her face as she did so. Jennifer gathered up Autumn's possessions—the iPod, a magazine, a paperback book, the half-empty bag of trail mix—and stuffed them in a backpack, which she passed over. The steward ushered Autumn down the aisle, passing the doctor who was already returning to his granddaughter. He paused in the aisle, extending his hand to Lucy.

"We're going to be neighbors for the duration," he said. "I'm Randall Cope. This is my granddaughter, Jennifer Fain. I recognized you from the airport. You're on the Winchester College tour also, aren't you?"

"Yes, I am." Lucy took his hand, finding it strong and warm and very reassuring. "My name's Lucy Stone. This is my friend Sue Finch."

"Delighted to meet you both. And I am sorry about the, uh, situation."

"You did everything you could," said Lucy.

His expression was a combination of regret and caring, and Lucy understood that he'd faced the same situation many times in his medical career. "Well, yes, but it wasn't enough."

Turning and moving quite easily for a man of his age, he stepped over Temple's body, eased himself into Autumn's vacated seat, and fastened his seat belt. Once settled, he placed his big, comforting hand over Jennifer's tiny white one. She leaned her head against his shoulder, and he reached across his chest with his free hand and smoothed her long, wavy hair.

The motherly flight attendant returned, holding a tray with a number of miniature liquor bottles. "This has been a bit of an upset," she said in a soothing nanny voice. "Would you care for a bit of brandy to soothe your nerves?"

Lucy certainly did, and so did Sue.

"What's going to happen?" Lucy sipped the fiery brandy, feeling its warmth spread through her body. "He was our leader."

Sue had polished off her brandy in a single gulp. "I don't know. I can't think that far ahead. Right now, all I want is something to eat."

Crew members were already working their way down the aisles, distributing dinners, and it wasn't long before their meals were placed in front of them and they tucked into their Tuscan chicken and pasta.

"It's not bad." Lucy stabbed a tiny square of chicken.

"It's horrible, but it beats starving." Sue was polishing off her tiny bowl of salad. "I can't believe I have any appetite at all."

"They say death has that effect." Lucy lowered her voice. "It makes people hungry—and not just for food. Sex, too."

Sue gazed at the blue lump on the other side of the aisle. "Survival instinct, I suppose."

Lucy followed her gaze and saw that while Dr. Cope was eating his dinner, Jennifer had refused her tray and was staring at the blank TV screen in front of her. She remembered how happy the girl had seemed only a short time before, bouncing around to her iPod with Autumn and sharing the trail mix snack. Now, Temple's sudden death had changed everything, and a carefree jaunt had turned tragic.

This was supposed to be the trip of a lifetime, thought Lucy, her first trip abroad, and now it was spoiled. She remembered how excited she'd been when Pam had told them all about the tour and how she'd almost rationalized her way out of going. "It's too expensive; I'll be away too long; I can't leave you all," she'd told Bill. But he had brushed away her objections. "You were an English major in college. You've always wanted to go to England. You should go."

Lucy's friends had backed him up. "You're the mom and grandma. You've been taking care of everybody else for twenty-five years. It's time for you to do something for yourself," Rachel had told her when they had lunch together one day at Miss Tilley's antique Cape-style cottage.

"You don't think it's selfish?"

"They'll be glad to be rid of you," said Miss Tilley with a wave of her blue-veined hand. "That's what I told

Rachel. We all need a break from each other once in a while. I'm looking forward to putting real cream in my coffee and eating potato chips." She scowled at Rachel. "My keeper here never lets me have potato chips."

"It's for your own good," said Rachel, placid as ever.

Lucy suddenly felt homesick, thinking of Miss Tilley and her cozy house and her own comfortable old farmhouse on Red Top Road and Bill and the girls and Libby the Labrador and little baby Patrick. She missed them all, she thought, as the flight attendant removed the remains of her meal. She latched the little folding table back in place and leaned back in her seat, letting out a big sigh. It seemed she'd been right: This trip was a big mistake.

She checked the progress of the flight on the little screen, discovering that the tiny plane icon was about a half inch into the blue Atlantic and they had more than three hours of airtime left. The lights were dimmed, and she decided to try and get some sleep, imagining she was back in bed at home, spooning with Bill.

Next thing she knew, the lights were flicked on, the scent of coffee was in the air, and the flight attendants were distributing breakfast packs containing crisp fruit salad and soggy apple pastry.

"Good morning, sunshine," said Sue, looking at her with dark-rimmed eyes.

Lucy yawned. "Didn't you sleep?"

"Not a wink."

"I'm surprised I did." Lucy glanced at the body and the sight depressed her. Dr. Cope was still sound asleep, his head thrown back and his mouth slightly open, and Jennifer was sitting in the same position as before, staring straight ahead and rigid with tension.

Lucy still felt uncomfortably full from dinner, which

seemed to have settled like concrete in her tummy, so she only ate a few bits of fruit and sipped her coffee, then made a trip back to the toilet. There she splashed a little lukewarm water on her face and attempted to brush her teeth with the toothbrush and tiny tube of toothpaste provided by British Airways. When she returned to her seat, it seemed that the pace was picking up—the breakfast packs were collected, and the pilot soon announced it was time to prepare for landing. Lucy checked her watch and discovered it was 3:40 a.m. She fastened her seat belt, sniffing the refreshing green tea scent of the moisturizer Sue was applying to her cheeks and hands. The plane gave a shake and a rattle, landing with a big thump, and they were in England.

Once again, the captain's voice came over the PA system. "Welcome to London. It's 7:50 a.m. and the temperature is ten degrees Celsius with clouds and passing showers." He paused. "And now I'm going to turn this over to our head steward, Ron Bitman, who has a special announcement."

"I want to remind you to remain seated with seat belts fastened until the aircraft comes to a complete stop and the fasten-seat-belt light is turned off. And we must ask the following passengers to remain in their seats: Laura Barfield, William Barfield, Randall Cope, Jennifer Fain, Sue Finch . . ."

Lucy's and Sue's eyes met and the voice continued: "Rachel Goodman, Autumn Mackie, Ann Smith, Caroline Smith, Thomas Smith, Pamela Stillings, and Lucy Stone. Thank you."

"It's everyone on the tour," said Sue as the jet taxied to the gate.

"Looks like there's going to be a police investigation," said Lucy, looking past Jennifer through the oval window and glimpsing a cluster of police cars and an ambulance on the ground.

The plane stopped, the fasten-seat-belt light went off with a ding, and people all around them were stretching and getting to their feet and opening the overhead compartments to retrieve bags and coats. The aisles were packed with people, and then suddenly everyone was gone, leaving behind crumpled pillows and blankets and newspapers—and the twelve people whose names had been called. They were all told to please move forward into the first-class cabin.

"I was hoping for an upgrade," quipped Sue. "But I would have appreciated it earlier in the flight."

When they entered the first-class cabin, which was every bit as rumpled and untidy as their own, although much roomier, they found a pair of uniformed police constables with checked caps tucked under their arms blocking the exits, as if the group was comprised of dangerous prisoners who must be kept under guard.

"What happened? Why are we being kept on the plane?" asked Rachel as they gathered in a little group.

Pam was looking around. "Where's George? How come they didn't call his name?"

Lucy cast a questioning look at Sue, who delivered the bad news. "He's dead."

Pam was stunned. "What?"

"How on earth?" asked Rachel.

"I knew something was wrong. There was a fuss, but I never imagined. . . ." said Pam.

Rachel was clasping her hands together. "Was it the asthma?"

"He was having trouble breathing at the airport," recalled Pam, stepping aside to let a young woman in a white disposable overall pass. She was snapping on a pair of latex gloves as she hurried to the economy section.

"Probably the medical examiner," said Lucy, whose job as a reporter had given her some familiarity with the procedures surrounding unexpected death. She watched as a tall, rather distinguished-looking man in a gray suit entered the cabin, receiving nods from the two uniformed officers. He was soon followed by a shorter, sturdier man wearing a tweed jacket and a rather stout, red-faced man wearing a beautifully tailored suit.

"If you'll all take a seat, we can begin, and hopefully we won't delay you for very long," said the man in the gray suit. "I am Inspector John Neal of the Metropolitan Police. It is the responsibility of the Met, which you may know better as Scotland Yard, to investigate any unexplained deaths." There was a little stir from several tour members, and he quickly explained. "Due to the configuration of the aircraft, you may not know that the leader of your tour, George Temple, expired in midflight." He paused a moment, waiting for this information to be absorbed, before continuing. "My colleague"—he indicated the sturdy man in the sport coat—"is Sergeant Chester Luddy. Mr. William Bosworth is the coroner." He indicated the man in the expensive suit. "Mr. Bosworth will determine from our investigation here today whether an inquest is required." He paused again, his gaze moving from one person to another. "I need hardly point out to you all that the more helpful and open you are at this time, the sooner we can wrap this up and you can carry on with your travel plans."

Sergeant Luddy passed a sheet of paper to the inspector, and he began reading names. "Laura and William Barfield, please identify yourselves."

A slight woman with wispy, chin-length brown hair

raised her hand. She was dressed in a pair of beige wool slacks and a brown leather jacket with a gold paisley scarf tucked into the neckline. "I'm Laura Barfield and this is my son, Will."

Will was a tall kid who needed a haircut, his streaky blond hair flopped over his forehead. He was dressed in jeans, a white Oxford button-down shirt that wasn't tucked into his pants, and a bright blue sweater.

"I understand you are a student?" Neal was looking at Will.

"That's right. I'm a freshman at Winchester College."

Neal nodded and went on to the next name on his list. "Dr. Randall Cope."

The doctor stood up. "I am a medical doctor, and I attended George Temple in his final moments."

"I see." Neal made a tick next to his name. "Jennifer Fain."

"That's me." Jennifer lifted her hand. She looked quite tiny and vulnerable in the roomy club chair.

"And you are also a student at Winchester College?"

She nodded.

Dr. Cope was seated beside her and patted her knee protectively. "Jennifer is my granddaughter."

The inspector was consulting his list. "Sue Finch."

"Here." Sue raised her hand with a decisive motion.

Neal's eyes seemed to flicker briefly as if he found her worth a second look. "Are you connected to Winchester College?"

"No. The tour was open to anyone, so I signed up with three friends. Just a little vacation."

"I see." Neal passed his eyes over the group. "Rachel Goodman."

Rachel spoke up in a low, clear voice. "That's me. I'm one of the friends."

Neal didn't smile but went on to the next name. "Autumn Mackie."

"I saw the whole thing," said Autumn, sounding defensive. "It was disgusting."

The sergeant passed another paper to Neal, indicating something with his finger.

"You were seated next to the deceased gentleman?"

"They were going to make me sit next to a corpse!" declared Autumn, outraged. She pointed to Dr. Cope. "He changed seats with me."

"I see." Neal consulted the list. "Ann, Caroline, and Thomas Smith. Are you all the same family?"

"Yes," said Tom Smith, a fortyish man with a brush cut and a beer belly spilling over his Dockers. He and his daughter were standing behind his wife, who was seated. "My wife, Ann," he said, tapping her on the shoulder. "And my daughter, Caroline."

Ann, Lucy saw, was painfully thin, with a pinched face and unattractively short gray hair. Caroline, on the other hand, was overweight, with a bushy mop of curly orange hair.

"This is the first we even knew about Mr. Temple's, um, death," said Tom.

"Quite so," said Neal. "Pamela Stillings."

Pam gave a little bounce in her chair, half standing. "I'm Pam," she said. "One of the four friends. I didn't know anything about this. I was sitting in the front, you see, in a middle seat. I couldn't see what was going on in the rear of the cabin."

Neal exchanged glances with Luddy, who shrugged. "Lucy Stone."

Lucy raised her hand. "I was sitting across the aisle from Mr. Temple."

"I guess we'll begin with you, then," said Neal. "Come with me."

Me and my big mouth, thought Lucy, following the inspector to the far corner of the cabin. The coroner and Luddy joined them, making a tight little circle around her chair. She felt hemmed in.

"When did you first notice Mr. Temple was having difficulty breathing?" asked Neal after he had taken down Lucy's address and studied her passport.

"At the airport, actually, in Boston."

Neal raised an eyebrow. "Really?"

"Yes. I happened to be behind him when he went through the security screening. For some reason they took him away, and when he returned and joined us at the gate, he was breathing heavily." Lucy was thinking hard, trying to recall any detail that might be important. "His breathing was ragged. With a little wheeze. But when he used his inhaler, he seemed to improve. Then he took a roll call and discovered somebody was missing—that kid Will—and his breathing got worse again. We were all quite concerned, and that lady, Ann Smith, I think, urged him to stay calm and relax. She tried to teach him some relaxation technique and even attempted to cover him with a shawl she had, but he refused it. He was almost angry—*flustered* is maybe a better word. Then we lined up and boarded. I sort of lost track of him until I found my seat and he was on the other side of the aisle. Will made it to the gate in time, obviously, but I didn't see that."

"And who was sitting on the other side of Mr. Temple?"

"Autumn, the dark-haired girl who is so upset, and Jennifer, Dr. Cope's granddaughter, had the window."

"How did Mr. Temple react to takeoff?"

"He seemed fine. He used the inhaler again, and he was sitting forward a bit, quite calm and quiet. I thought he was improving."

"And how long was this?"

"Quite a while. We were well into the flight—they were serving drinks—when he kind of reached over and grabbed me. He was trying to say something. I could see he was in distress and rang for the flight attendant. Then they called for the doctor, and he came and gave him an injection but it was too late." Lucy was exhausted. She felt quite empty as she recalled the horrifying chain of events. "It was so unexpected. The last thing you'd think would happen."

"What about his seatmates? Did they try to help him?"

Lucy hesitated for a moment before answering. "They're only kids. They didn't seem to realize he was in distress. They were listening to music on their iPods and kind of dancing in their seats."

Neal's and Luddy's eyes met.

"In fact," recalled Lucy, "Autumn accidentally knocked his inhaler out of his hand. It fell into his drink."

"Anything else you can remember?"

"Well, they were eating something. They had a bag of nuts and raisins they were sharing."

"What sort of bag?"

"One of those zip bags you're supposed to use for liquids."

Neal nodded. "Thank you. You've been very helpful."

Released from the hot seat, Lucy went back to join the group, feeling oddly guilty, as if she'd ratted on the girls. But they hadn't done anything terrible. They were just young and full of energy, caught up in themselves.

She was just sitting down when the inspector called Dr. Cope. He got to his feet rather stiffly, not quite as nimble as he'd been earlier, and made his way to the other side of the cabin. His granddaughter, Jennifer, watched anxiously, biting her lip.

"What did you tell them?" whispered Sue.

"Just what I saw. What else could I do?"

"You told them about the girls and the inhaler?"

Lucy was a bit defensive. "Yeah. Wouldn't you?"

Sue shrugged and checked her watch. Time, Lucy realized, was crawling by. She was stiff and tired, and she felt grubby and wanted to wash her face properly. Instead, she was virtually a prisoner on this airplane while the inspector systematically questioned each member of the tour. She wouldn't have minded quite so much, if only she could hear what they were saying. But even though she strained her ears, she heard very little. Autumn was the loudest, and Lucy heard her proclaim something about "How was I supposed to know?" but that was all.

The inspector was interviewing Rachel, the last member of the group, when a sharp snap indicated the medical examiner had finished her examination and was removing her gloves. She stood in the rear of the cabin, not far from Lucy, and the coroner went over to her.

"What have you got?" he asked.

"I was only able to do a superficial exam, but my observations are consistent with anaphylactic shock."

Lucy remembered Dr. Cope using the phrase when he examined Temple.

"That accords with the witnesses' reports," said the coroner.

"Of course, I'll know more when I get him back to the morgue."

"Do you really think that's necessary?"

"It is customary."

"That's not what I asked you," snapped the coroner. "Do you have any reason to think it wasn't anaphylactic shock?"

The woman spoke slowly. "Uh, no."

"Well, then I guess we can save the rate payers some money."

"Whatever you say." She proceeded through the cabin, stripping off the overall as she went and shaking her head.

The inspector was now standing at the front of the cabin, addressing the group. "Thank you all for your co-operation. You're free to go, and I hope there will be no further unpleasantness to spoil your visit to the UK."

They were starting to stand up when a rosy-cheeked man with slicked back hair suddenly appeared. "I'm Reg Wilson from British Airways, and I, too, want to thank you for your cooperation. Furthermore, I have arranged transport for your group to your hotel. Now, if you will gather up your things, I will escort you to immigration and on to the baggage area."

Pam was bouncing on the balls of her feet, itching to go. "Let's get this show on the road," she said.

Lucy smiled, resolving not to let Temple's death ruin her vacation. After all, she hadn't really known the man. And she was finally here in England. "Tallyho," she said.

Chapter Three

The group was quiet as the minibus crept along in heavy traffic on the M4, a highway Lucy recognized from those BBC mystery dramas she loved to watch. It was a lot like the Maine Turnpike, except all the cars were driving on the wrong side of the road. Lucy peered out the window at the passing scenery, fascinated by everything she saw. The houses were subtly different from houses in America, she thought. They were mostly built of brick, instead of the shingles or clapboard used in Maine, and they were tightly packed together in rows with tiny, fenced backyards instead of the spacious lawns she was used to. They were passing an old brewery that seemed oddly familiar—had it been a set in a costume drama?—and then the highway ended and they were on a London street, passing shops and museums and more row houses. These were taller and more imposing than the ones they'd seen from the highway and didn't have front yards. Some had flower boxes at the windows or a plant in a tub set on the front steps. The street widened, and there was the giant flickering TV screen at Piccadilly Circus. They continued weaving through narrow streets, past theaters and restaurants, until they suddenly broke into a square with a leafy green park in the center. A few more turns through streets that were now arranged in a series of neat squares and the bus stopped in front of yet another tall brick row house. The gilded letters in the transom above the shiny black front door announced they had arrived at the Desmond Hotel.

"What happens now?" asked Tom Smith, as if only now realizing the group had lost its leader. "Who's in charge?"

"I'll fill in for George, for the time being," said Pam, rising and moving to the front of the bus. "I work at the college part-time, so I know the president. I'll call her and explain the situation." She checked her watch. "It's eleven here. That means it's seven in the U.S. That's awfully early for a Saturday morning. I'll wait a bit—I should have some information for you by dinnertime."

"What do we do in the meantime?" asked Laura, looking a bit lost.

"For the time being, I guess we're all on our own," said Pam. "We might as well get settled here at the hotel. I'm sure the hotel staff can suggest some things to do. After all, this is London." She smiled at the bus driver. "You can start unloading the luggage, and I'll go in and see about checking in."

The bus driver had just pulled the last bag from the luggage compartment when Pam reappeared with a piece of paper and a handful of keys. "We're all set. George took very good care of us," she announced, standing on the steps in front of the hotel. "Barfields, you're in room seven," she said, handing over two keys. "The larger one is for the outer door, the smaller for your room."

The bus drove off and the group on the sidewalk

gradually dispersed as Pam distributed the keys until only the four friends remained. "Here you go," she said, handing a set of keys to Sue. "You and Lucy are in room twenty-seven and Rachel and I are in twenty-six. I think that means we have a bit of a climb."

Once inside, Lucy found herself in a small hall with a steep flight of carpeted stairs directly opposite the front door. The entry was homelike with a small console table holding a lamp, guestbook, and vase of fresh flowers. A narrow hallway ran alongside the stairs, ending in a small office, where a middle-aged man was talking on the telephone in a Cockney accent. Following Sue, Lucy began climbing, dragging her suitcase behind her up four flights of stairs until they reached the top floor and their rooms.

Room 27 was small, but it had two large windows overlooking the street, two twin beds with white coverlets, and a very tiny bathroom with a shower. It was also very hot, so Lucy headed straight for one of the windows, which was sealed with an inner storm panel. She'd never seen anything like it before, but it opened easily and soon a cool breeze was lifting the white net panels that hung behind the wildly flowered drapes.

Sue emerged from the bathroom. "Good thing we're both slender," she said. "Otherwise we couldn't fit between the sink and shower to get to the toilet."

Lucy poked her head inside the bathroom and discovered Sue wasn't exaggerating. "It's a tight squeeze but very clean."

"And we each get a whole towel to ourselves," said Sue, pointing out the neatly folded bath towels resting on the foot of each bed. Extremely small, thin towels, judging from their flatness.

"And we share the soap." Lucy was holding up the tiny pink rectangle she'd found on the tiny white sink.

"It's not exactly the Four Seasons," said Sue.

"It's not even a Holiday Inn," said Lucy, sitting on the end of a bed.

"Well, sweetie, when the going gets tough, the tough get going. Shopping, that is. And since it's Saturday, we can go to Portobello Market!"

"But I want to take a nap," said Lucy, falling backward onto the bed.

"Worst thing you can do. Come on, up you go! We're in London! You can sleep tonight."

Slowly, very slowly, Lucy dragged herself to her feet. From the street outside, she could hear the roar of traffic, the voices of passersby. It was true. She wasn't in quiet little Tinker's Cove anymore.

Downstairs, they met Pam and Rachel. In response to Pam's inquiry, the proprietor, a short and stocky fellow in a worn olive-green sweater vest, gave them directions to Portobello Market. "Just walk up the street to the Euston Square tube station, take the Circle Line to Notting Hill Gate, and follow the Pembridge Road to Portobello Road. You can't miss it."

"I'm so excited," declared Sue as they headed up Gower Street. "I'm so glad you're not going to miss Portobello."

"What is it exactly?" asked Pam.

"A giant street fair. There's antiques and junk and all sorts of stuff. Kind of like a giant flea market."

Rachel was consulting her guidebook as they walked along. "It says here you shouldn't be afraid to bargain. The dealers expect to come down at least ten percent."

"Sounds like my kind of place," said Lucy as they descended the stairs to the Euston Square station.

There they gathered in front of the machines that sold tickets and tried to figure out the system for payment.

"In Boston you have to buy a CharlieCard," said Pam, who often returned to her hometown to visit her mother.

"This Oyster card is new—they didn't have it last time I was here," said Sue.

Looking around, they found a cashier sitting in a booth behind a thick Plexiglas window who sold them the cards, collecting twenty-three pounds from each of them.

"Seems expensive," complained Lucy.

"No, no," said Sue, repeatedly tapping the card on the yellow disk that was supposed to operate the entry gate, but to no effect. "The Tube is fantastic, you'll see. It will take us everywhere."

"If we can get in," said Rachel.

"May I?" A tall gentleman togged out in a suit and tie took the card from Sue. "You just touch the back of the card to the disk, like so," he said, demonstrating. The gates opened.

A train could be heard arriving at the platform below, so they hurriedly thanked him and dashed for the stairs—a very long flight of stairs. "It's hopeless. We'll have to wait for the next one," said Pam in a resigned tone. But when they reached the platform, an illuminated sign informed them that the next train would arrive in two minutes. "Could that possibly be right?" asked Pam, pointing at the sign.

When the train pulled in, exactly on schedule, Rachel was impressed. "This is amazing," she said.

The train ground to a halt, the doors slid open, and a mellifluous female voice reminded them to "Mind the gap" as they boarded. They were seating themselves on upholstered benches and noting the clean carriage when the voice continued. "This is a Circle Line train. The next stop will be Great Portland Street."

Stunned by British efficiency, they rode in silence to Notting Hill Gate, where they were once again urged to mind the gap.

"Why can't we have trains that run on schedule in America?" asked Rachel as they emerged from the dim station into the sunny street.

"And actually let you know where you're going in clearly understood announcements. The last time I was in Boston, I got the last train of the evening, which I thought was lucky, but unfortunately it didn't go where I thought. I ended up at the end of the line on some deserted street trying to get a taxi at one in the morning." Pam's expression was dark. "Not much fun at all."

They were walking past neat white row houses with tiny front gardens behind black-painted iron railings in what seemed to be a very nice neighborhood. Lucy wondered what it would be like to live in one of these houses.

"Up and down stairs all day," said Sue, reading her mind.

It was true, she realized. The houses seemed to be one room wide but were three or four stories tall. You'd get plenty of exercise just getting out of the house in the morning, especially if you forgot something in an upstairs bedroom.

When they turned the corner onto Portobello Road, they were confronted by a colorful riot of activity. The narrow street was packed with people who jostled their way along the sidewalks and squeezed between the shops and the temporary stalls that filled the street.

Most of the shops sold antiques, but there were also restaurants and clothing boutiques, even a Tesco supermarket. The stallholders sold everything from crafts and cheap imports to all sorts of fruits and vegetables, baked goods, meats, and even fish. One enterprising man had set up three enormous paella pans and was browning chicken pieces in sizzling oil; on the ground beneath the huge braziers, plastic bins full of shellfish were ready to hand. The air was full of scents: cooking chicken, fish, fragrant flowers, incense. Suddenly, Lucy felt quite dizzy and stumbled against a T-shirt stall.

"Whoa, there," exclaimed Sue, reaching out to steady her.

Rachel took one look at Lucy's white face and made an executive decision. "We need lunch."

Fortunately there was a nearby café, and they took an outside table. Pam kept Lucy company, basking in the warm March sunshine, while Rachel and Sue placed orders for tea and sandwiches.

"I feel so foolish," said Lucy, who was still a bit dizzy.

"Don't be silly." Pam sounded tired. "We've all had a terrible shock, but you were right next to George. You saw the whole thing. It's no wonder you're a bit fragile."

"It's probably just low blood sugar." Lucy felt a surge of sympathy for Pam, who had assumed responsibility for the group. "Were you able to reach the college president?"

"My cell phone doesn't work here, so I sent an e-mail from the hotel—they have a computer for guests."

"You shouldn't feel as if you have to take charge. We're all adults. . . ." Lucy remembered the four students: Caroline, Will, Autumn, and Jennifer. "Well, almost adults."

"I still can't believe it happened." Pam looked up as

Rachel and Sue arrived with their food, distributing ploughman's lunches and cardboard cups of tea. "Poor George."

"What was he like?" asked Lucy, taking a sip of tea. She wasn't quite ready for the sandwich, which consisted of cheese, pickle, and lettuce on whole wheat bread.

"I only knew him from my yoga class," said Pam, pausing to chew. "He was very flexible, considering his age."

"Men aren't usually flexible," said Lucy, picturing Bill's struggle to touch his toes.

"George had a lovely downward dog, and his cobra was amazing."

"How old was he?" Sue took a tiny bite of her sandwich.

"Not old enough to die. Fifties maybe?" said Rachel. "This bread is very good."

"That's about right." Pam nodded. "This whole sandwich is excellent."

Encouraged, Lucy took a bite and experienced a revelation. "It's real cheddar," she declared. "And the bread is so wholesome-tasting. It's really good, and I always heard English food is bad."

"So was he a full professor?" asked Sue. Her son-in-law Geoff had recently landed a position as an assistant professor at New York University.

"No. He was only an adjunct," said Pam. "Paid by the course, no benefits or anything."

"Really?"

"Yeah." Pam crumpled up the cellophane sandwich wrap. "You know how it is—a lot of liberal arts colleges are struggling financially these days. Winchester has a lot of adjuncts, but I did hear something about an opening in the English Department. Professor Crighton is due to retire, so maybe George would have gotten his job. He always scored really high on the student evaluations, and he was devoted to Winchester. He put in all sorts of extra time. He was even published." She stood up. "I don't know about you guys, but I don't want to spend all day sitting here. That stall with the scarves is calling my name."

Rachel turned her big brown eyes to Lucy. "How are you feeling?"

"Much better. Let's go shopping."

Pam was willing to pay the ten pounds the vendor was asking for three scarves, but Sue intervened and haggled until he agreed to accept eight pounds. Lucy ventured inside some of the antique shops and found they extended far from the street front, winding through adjacent buildings in a higgledy-piggledy fashion, housing numerous dealers. She fell in love with a round breadboard that the seller assured her was a good value at thirty-five pounds. The woman had a number of them, ranging in price from ten to nearly one hundred pounds, so Lucy figured she could trust her expertise and paid the asking price.

Rachel had to be dragged away from the bread stall, where she insisted on buying four hot cross buns, and they all gathered in Tesco to buy the shampoo and body wash the hotel didn't supply. Sue lingered at the newsstand, stocking up on English magazines, while Lucy picked up a couple of tabloid newspapers. By then it was late afternoon and the market was winding down as stallholders began packing up their wares.

Sue glanced at her watch and yawned, setting off a little chain reaction among her friends. "I know. We should have afternoon tea and then head back to the hotel for an early night."

"I've always wanted to have high tea," enthused Pam.

"No, not high tea." Sue nodded wisely. "High tea is beans on toast, a working-class supper. What we want is afternoon tea with scones and cake and little sandwiches and a silver teapot."

Lucy was skeptical. "I don't think we'll find any establishments like that around here. These places all seem to use paper cups." She paused, remembering the many British mysteries she'd borrowed from the library, all aged and well thumbed by readers. "There's a chain called Lyons, or used to be."

Sue was thoughtful. "Maybe closer to the hotel," she said. But when they retraced their route back to the hotel and emerged, panting with exhaustion from the climb out of the Euston Square station, there seemed to be a surprising lack of tearooms. No restaurants at all, in fact, except for a dingy-looking Indian place. Coming to the end of their street, Sue admitted defeat. "How about some curry?" she asked.

Waking at two in the morning, Lucy tiptoed into the tiny bathroom and dug in her toiletries bag for the roll of antacid tablets she'd brought. She'd enjoyed the spicy Indian food, but now she had a terrible case of heartburn. She crunched a couple of the tablets while she peed, had a drink of water, and went back to bed, hoping she'd look better in the morning than she did now. Her reflection in the mirror over the sink wasn't encouraging; she had dark circles under her eyes, and she was certain she'd sprouted some new wrinkles.

Back in bed, she yawned and settled herself for sleep, but sleep didn't come. She was tired enough; there was no doubt about that. Her legs ached; her arms felt heavy. Every cell in her body seemed to be crying out for rest. All except her brain cells, which were annoyingly active and returned again and again to Temple's death, producing an image of his blanket-covered body whenever she closed her eyes.

Turning on her side, she stared at the windows, which were lighter patches of gray in the darkened room. She remembered how nervous she'd been going through security at Logan Airport, even though she'd checked the TSA Web site and packed according to the directions, filling a quart-sized ziplock bag with miniature versions of her favorite toiletries. She'd forgotten the water bottle she had tucked in her travel bag and had been forced to empty it, but the officer had been pleasant about it. George Temple hadn't been so lucky. The buzzer had sounded when he walked through the metal detector, and he'd actually been taken away by two officers, protesting loudly. "I never saw that before," he was saying as they hustled him along.

What on earth had they found? wondered Lucy, now staring at the white glass light fixture that hung from the ceiling, dimly glowing from the reflected light that came through the windows from the street. And what did they do to him? She'd been warned that TSA officers were empowered to conduct strip searches, and she'd made sure not to wear an underwire bra and had chosen elastic-waist pants without a zipper, just to be on the safe side.

No wonder Temple had seemed flustered when he returned and began rounding up the group and making sure everyone was there. Of course, Will Barfield was late and his mother's fretting had driven them all to distraction. "This isn't like him," she kept saying. "I hope he hasn't had some sort of accident."

By then Temple had begun coughing and sneezing

and had used his inhaler at least once. Ann Smith had noticed and urged him to sit down and relax, taking deep regular breaths. He had complied and seemed to be recovering, until she tried to wrap him in her pashmina shawl so he'd be nice and warm. He'd protested and that had started a new fit of coughing.

Then the gate attendant had announced boarding and there was a great deal of movement, and Lucy lost track of Temple as she waited for her row number to be called. Dr. Cope had been right next to her at one point, she remembered, but if he noticed Temple's condition, he hadn't seemed concerned. Now that she thought about it, it seemed a bit odd. Temple's coughing had been very noticeable, and he'd attracted a lot of attention. At one point, a uniformed airline representative had even approached him, but Temple had produced his inhaler and apparently assured the official that he would be all right.

Of course, thought Lucy, embarrassment had no doubt played a part in Temple's refusal to accept assistance. She knew how silly she'd felt that afternoon, when she nearly fainted at the Portobello Market. The last thing she'd wanted was to make a scene.

Sighing, Lucy checked her watch. Three in the morning. Hours to go before it was time to get up. She should have accepted Sue's offer of a sleeping pill. Sue, who'd taken two, was sound asleep while Lucy was tossing and turning and burping up chicken korma. She rolled over, closed her eyes, and suddenly remembered Sue telling her the pills were on the sink in case she changed her mind. She had indeed changed her mind, she decided, throwing back the covers.

Chapter Four

When Lucy and Sue descended *six* flights of stairs to the little hotel's basement breakfast room on Sunday morning, they found that everyone from the group was already there, as were a smattering of other guests, sitting in twos and threes at little tables covered with red and white checked cloths. They nodded and smiled as they wound their way through the dining room to the table for four where Pam and Rachel were waiting for them. As soon as they sat down, a young waitress arrived with pots of coffee and tea, and they both chose coffee, craving the caffeine. While they were drinking, Pam stood up and tapped her juice glass with a spoon.

"I have an announcement," she began in an official tone. "I received an e-mail from President Chapman this morning, and she sends her condolences to all of us. She was also able to find a substitute for George Temple—she is sending Professor Quentin Rea to take over the tour."

The name caught Lucy by surprise, and her empty cup rolled onto its side with a rattle as she set it on the saucer. She had taken a class in Victorian literature from Professor Rea some years ago and had found him terribly attractive. Of course, he was much younger then—they both were—but she'd always been a sucker for that preppy look of worn tweed jackets, frayed button-down shirts, and sun-streaked hair. She wondered if she'd still be attracted to him, not that she planned to do anything about it, she vowed, straightening the cup.

She hadn't done anything then, but she had been tempted, and she was sure that he had also found her attractive and smiled at the memory.

"Lucy! Stop daydreaming!" It was Sue, hissing at her. "Our server wants to know if you want cereal."

Lucy blushed and turned to the girl who offered bran flakes, corn flakes, or Cheerios. Cheerios, here in England. Who knew? But Lucy chose bran flakes, taking the state of her digestion into account.

Pam was continuing her speech to the group. "Professor Rea won't arrive until tomorrow morning, so Dr. Chapman suggests we follow the itinerary George planned on our own. That means we go to the Tower of London this morning, break for lunch, and visit St. Paul's Cathedral in the afternoon. I suggest those who are interested gather in front of the hotel at nine-thirty and we'll go together on the Tube."

Pam was seating herself when the server arrived with Lucy's bowl of cereal. "This morning's breakfast is egg, bacon, and beans," said the girl.

"Okay," said Lucy, figuring that she might as well try the traditional English breakfast. Pam and Rachel declined the beans and Sue opted for nothing but toast.

The Smith family was seated at the table next to Pam, and Ann reached across and tapped her on the arm. "Since it's Sunday, I think we'll opt out of visiting the Tower," she said. She had dark circles under her eyes, and the gray sweater she was wearing only added to her careworn appearance. "We'll attend services at St. Martin in the Fields and then go on to the National Gallery." She paused. "Caroline loves art."

Lucy glanced at the red-haired girl, who seemed more interested in using a triangle of toast to mop up the egg and bean juice that remained on her plate than in discussing the day's program.

Her father, Tom, stabbed the map spread open before him on the table with a stubby finger. "We can take the Northern Line from Goodge Street. It's just a few stops. Ann doesn't feel up to much today, what with this jet lag and all."

Lucy thought he seemed a practical, take-charge sort of guy, rather like Bill, and she suddenly missed her husband.

"Fine with me," said Pam as their breakfasts arrived. She poked her fork at the generous slices of pink meat that were arranged alongside her fried egg. "This doesn't look like bacon."

"English bacon's different," said Sue, looking as if she wouldn't touch it with a ten-foot pole. As far as Lucy knew, Sue rarely ate solid food and seemed to exist on little more than black coffee and cocktails.

Rachel wasn't so fussy; she was digging right in. "It's very good."

Lucy tasted a forkful of beans and found them not so good. "Live and learn," she said with a grimace. In the future, she decided, she'd skip the beans.

"Don't like the beans?" It was Will Barfield, who was seated with his mother on the other side of their table, next to the wall. "I'll take them."

"Will!" protested Laura. She was dressed today in the same ladylike caramel-colored leather jacket she'd worn on the plane but had added a different scarf, green this time. "Don't be rude!"

"He's not rude," laughed Lucy, thinking of her son, Toby, and the huge amounts he ate as a teenager. "He's still growing." She spooned her beans onto her bread plate and passed it over. "It's a shame to waste them, and I'm certainly not going to eat them."

"Thanks," said Will, diving in. "You know, I'm not all that interested in this historical stuff," he said, raising a fork dripping with juicy beans and popping it into his mouth. "I heard the London Eye is really cool. I think I'd like to do that."

"Fine with me," said Pam.

"But, Will," protested his mother, slipping a pair of schoolmarmish wire-rimmed reading glasses on her nose and preparing to consult her guidebook. "You can't come to London and miss the Bloody Tower. I think you'd really like it—they say it has suits of armor worn by Henry the Eighth."

Will had plucked a tiny jar of marmalade from the little silver rack and was slathering it onto a triangle of toast. "Nah. I wanna do the Eye and then maybe hike over to the Tate Modern and that Millennium Bridge over the river. I saw it in a movie—it was neat."

Laura was studying the map in her guidebook. "Maybe you're right. The Millennium Bridge is next to the New Globe Theatre. I'd love to see that. It's a copy of Shakespeare's theater. Maybe we could even see a play there."

Will's face stiffened. "It's a pretty long walk, Mom." Lucy and her friends exchanged glances. It was clear to them that Will was trying to get away from his mother for the day. "Probably too much for you," he added.

"I walk all the time," she said, squashing his rebellion with a look as she removed her glasses and tucked them into a quilted case. "I walk miles every week with the dog."

"Okay," he said, accepting defeat with a sigh and pushing his chair back. "Let's go."

Laura popped happily to her feet. "Have a nice day," she said to the group in general before following her tall son out of the room.

Lucy watched them go, spreading a dab of butter on her toast and wondering how this little struggle would play out. It was only the second day of the trip and Will was already chafing at his mother's attempts to control him. He was obviously a kid who enjoyed his independence, and it seemed odd that he'd agreed to a trip with his mother. Most boys his age would choose to spend spring break in Mexico or Florida, or in a worst-case scenario, at home, where they had developed ways of deluding and eluding their parents and could hang out with their high school friends.

"He's a cute kid," said Rachel. "Reminds me of my Richie."

"Have you heard from Richie lately?" asked Lucy, who knew that Rachel's son was in Greece, working on an archaeological dig.

"Come to think of it, not since last month." She laughed. "He wanted income tax forms."

"That's something at least," complained Pam. "I haven't heard a word from Tim since Christmas." She paused. "Lucy's so lucky to have Toby living in town."

"It's true. I am lucky." Lucy put down her fork and dabbed at her mouth with her napkin. "But I have to remind myself not to hover. They may be nearby, but they need their own space." It was a lesson she thought Laura Barfield would have to learn, too, if she hoped to maintain a healthy relationship with her son.

Dr. Cope and Jennifer Fain were already waiting on the sidewalk in front of the hotel when Lucy and her friends stepped outside at nine-thirty. The sky was overcast but the TV weatherman had promised later clearing, and the temperature was forecast to rise to twelve degrees Celsius—around sixty degrees Fahrenheit.

"Are we all here?" asked Pam, consulting her list.

"Autumn's still upstairs," said Jennifer.

"We'll wait for her, then," said Pam, unfolding her map of the Underground. "It looks like we can take the Northern Line from Euston Square."

"Lead on," said Lucy when the door of the hotel opened and Autumn clumped down the steps in her Dr. Martens. Today she was wearing black leggings that stopped at her ankles, a short black jersey dress, and a torn fishnet sweater.

"Do you think you'll be warm enough?" asked Pam, unable to stifle her motherly instincts.

Autumn's back stiffened and she glared at Pam as if she'd been accused of some dastardly crime. "I'll be fine."

"Okay," said Pam, backing off. "It looks like we're all here. The others have made separate plans."

"Well, this is nice," declared Dr. Cope. "I feel like Henry the Eighth, accompanied by six lovely ladies."

"Just as long as you treat us better than he treated his wives," said Rachel, falling into step beside him as they walked along Gower Street to the Tube station.

Crowds were already making their way to the Tower of London when they emerged from the Tower Hill Tube station into what had become a sunny day. As they joined the throng walking along the outer walls that ringed the spacious grassy moat, Lucy thought it must have been much the same throughout the centuries, especially when traitors and criminals were publicly executed on Tower Hill. Today's crowds weren't out for blood, however, but were drawn by the Tower's various attractions, including the crown jewels.

Despite the sunshine, it was chilly when they passed through the Middle Tower entrance into the castle complex. Lucy wasn't sure what she had expected but was somewhat surprised to find the Tower of London wasn't a single structure; rather, it was a number of buildings collected inside a double ring of walls that would frustrate an attacker. It was a true medieval fortress and reminded her of books about knights and castles she had read to Toby when he was small. Even today, she thought as they strolled along the shadowed path between the two walls, there was something grim about the place.

"The Traitor's Gate," said Dr. Cope, pausing in front of a semicircular opening in the outer wall, blocked with forbidding bars, that connected to the Thames beyond. It was here that prisoners had been delivered by boat.

"Imagine being brought through there, knowing you'd never get out," said Rachel.

"They used to put the heads of people they executed on top of the walls," continued Dr. Cope. "A grim reminder of the price of treason." He lifted his shoulders in a shrug. "And in those days, treason was whatever displeased the king."

"This is a terrible, evil place," said Jennifer, drawing the lapels of her pale blue jacket together with a delicate, ringed hand.

"Not really," said Rachel, who was studying her guidebook. "It says here it's like a little village. People actually live here. The Yeoman Warders—those are the guys in the funny red outfits—live here with their families."

"That's too cool," said Autumn, breaking her usual bored attitude to express a flicker of interest. "Look at that bird!" She was pointing to a super-sized crow, perched above the entry gate.

With its feathers fluffed out, it reminded Lucy of Autumn's spiky black hairdo and she smiled.

"That," said Rachel, "is a raven. The legend is that if the ravens ever leave the Tower, the kingdom will fall."

"I'd be worried if I were Prince Charles," said Sue.

Rachel smiled. "They're taking no chances—their wings are clipped."

"Seems like cheating to me," observed Lucy as they passed through yet another dank and chilly portal to emerge into a spacious green, grassy court. The gleaming White Tower, a large square fortress with a domed and turreted tower at each corner stood before them.

"It was built by William the Conqueror," said Rachel, amazed.

Lucy didn't know many dates but she did know this one. "In something like 1066?"

"Yeah. That's old," said Pam.

"The Hallett House, the oldest building in Tinker's Cove, was built in the eighteenth century," said Sue. "That White Tower is nearly a thousand years old."

"This is really something," said Rachel. "So where shall we start?"

Sue didn't hesitate. "The jewels, silly. Where else?"

A short line was already forming at the building housing the crown jewels, but the group happily joined it. Once inside, they discovered it was a bit like Disney World with a convoluted route that hid the length of the wait. The queue snaked past a flickering old black-and- white newsreel of Queen Elizabeth II's coronation, where she was decked out in a crown and ermine robe, as well as a number of other jewels, and carried an orb and scepter. Eventually they found themselves in a darkened room where a moving pathway carried viewers past the illuminated glass cases containing crowns and scepters glittering with thousands of diamonds, pearls, sapphires, emeralds, and rubies.

It all left Lucy rather cold, except for Queen Victoria's dainty little diamond topper, which looked like a miniature crown designed for a doll, but Sue was enthralled. When she came to the end of the people mover, she quickly ducked around and hopped on for another viewing.

"Pardon me," she said to the startled gentleman she stepped in front of.

"Not at all," he replied with famous British politeness.

But when she tried the same trick a second time, one of the Yeoman Warders stepped forward. "Madam, if you wish to see the jewels again, you will have to go to the end of the queue."

"Busted," announced Autumn, who was waiting with Lucy at the end.

"I don't care. It was worth it," insisted Sue. "If diamonds are a girl's best friend, the queen sure has a lot of friends."

Dr. Cope and Jennifer had drifted away from the others and were standing by a plaque embedded in the pavement, near a small stone church building, gazing at a withered bunch of roses that had been placed there. Lucy and the others went over to join them, and she realized the plaque marked the spot where the scaffold used for royal executions had once stood.

"Only very important prisoners were executed here," Dr. Cope was saying. "Or more controversial ones. It was more private since the public wasn't allowed in."

Lucy was reading the names embedded in a circle around the plaque: "Margaret Pole—Lady Salisbury; Catherine Howard; Anne Boleyn; Lady Jane Grey—"

"That poor girl was only seventeen . . . ," said Rachel, who devoured historical novels.

"Whatever did she do?" asked Jennifer.

"Nothing really," said Rachel. "She was the victim of an ambitious family. They managed to get her on the throne, but in the end they lost a battle and somebody else got the job—Mary Tudor, fondly known as Bloody Mary."

"They didn't have to kill her!" exclaimed Jennifer, looking pale.

Autumn had spotted one of the ravens, perched on a nearby fencepost, and waved her sweater at it, causing it to flap its wings and rise a few feet into the air, only to brush Jennifer's shoulder with its wing. Startled and frightened, Jennifer shrieked as the bird made a clumsy landing on the memorial plaque, where it stood like a grim reminder of the gruesome beheadings that had taken place there.

"Get it away!" she begged as tears rolled down her cheeks. "Make it go away."

"I don't think you're supposed to interfere with the ravens," said Lucy, reproving Autumn. "Let's check out the Medieval Palace and see what life was like back then."

"Yeah," said Autumn cynically. "If you managed to keep your head."

Chapter Five

"Now this is better," declared Sue as they wandered through the sparsely furnished but brightly decorated rooms of the Medieval Palace. A scratchy recording of lute music provided atmosphere.

Sue's interest was caught by a display case containing jewels and perfume bottles. "These things are pretty, but we can't really know what life was like back then, can we?"

"Not very pleasant, even at the best of times," speculated Rachel as they passed through the room where Sir Walter Raleigh wrote *History of the World* during his long imprisonment. "Imagine what this place was like in winter, with only a small fireplace to heat it."

Indeed, even though it was sunny and warm outside, it was chilly inside, where the stone walls held the cold and where sun couldn't penetrate the small windows. And these accommodations were deemed comfortable, a great improvement over those provided for less illustrious prisoners.

"I once read somewhere that life was so painful in the Middle Ages that tortures had to be really drastic to make an impression. Remember, this was before antibiotics and modern dentistry. There were no painkillers or anesthetics like we have now," said Dr. Cope. "Childbirth and infancy were perilous for women and children, and the men were fighting and riding horses and generally living dangerously. There was plague, I don't imagine the food was terribly wholesome, and the water wasn't fit to drink. People didn't bathe much. Their lives were short and painful. It's no wonder they put so much faith in religion and hoped for a better afterlife."

"It still seems terrible, the way those kings treated people. Poor Sir Walter was kept here for ten years." Jennifer had paused to read the explanatory placards.

"He committed treason," said Autumn. "It seems like everybody was committing treason."

Pam nodded. "They didn't have government like we do now, with an orderly transfer of power. Whoever was strongest and had the best army got to be king. There were plenty of people with a drop or two of royal blood, and they didn't have any trouble finding ambitious backers to support their claims."

"And if you backed the wrong guy, you lost your head," said Autumn as they paused inside a chilly tower with whitewashed walls whose signs pointed out inscriptions carved by prisoners.

They all fell silent as their eyes wandered over the carvings. It was too easy to imagine the prisoners' despair as they waited day after day to learn their fates, and their desire to leave some little scrawl proclaiming that they once lived and suffered for their beliefs.

It was a relief to emerge into the warm sunshine of the Wall Walk, which ran along the top section of the fortifications.

"Have we had enough of the Tower?" asked Rachel. "I believe there's a café down by the river."

Lucy was thoughtful as they made their way through the complex toward the river exit. Pam and Rachel were leading the way. Dr. Cope had fallen into step with Sue, and they were having a lively discussion. Autumn and Jennifer followed. Autumn was striding along in her thick-soled shoes, but Jennifer kept glancing at her companion anxiously, almost as if expecting a blow.

Maybe she was reading too much into Jennifer's body language, thought Lucy. Maybe she had bad posture from scoliosis or something, or maybe she was simply nervous and high-strung or had a blood-sugar problem. There could be lots of explanations for her extreme thinness, she told herself. Nevertheless, the way Autumn was dressed all in black with her spiky hair reminded Lucy of the Tower's nasty ravens, while Jennifer was like one of the little brown sparrows that flitted about nervously after crumbs, always keeping an eye out for the predatory ravens.

When Lucy joined her three friends at one of the riverside café's green-painted picnic tables, she realized she'd been on her feet for more than four hours. It felt good to sit with the sun warming her back and the River Thames sparkling in front of her. The view was splendid, featuring Tower Bridge with two tall stanchions that mimicked the nearby Tower of London. "It's hard to believe I'm really here," she said, feeling a sudden sense of dislocation. "I'm really in London."

"I know exactly what you mean," agreed Sue, taking a tiny bite of her panini. "I remember the first time I went to Paris. Sid and I were taking a taxi from the airport, and we drove right past the Eiffel Tower and the Louvre and Notre Dame, and I could hardly believe my eyes.

I'd seen those things in books and movies, but it's quite different to see them in real life."

"I feel really lucky to be here," said Lucy, finding her thoughts turning to George Temple. "To be alive to see this, I mean."

"I wonder if George Temple had been to London before," said Rachel, echoing her thoughts.

"Oh, yes, I'm sure he had," said Pam. "He was quite a traveler. He led a trip like this every spring break, to different places, but quite often to London."

"That makes me feel a bit better, knowing he had a rich life," said Lucy.

Dr. Cope, who was seated at the next table, let out a harsh, barking laugh, and Lucy's eyes met Pam's. It seemed an odd reaction if he'd overheard them, but they had no reason to think he had. Maybe he was laughing at something his granddaughter said.

Lucy was so tired when they finally reached St. Paul's Cathedral that she headed straight for one of the chairs that filled the nave. Sue had assured them it wasn't worth taking the Tube, since St. Paul's was only one stop away from Tower Hill, but she had been deceived by the distortions of the Underground map. It was a different story aboveground, where they had to make their way through what seemed like miles of confusing streets, albeit with charming names like Fish Street Hill and Ironmonger Lane. This was the oldest part of London and still reflected the haphazard layout of the medieval town.

"We got quite a tour of the city," said Dr. Cope, lowering himself stiffly onto the seat next to her. He was breathing heavily as he cast his eyes around him, taking in the huge cathedral with its immense dome. His hands, holding the plan of the building, were resting on his thighs. "My goodness," he finally said.

"It's very grand," agreed Lucy, taking in the immense white and gold cathedral. "The dome is magnetic—you have to keep staring at it."

"I imagine that's the idea: to draw your eyes and your mind heavenward." He opened the brochure and began reading. "Well it's quite a climb to the top of the dome. I don't think I can do that."

"Me neither," said Lucy. "Not yet anyway. Shall we explore a bit around here?"

"Sure," said the doctor, rising with a grunt. "There are supposed to be carvings by Grinling Gibbons in the choir."

Looking around as they crossed the transept beneath the dome, Lucy saw the other members of the group dotted here and there in the cathedral. Autumn and Jennifer were also in the transept, staring up at the paintings in the dome. Rachel and Pam were admiring the elaborate carvings on the pulpit, and Sue was marching purposefully toward an aisle; Lucy suspected she was looking for a ladies' room.

Lucy found the choir a cozy contrast to the immense emptiness of the cathedral. Here in the enclosure behind the organ, there were wooden pews and carvings of fruit, flowers, and cherubs. Unlike the cathedral proper, which inspired awe, the choir encouraged reflection. Here your thoughts turned inward and you could assess the state of your soul.

"Are you a man of faith?" asked Lucy, turning to Dr. Cope.

"Not really. Medicine is a science, after all." He paused. "I guess I believe in the scientific method of hypothesis, tests, and conclusions based on evidence. I haven't seen any evidence of God. Quite the contrary, in fact."

Lucy was studying the adorable face of a Grinling Gibbons cherub puffing away on a trumpet. Though carved of wood, it seemed plump and soft enough to stroke. "Some scientists believe in God."

"Yes. They see the natural order of the universe as evidence of a master plan and conclude there must be a master inventor somewhere."

"Where is the question, I suppose," said Lucy with a smile.

"Exactly," agreed Dr. Cope. "It seems that you are also a doubter."

"I am. I don't believe in a higher power who judges what we do on earth. I think we must each make of our lives what we can. We must do the very best we can."

"In that case, we must each answer to our own personal conscience," said Dr. Cope. "That's quite radical, isn't it?"

"I guess it depends on each conscience," said Lucy. "Mine is actually rather conservative. I believe in the Golden Rule: Treat others as you wish to be treated."

"I used to think I had a clear understanding of right and wrong, but now I'm not so sure." Dr. Cope was staring at a faceted golden cross, whose trident-shaped rays caught the light and made it look like a radiant sun. His brow was furrowed and his expression troubled.

Lucy suspected he felt guilty about his failure to save George Temple. "You did everything you could to save him," she said.

He turned and looked at her, his blue eyes bright in his wrinkled, weathered face. "Did I? Do you really think so?"

"I do," said Lucy. "I blame myself. I should have realized he was in trouble much sooner and called for help."

The doctor raised his white, bushy eyebrows. "You do have a conservative conscience, but you shouldn't blame yourself. If I've learned anything at all in thirty-odd years of practice, it's that you can't save everybody. Death comes to us all, eventually. And you never know, perhaps his death was actually a blessing. Perhaps he would have developed Alzheimer's or cancer." They were walking back toward the transept and paused once again under the dome. "So now we have a choice: Shall we ascend to heaven or descend to the crypt?"

Across the way, Lucy saw a booth where tickets to the dome were sold. "I think I shall pay my money and attempt the ascension," she said.

"I, on the other hand, shall accept my fate as an unrepentant sinner and descend to the realm of the wicked and the doomed," said Dr. Cope.

According to the sign, there were 259 steps to the Whispering Gallery; 378 to the Stone Gallery on the outside of the dome; and 192 more steps to the Golden Gallery at the very top, which also offered 360-degree views of London.

"How high do you want to go?" asked Sue, joining her at the ticket window.

"In for a penny, in for a pound," declared Lucy, wondering how that particular phrase had popped into her head. "Might as well go all the way."

"Or die trying," said Sue, counting out the confusing coins that looked so much like American money but had entirely different values.

* * *

"People have been climbing these steps for hundreds of years," gasped Sue when they emerged at the Whispering Gallery. The stone steps were shallow, but they'd still had to pause several times on the way up to rest their legs and catch their breath. Even so, Lucy's thighs were burning and her left knee felt as if one of the Tower's torturers had inserted a red-hot skewer or two into it.

"This is it for me," declared Lucy, feeling a bit dizzy as she looked down at the cathedral's black-and-white checked floor so very far below.

"Well, I'm going on up," said Sue. "I want to get my money's worth."

"I'll wait for you here," said Lucy, eager to study the paintings and mosaics that decorated the dome. The paintings, on the upper portion of the dome, were sepia monochromes, rather like old photographs. She wasn't exactly sure who or what they portrayed: Moses? Isaiah? St. Paul? Whoever they were about, there was plenty of movement from flowing draperies and pennants, and there was a stirring scene of a shipwreck.

Also above her head, but below the paintings, were a number of white marble statues. From below they had seemed little more than chess pieces, but from up here they were huge. She dreaded to think what would happen if one of them toppled from its lofty perch to land on the cathedral floor below, and hoped they were fastened firmly in place.

From her vantage point in the gallery, she could look across to the opposite side and see the colorful mosaics tucked beneath the gallery. These were labeled, and she made out Ezekiel, apparently laying down the law on a stone tablet, and Jeremiah, consulting with an angel, as she proceeded around the gallery. She was just opposite St. Mark, seated on a lion and accompanied by two beautiful angels, when she heard a female voice, clear as a bell, from the other side of the dome. It was true, she realized—the Whispering Gallery was aptly named. You could hear people talking on the other side.

Curious about this phenomenon, she stood in place, listening intently.

"I saw what you did," said a voice that sounded a lot like Jennifer's. The wall blocked her view, so she couldn't quite make out the people on the other side, but she could see two little heads resembling Jennifer and Autumn.

The reply was hissed, little more than a whisper. "Like you're Little Miss Innocent! Give me a break!"

This time Lucy was sure the speaker was none other than Autumn, once again taunting Jennifer. The more she thought about it, the less she liked it and she wondered if she ought to have a word with Autumn. Not in a scolding way; maybe in a joking way. "Little birds in their nests agree," or something like that, a silly phrase that had suddenly popped into her head. From a movie perhaps, she wondered as she walked along the gallery. *Mary Poppins* maybe? But when she reached the other side, the girls were gone and Sue was waiting for her.

"You should have gone up, Lucy! The view was amazing and the guard said it's the clearest it's been in months."

"That's okay," said Lucy, whose knee was still bothering her. "Besides, this Whispering Gallery is pretty amazing. You really can hear people whispering on the other side."

Sue grinned wickedly. "What did you hear? Something naughty?"

"Maybe," said Lucy as they started down the stairs.

Lucy found herself seated next to Autumn and Jennifer as they took the Underground back to the hotel, but she hesitated to take a nannyish tone with them. Instead she made small talk, asking if they were roommates at college.

"No, we met at group," said Jennifer.

Lucy was puzzled. "What sort of group?"

Autumn leaned forward, speaking across Jennifer. "Not what you think. It's no big deal, just something they have for freshmen. We get together once a week and talk about how we're adjusting to school, time management, study skills, stuff like that."

"Sounds good," said Lucy, rising as the train pulled into Tottenham Court Road station, where they would change to the Northern Line. "I wish my daughter's school had something like that."

When they emerged at Goodge Street, Lucy noticed that Jennifer and Autumn were once again best of friends. They were walking with their heads together, and Autumn had her arm around Jennifer's waist.

"What's with those two?" asked Sue, falling into step beside Lucy. "One minute they're fighting and the next they're best friends."

"I noticed that, too," said Lucy, pausing to peek through a gate to admire the fenced gardens running behind the row houses. "Very weird."

"What's weird?" asked Rachel, joining them. "Hyacinths in March?"

"No, we were talking about the relationship between Jennifer and Autumn." The girls were well out of earshot, far ahead of them on the sidewalk and turning the corner onto Gower Street.

"It's almost a dominant-submissive sort of thing," said Sue.

"I don't think it's so odd," said Rachel, who was a psych major in college and never got over it. "College is a time for experimentation, discovering your real identity, and that includes your sexual identity."

"Do you think they're gay?" asked Pam, joining the group.

"Could be," said Rachel. "It wouldn't be the first time two women fell in love." She pointed to a hyacinth that had escaped the neat border and sprouted in the middle of a lawn. "Or maybe they're two outsiders who've found each other."

Chapter Six

There were no beans for breakfast on Monday; the menu was egg, bacon, and grilled tomato. Lucy discovered she loved grilled tomatoes, but Pam and Rachel were less enthusiastic. Sue stuck with black coffee and a triangle of toast.

After breakfast, the group lingered in the lounge, waiting for Quentin Rea, who was due to arrive at any moment. Lucy checked his flight on the computer the hotel provided for guests' use in the lounge and learned he had landed at Heathrow over two hours ago.

She also checked her e-mail, replying to Bill's update that all was well at home but everyone missed her with a chatty summary of her visit to the Tower and St. Paul's. When she sent it off, she noticed a new e-mail in her folder from Elizabeth.

News from Elizabeth was rarely good. Like most college students, she only bothered to contact her parents when she was in trouble or needed money. Lucy opened the message only to learn with dismay that the new dean at Chamberlain College was, in Elizabeth's words, "a stupid Fascist" who was threatening to remove Elizabeth from her post as a resident advisor. While

Elizabeth was outraged at what she believed was the dean's unfairness, Lucy had a different reaction. She was concerned about her bank balance, because the position provided free room and board, which amounted to several thousand dollars. If Elizabeth lost her job, they would have to come up with the money. Just the thought of such a large, unexpected expense was enough to put a damper on her vacation.

Hearing voices in the hallway, Lucy wrote a quick reply asking for more information, then glanced up as Quentin Rea entered the lounge accompanied by a tall young woman. She had the sort of looks that turned heads, not so much because her features were outstanding—her nose was a bit too big, her lips thin—but because she knew how to present herself. Her black tailored pantsuit not only fit her slender figure to perfection but it also set off her buttery, shoulder-length blond hair. If she was wearing makeup, it was so expertly applied that you couldn't tell, apart from a dab of lip gloss and a swipe of mascara on her wide-set brown eyes. Remembering how tired she'd felt when she finally arrived at the hotel, Lucy wondered how this woman could look so remarkably fresh after spending the night on the red-eye from Boston.

Turning her attention to the professor, Lucy decided he hadn't aged well. He'd put on some weight in the years since she'd taken that course in Victorian literature, and his rumpled khaki pants and Harris Tweed jacket couldn't stretch to cover the round belly that stuck out like a baby bump. The longish, streaked hair that Lucy had found so attractive all those years ago had darkened into a slatey gray and had thinned as well, leaving a circular, pink bald patch at his crown. Of course, everybody got older, everyone aged, thought Lucy. The unfortunate thing in Quentin's case was that he hadn't accepted the fact and was still sporting the same look he'd adopted straight out of grad school as a young assistant professor. It had been devastatingly effective back then, but it didn't work now. He needed to buy pants with a larger waist; he needed a good haircut and a new pair of shoes. Long, bushy sideburns and loafers held together with duct tape looked ridiculous on a man approaching his fifties.

"There's nothing worse than preppy gone to seed," said Sue, leaning down to whisper in her ear.

Lucy laughed, closing out her e-mail account and pushing back her chair. Standing up, she caught Quentin's eye.

"Lucy Stone!"

Lucy was chagrined to feel her cheeks warming. All that had been long ago and had mostly been in her imagination. "Meet my friends," she said, quickly introducing Pam, Rachel, and Sue.

"Terrific, terrific," he murmured, glancing around the crowded lounge. "Is everyone here?"

Lucy did a quick head count. The Smith family were seated together on a big sofa; Caroline, ever the well-behaved daughter, was in the middle between her watchful parents. Dr. Cope and Laura Barfield were standing by the window, and Laura's son Will had taken Lucy's seat at the computer. Autumn and Jennifer had squeezed together into an armchair where they were giggling and looking through some of the tourist brochures provided by the hotel.

"We're all here," said Pam. "And we're very glad you could come and take over for George."

"Not at all," said Quentin. "I'm very happy to be here with you all, though of course I regret the circumstances that brought me here. This is Emma Temple," he said, indicating his companion. "She has come to make arrangements to return her father's body to the States."

If he'd announced he'd brought along an auditor from the Internal Revenue Service to inquire into their tax returns, he couldn't have gotten a more awkward reaction. The room fell silent and eyes were averted until Pam stepped forward and grabbed Emma's hand. "I think I speak for everyone when I say how very sorry we all are for your loss. If there's anything we can do to help, please don't hesitate to ask."

"You're very kind," said Emma, her glance passing to each of them, as a lawyer might assess a jury. "I don't anticipate any problems. I'm an attorney, so I'm familiar with situations like this. I expect to wrap things up fairly quickly."

"Dealing with the death of a parent is always difficult . . ." began Rachel.

Emma cleared her throat, eager to set the record straight. "My parents were divorced and I hadn't seen my father for many years. I can't pretend to be grief-stricken, but I do appreciate your concern." She turned to Quentin. "If you'll excuse me, I'd like to get settled in my room and leave you all to your tour. I have some phone calls to make."

As Emma left the room, there seemed to be a general relaxation of tension. People were uncomfortable with death, Lucy reasoned, and it was awkward to confront grieving family members. Even worse, perhaps, when the family member wasn't grieving.

"Well, then. Onward and upward as my dear mother likes to say." Quentin was ready to take charge. "I believe George made arrangements for an excursion to

Hampton Court today. In fact, I noticed a minibus parked outside, and I spoke to the driver, who is waiting for us. So if you all want to get your things for the day, we can get this show on the road."

As always in London, the road was crowded and the minibus crawled through town. Lucy didn't mind the slow pace, because it gave her an opportunity to get the lay of the land. Passing through busy Leicester Square, she spotted the TKTS booth where theater tickets were sold for half price, and passing Green Park, she noticed a sign pointing the way to Buckingham Palace. This was all useful information that she filed away for future reference.

Sue was also taking notes. "That's the Wolseley," she said, pointing out a restaurant on Piccadilly. "Very fashionable."

"Looks expensive," said Lucy, noticing the Ritz Hotel on the next corner and the well-dressed men in bespoke suits with slim briefcases striding along purposefully on the sidewalk.

Sue had also noticed them. "Don't you wish people in America dressed better? All anybody seems to wear anymore is jeans."

"Jeans are just fine with me," said Lucy, looking down at her denim-clad legs, "and I've noticed plenty of people wearing them here in London, too."

"Only tourists," sniffed Sue.

Lucy laughed. "We're tourists. There's nothing wrong with that."

"Even Jane Austen was a tourist," said Quentin, joining the conversation. "It was quite the fashion in nineteenth-century England to tour the countryside and visit the stately houses. Elizabeth Bennett goes sightseeing in *Pride and Prejudice*. In fact, it's the sight of Mr. Darcy's impressive estate that prompts her to revise her previously unfavorable opinion of him and decide he's marriage material." He paused. "I think you will discover that Hampton Court is well worth a visit. It was built by Cardinal Wolsey and was the finest palace in England, a fact that didn't sit well with Henry the Eighth. He complained that the cardinal's home was far nicer than anything he had, compelling the cardinal to offer it to him. Henry didn't hesitate to seize it. He wanted something that would impress his new lover, Anne Boleyn." Quentin paused. "I guess we all know how that turned out."

"She was beheaded, wasn't she?" said Autumn. "We saw the monument at the Tower of London."

Quentin nodded. "Henry soured on the relationship when she failed to produce a male heir."

"Typical!" snorted Autumn. "Like that was her fault."

"Nowadays we know it's the father's sperm that determines the sex of the child," observed Dr. Cope. "They didn't know that in the sixteenth century."

"Was that why she died?" Jennifer's voice was low and her face pale. "Just because she didn't have any sons?"

"It was a bit more complicated than that. She was accused of treason and fornicating with her brother and just about anything her enemies could think of. But Henry had it done in true royal style." Quentin spoke with relish, enjoying showing off his knowledge. "Instead of letting the usual executioner go at her with an ax, which sometimes took more than a few whacks, he hired the famous swordsman of Calais to do the deed in the French manner. One quick swing of the sword and the problem was solved."

"I hated the Tower," whispered Jennifer. "It's a horrible place. You can almost hear those poor souls screaming."

"I imagine more than a few got exactly what they deserved," said Tom Smith.

"And others were sacrificed to royal whims," said Quentin. "At Hampton Court, they say, visitors sometimes encounter the ghost of Katherine Howard, still protesting her innocence."

"What happened to her?" asked Caroline, rousing from her usual lethargy and taking an interest.

"She was Henry the Eighth's fifth wife." Quentin ticked them off on his fingers. "Divorced, beheaded, died, divorced, *beheaded* . . ."

"Oh, no, not another," moaned Jennifer.

"Afraid so. She not only failed to produce an heir but she was also judged unfaithful to the king."

Sue raised a perfectly shaped eyebrow. "Seems a risky sort of thing to do with a husband like Henry."

"Who knows?" Quentin shrugged. "The court was full of rumors. It may not have been true. Unfortunately, Henry believed it, so it was 'Off with her head!' and this time there was no fancy French swordsman."

Jennifer was so pale Lucy was afraid she might pass out. "Tell us about the sixth wife," she suggested. "She outlived Henry, didn't she?"

Quentin smiled. "Catherine Parr. She did indeed. As the rhyme goes, she survived. She married again after Henry's death but unfortunately died of puerperal fever."

"A common occurrence in those days," said Dr. Cope.

"But don't think Hampton Court is anything like the Tower—it's a beautiful Tudor country estate that's been enlarged by subsequent kings and queens. It's situated

on the Thames and has beautiful gardens, which I en-
courage you to explore. Because, it seems, we've arrived."

The driver swung the minibus into a drop-off area,
and they disembarked, gathering in a small knot on the
gravel pathway to wait while Quentin bought the tickets. Lucy found herself enjoying the fresh air and sunshine as she took in the splendid view. The gravel drive,
which bisected a bright green lawn edged on one side
by the meandering river, led to the quaintly towered
and turreted structure of age-darkened red brick. It
didn't seem very large or impressive from this angle,
but rather like a castle you might see pictured in an il-
lustrated book of fairy tales. Rapunzel would not have
looked out of place letting her hair down from one of
the twin towers that flanked the central gate.

When Quentin returned and distributed plans of the
palace, she discovered it was a vast complex of buildings
extending far beyond the Tudor façade and included a
chapel, numerous enclosed courts, a Tudor kitchen,
picture galleries, an orangery, halls for receiving state
visitors, and once-private royal apartments.

"I'm afraid we got off to a rather late start this morning, so we don't have as much time as I'd like," said
Quentin after checking his watch. "I suggest we stick together for a quick tour of the interior and then go our
separate ways to the garden, lunch, the maze, whatever
you like. We must all meet back here at exactly this spot
at three o'clock. And I mean three o'clock and not a
minute later because our driver has warned us that traffic will most likely be heavy and we must get back to
London before our minibus turns into a pumpkin on
the stroke of five."

This was met with nods and bemused smiles as they

began making their way to the entrance with Quentin leading the way. Once inside, he led them upstairs and down through vast halls with elaborately plastered ceilings and along dark and chilly bricked corridors to the vast, smoky kitchens where two meals a day for hundreds of members of the royal household had been cooked every day on open fires. Lucy found it all fascinating and hung on to every word, but after they'd viewed the Chapel Royal and entered the Georgian area of the palace, she began to lose interest. All those Williams and Georges confused her, and she found herself longing to get outside to explore the garden and find the Great Vine. She'd recently read about it in a gardening magazine and was eager to see the famous old survivor for herself.

"These rooms were originally intended for Queen Mary the Second. She was coruler with her husband, William the Third, but they are better known to us as William and Mary, who the college is named after but were later used by Queen Caroline, George the Second's wife . . ." Quentin was rambling on, absorbed by a subject that he alone found fascinating. Without the titillation of sexual misalliances and royal beheadings, the group was becoming restless, and when Lucy saw Autumn and Jennifer slip away, she tapped Sue on the shoulder. "Let's go," she whispered. "I want to see the Great Vine."

When the group turned a corner into a little room with original linenfold paneling, Lucy and Sue headed in the opposite direction. By following a few signs, they soon found themselves outside, standing in front of a classically proportioned Georgian façade that bore no resemblance at all to the Tudor side of the building. This part of the redbrick palace had white trim and even rows of large windows that wouldn't have looked out of place on a New England college campus. It could even be a high school or a town hall.

"Whoa," said Sue, putting on her sunglasses, "talk about a time warp."

"Yeah," agreed Lucy, spotting a sign pointing to the Great Vine. "This way, come on. We can't miss this. It's hundreds of years old."

Sue was poring over the plan. "What exactly is it?"

"A grapevine. It was planted three hundred years ago."

Sue's eyebrows rose over her DKNY sunglasses. "So?"

"That's amazing. Just imagine. Three hundred years and it still produces grapes."

"Poor thing." Sue was marching along the walkway. "They ought to let it retire."

"Nope, it's like the queen. It has to carry on until it dies." Lucy waved her arm. "Just look at these gardens. They're beautiful."

As they walked along the side of the enormous palace, they could see various formal gardens laid out before them, many with lavishly planted beds packed with hyacinths and pansies, outlined by neatly clipped boxwood hedges.

"Their spring is way ahead of ours," said Lucy. "I haven't even seen a crocus at home."

"We don't really have spring in Maine," observed Sue. "We go straight from winter to mud and then it's summer and black flies."

Lucy had paused in front of an old-fashioned little greenhouse, surrounded by a patch of freshly turned earth. "This is it," she exclaimed, her voice full of awe. "The Great Vine."

"I only see dirt," said Sue.

"They don't plant anything here. The roots are beneath this soil, and they don't want anything to compete with the vine. Come on." She grabbed Sue's hand and pulled her toward the door.

Inside it was warm and humid, and the Great Vine was bare and leafless, its tendrils rising from a thick and knobby trunk and spreading beneath the greenhouse's glass roof.

Lucy exhaled slowly. "Isn't it magnificent?"

Sue was peering over her sunglasses, staring at the vine's rough brown bark. "I don't see it myself, but, then, I'm not much of a gardener. I suppose it's quite nice when it has leaves and grapes."

Lucy was crestfallen. "You don't like it?"

"I love it," said Sue, stifling a smile. "Now let's find this famous maze."

The walk to the maze took them past spacious lawns filled with thousands of naturalized daffodils, all in bloom. "Now this is more like it," said Sue. "I like a bit of color, and look at the way they all nod in the breeze. When I get home, I'm going to plant a whole lot of daffodils."

"You'll have to wait till fall," said Lucy.

Sue was doubtful. "Really?"

"Really. You plant them in the fall and they come up in the spring."

Sue chewed her lip. "I'll probably forget by then."

"I'll remind you." Lucy had stopped before a wall of living green. "This is it. The maze. The entrance must be around the side."

"It's bigger than I thought," said Sue. "What if we get lost and can't get out?"

"I have an excellent sense of direction," declared Lucy, stepping through the turnstile. "Follow me."

Once inside the maze, Lucy found she'd spoken too soon. The twists and turns of the paths soon confused her, and they came to several dead ends that required them to retrace their steps through the narrow alleys between the clipped hedge. The hedge was too tall to see over, but they could hear voices as other visitors laughed and called to each other. They recognized Autumn's voice, calling, "This way, come this way," and followed it to the center of the maze. But when they got there, they didn't find Autumn, only Jennifer, who was wiping tears from her eyes with her hands.

Lucy's motherly instincts were aroused and she produced a tissue from her bag. "What's the matter?"

"Nothing." The girl smiled wanly. "I had a little panic attack, but now that you're here, I'll be fine."

"Where's Autumn?" Sue gestured at the enclosed space, empty except for the three of them. "I heard her voice."

"She was here but she ran off." Jennifer's face was an angry red, in marked contrast to her usual pallor.

"Why did she do that?" asked Lucy, suspecting the girls had quarreled.

Jennifer licked her lips nervously and shrugged her bony shoulders. "You know how she is. She thought it would be fun to frighten me. She knew I was afraid I couldn't find my way out."

"That's rather mean," said Sue.

Jennifer was quick to defend Autumn. "Oh, she didn't mean anything by it." She tucked the used tissue into her pocket. "What does happen if you can't figure it out? Do they leave you here all night?"

"I don't think so." Sue was leading the way. "I imagine they keep count. That's probably what the turnstile is for."

"Oh." Jennifer giggled nervously. "Now I feel foolish. Why didn't I think of that?"

"They don't call it a maze for nothing," said Sue, pausing at a fork and trying to decide which way to go. "It's very disorienting."

"Go left," said Lucy. "When in doubt, go left."

Sue was doubtful. "Why?"

"Because it's natural to go right and the maze designer knows that."

"Okay," agreed Sue, turning the corner and discovering a sign pointing to the exit. "Look at that! Easy as pie."

"Pie!" exclaimed Lucy. "Do you realize we haven't had lunch yet? I'm starving."

"I could do with a bite myself," said Sue. "Let's head back to the entrance. I saw a sign for a café there."

Jennifer walked along with them. "Do you mind if I come, too?"

Lucy was impressed by her politeness and gave her a little hug. "Not at all."

It was quite some distance through the palace and back to the entrance gate, and then even farther to the Tiltyard Café, which was tucked behind a formal garden outside the palace. When Lucy saw the sign advertising Devonshire cream teas, she was encouraged.

"Look!" she exclaimed. "We can have afternoon tea."

The little café was packed. Every table inside and out was occupied by people of every size and description, speaking numerous languages, and all of whom seemed to be tucking into their afternoon snacks.

Jennifer's eyes were enormous as she watched the servers dipping out big scoops of Devonshire cream and strawberry jam that they arranged on plates alongside freshly baked scones. Even Sue was taking an interest. "When in England, do as the English," she said, joining the queue and taking a tray.

She'd no sooner picked it up than Quentin hailed them from the exit, where he was returning his empty dishes to the rack by the door. "Lucy!" he called. "It's three o'clock!"

Lucy's stomach growled in protest. "We'll get it to go," she promised.

"You don't have time! The bus is leaving!"

Jennifer was already hurrying across the café to Quentin, who was waiting for them by the door.

Sue replaced the tray with a thunk. "Just as well," she muttered. "Those things must be loaded with calories."

As they departed, Lucy's eye was caught by a pleasantly plump Indian woman in a sari who had bitten into a scone and was licking cream and jam off her lips, a blissful expression on her face. "We're zero for three," she reminded Sue as they followed Quentin and Jennifer down the gravel path toward the waiting minibus. "We couldn't find a tea shop on Saturday, we had a late lunch on Sunday, and today we didn't have time for tea. You wouldn't think it would be so hard, would you?"

"There, there." Sue was using her nanny voice. "This is England. I'm sure there will be lots more opportunities for afternoon tea."

"I sure hope so," grumbled Lucy, climbing aboard the minibus.

Chapter Seven

When Lucy took a seat on the minibus, she noticed Jennifer had spurned Autumn and was sitting with her grandfather. Autumn was sitting by herself, but when Quentin boarded, he took the seat next to her. Lucy was seated just behind him, which gave her a clear view of his pink and freckled bald spot.

Lucy knew that some women found baldness sexy—it was even fashionable for young men to shave their heads—but she wasn't a big fan of the look. She was glad that Bill still had a full head of hair and a thick beard, albeit dusted with gray. She thought of him fondly and wondered what he was doing at home and checked her watch. He was probably at work, she decided, and thinking about lunch. The thought made her feel a bit guilty since she wasn't home to pack that lunch for him. She wondered how he was managing with the girls, the dog, and the household chores, in addition to the remodeling job he'd taken on in one of the big shingle-style cottages on Shore Drive. The owners were very wealthy—and very demanding.

It was noisy in the minibus as the driver accelerated and turned into the road. The engine was loud and everybody was talking, comparing their experiences at Hampton Court. In the seat in front of her, Quentin was chatting with Autumn about Winchester College, and when there was a sudden drop in the general noise level, Lucy heard him offer to give her some career counseling. "It's not easy to decide what you want to be when you grow up," he was saying.

Ohmigosh, she thought, *he's up to his old tricks.* He'd used the same line with her, all those years ago, when she had taken that Victorian literature class. It all seemed foolish now, but she'd been a young mother then and had felt her sense of self slipping away as she struggled every day to meet her children's needs. When she'd decided to go back to school, it wasn't to satisfy her intellectual curiosity as much as to have something for herself. She'd enjoyed the course, had even liked writing papers, but what had kept her coming back week after week was the opportunity to see the handsome young professor.

It was nothing more than a crush, but he noticed her interest and invited her to lunch at the town's poshest restaurant, the Queen Victoria Inn. Another thought popped into her head—the image of the woman in the café licking cream off her lip. Quentin had done the same thing then, and she'd found it exciting. Much to her shame, she remembered, she accepted his invitation to go to his apartment. He said he wanted to show her some photos he'd taken of Elizabeth Barrett Browning's flat in Florence. She never got a glimpse of the photos, but he had kissed her, more than once.

The memory made her squirm in her seat, earning her a curious look from Sue. "Ants in your pants?" she asked.

"I've got a backache." It was true, she realized. Being

a tourist was hard work, and all that walking and standing was taking a toll.

"Me too." Sue raised her arms above her head and stretched, arching her back. "And I'm really hungry."

Quentin overheard her and made an announcement. "I've made reservations for dinner tonight for all of us at Ye Olde English Roast Beef," he told the group. "I've invited Emma Temple, too. I thought eating dinner together would give us all an opportunity for closure. We can share our thoughts and feelings about George's unexpected and tragic death and, hopefully, move on."

"I don't know," objected Ann Smith in a quavery voice. "There was that, well, I don't quite remember what it was about, but there was something about English beef not being safe to eat."

Rachel remembered. "Mad cow disease."

"That's right!" Autumn was eager to share the gruesome details. "You eat the meat and forty years later your brain turns to mush and you become a drooling idiot. We can't eat there."

"We certainly can," said Dr. Cope. "The British government dealt very effectively with that outbreak, and British beef is now one hundred percent safe to eat."

Laura Barfield was retying the blue scarf she had tucked into her jacket. "I know somebody who can't give blood because he was in England during that outbreak."

"A wise precaution, I'm sure," admitted Dr. Cope. "But the actual chance of infection was very low, even during the height of the outbreak. You have more to fear from the flu that arrives every winter."

"Well, then, we'll go ahead to the steak house." Quentin paused and, hearing a murmur of dissent, continued. "I'm sure they serve fish and chicken as well as beef."

Tom Smith raised a hand, as if in school. "Is the dinner included in the tour or will we have to split the check?"

"Good point. We'll split the check." Quentin was already turning his attention back to Autumn, who was bent over her iPhone. "Those are fantastic, aren't they? Super for e-mail."

Autumn was focused on the screen. "I'm not e-mailing. I'm tweeting."

"Tweeting? What's that?"

She turned and looked at him, her expression a mixture of shock and dismay. "Don't you know about Twitter?"

Oh, dear, thought Lucy. *Poor Quentin. His age is showing.*

When they all gathered at the long table that had been reserved for them at Ye Olde English Roast Beef, Lucy discovered Quentin was an equal-opportunity flirt. As soon as he spotted her coming through the door with her friends, he invited her to sit beside him. There was room for all four of them, so she could hardly refuse. Pulling out the chair, she noticed a couple of aged French fries curled up on the leatherette seat and brushed them off with her napkin.

Once seated, she took a look around and discovered the place had seen better days. Dated Tiffany lamps hung over the scuffed tables, the mirrors that lined the walls were streaked and dirty, and the stuffed head of an Aberdeen bull that hung over the bar seemed to have a bad case of mange, which was giving him a rather wild-eyed expression.

"The mad cow himself," said Sue.

"I need new silverware," said Rachel, holding up a fork for examination. If it had gone through the dishwasher, the dishwasher was in need of repair.

Lucy was checking her own place setting when Emma Temple arrived, seating herself in the last vacant seat, directly opposite Quentin. The rest of the group was arranged on Quentin's other side: Autumn was next to him, separated from Jennifer by Laura and Dr. Cope. Will was at the end of the table and the Smiths were seated between Will and Emma. As always, Caroline was positioned protectively between her parents, which struck Lucy as slightly ridiculous. The girl was every bit as big as her father and seemed quite capable of taking care of herself.

After a few pleasantries and greetings, everyone got busy studying their menus. There was no rush. Lucy had practically learned it by heart before the waiter appeared. He didn't seem old enough to be working—his face was spotty with pimples—but he quickly took charge.

"I'll replace that fork for you, madam," he said smoothly when Rachel displayed the offending piece of cutlery, and quickly moved on to the important business at hand. "Would you like to start with something from the bar?"

Once they'd all placed their orders, Quentin leaned toward Lucy in a rather intimate manner. "If I remember correctly, you're something of an investigative reporter."

Hearing this, Laura Barfield's head snapped around and she stared at Lucy. Conversation had stopped and

Lucy found everyone waiting for her reply. "Not really, although I do write a little bit for the Tinker's Cove weekly newspaper, the *Pennysaver.* Pam here is married to the owner."

"Don't be so modest." Quentin turned to the table at large. "Lucy cracked a case that had the police completely baffled. A murder."

Lucy could have killed him. The last thing she wanted was to be the center of attention. "It was a sad, tragic incident," she said, "and not really suitable for dinner table conversation."

"I quite agree," said Laura primly. "I was brought up to avoid controversy at dinner. Religion, politics, and money were all strictly banned at my mother's table." She paused, turning to Emma. "How was your day?"

Emma leaned to the side, making room for the waiter to put down her glass of white wine. "Thank you for asking. I'm afraid I encountered a bit more red tape than I expected."

"That is too bad." Laura seemed determined to keep the polite chatter going. "It's really the curse of the modern world, don't you think? Life has gotten so complicated. I recently changed my Internet service, and I can't tell you how confusing it was."

"Too many choices—that's the problem." Dr. Cope was twirling his old-fashioned, waiting for everyone to be served.

"You're exactly right," agreed Tom Smith. "First thing I have to do when I get home is my income tax. I'm not looking forward to that!"

The waiter had set down the last glass and Quentin was on his feet. "I'd like to propose a toast to our dear friend and colleague George Temple."

A few glances were exchanged but everyone raised their glass.

"*Requiescat in pace.*" Quentin took a big gulp of his red wine.

"Amen," said Rachel, prompting a responsive murmur and a few nods as everyone took a swallow.

Lucy felt badly for Emma, who she suspected might rather not be reminded of her father's death, but the young woman didn't seem upset. She joined the others in raising her glass and downed a hearty swallow before turning to Ann Smith, who was seated beside her, and referring to the menu. "What looks good?"

The next few minutes were spent placing their orders, but when the waiter ambled off to the kitchen, Lucy seized the opportunity to ask Quentin about George Temple. "Did you know George well?"

"Not well, no," he said, speaking slowly and making plenty of eye contact. "Although he had been at the college for some time. He arrived shortly after I started there, perhaps in the early nineties. He was middle-aged then. I think he had changed careers in midlife. He was popular with the students, and he led one of these trips every year, but he wasn't a true academic. His knowledge was wide but not deep, if you know what I mean." He smiled at Emma. "But that's not to say he wasn't a committed, caring teacher, quite competent to teach introductory-level courses. He was an adjunct, you know, not on the tenure track."

"That's not what I heard," said Lucy, remembering her conversation with Pam. "I heard he was being considered for some professor's job."

Quentin chuckled and promptly changed the subject. "What do you think of the English newspapers?"

"Pretty racy if you ask me," said Tom Smith with a leer. "Topless girls, right on page three."

Ann didn't approve. "Oh, Tom," she said. "Not in front of—"

"The kids?" Tom finished the sentence for her. "I imagine they could teach us a few things."

The food took a while to come, giving them all time to order a second round of drinks, which Lucy suspected might be intentional on the part of the restaurant. Quentin remained focused on Lucy, saying he'd followed her career in the *Pennysaver.*

"Not much of a career, really. I don't get to write as much as I'd like. I mostly edit the events listings." Lucy giggled; she was tired and that second glass of wine was going straight to her head.

"And what about your family?" Quentin was doing that thing again, running his tongue over his upper lip.

"The kids are growing up. Toby is married and has a baby boy."

Quentin's eyebrows lifted. "Don't tell me you're a grandmother?"

Lucy laughed. She had to admit it was nice to have someone paying attention to her. She loved Bill, but he did tend to take her for granted.

"And your husband?"

Lucy felt that Quentin was testing the waters, and it was time to let him know these seas were definitely chilly. "Bill is keeping the home fires burning, keeping an eye on our youngest girls."

Quentin gave her that half smile of his. "Sounds like you have the perfect family."

Lucy thought of Elizabeth's e-mail. "Not perfect." Quentin leaned a bit closer, apparently taking this as a sign of encouragement. "But okay," she added, pulling away from him.

She was relieved when he turned to his other side and began talking to Autumn. Conversation was lagging, despite Laura's gallant efforts at polite small talk, and more than one member of the tour was yawning when the waiter finally began delivering their dinners. Dr. Cope and Quentin had stuck to their guns and ordered steaks, which looked to be a mistake since the meat was overcooked. Ann Smith's broiled Dover sole, on the other hand, didn't seem to have more than a passing acquaintance with the flame and was still pink and glistening. When she asked the waiter to take it back for another pass under the broiler, he warned her that the chef would be insulted.

Ann wasn't about to insist. "Oh, dear, I guess it's all right." She was picking up her fork when her husband snatched the plate away.

"Don't be ridiculous," he told the waiter. "This hasn't been properly cooked."

The kid took the plate, perching it dangerously close to the edge of the tray, while continuing to distribute the other dishes. He finished passing out the chicken and pasta dishes the others had ordered before taking the fish back to the kitchen.

The younger members of the party immediately began eating, but the others sat waiting for the waiter to bring Ann's plate back.

"Please don't wait for me," she urged. "Your food will get cold."

"Have some of my pasta," offered Rachel, picking up her bread and butter plate and spooning some pasta primavera onto it.

"We didn't get any rolls," observed Lucy.

Sue had taken a bite of chicken, then put down her fork. "This chicken is weird. It's some sort of processed meat."

"Well, the steak is delicious," insisted Quentin, chewing energetically.

"I wouldn't go quite that far," said Dr. Cope.

"English food isn't supposed to be very good," said Emma, carefully cutting away the brown edges of a piece of broccoli.

The waiter returned with Ann's sole, which was now as brown and tough as a cedar shingle. "Can you get us some bread or rolls?" asked Lucy.

The waiter squinted. "Costs extra, you know."

"We'll pay," said Pam in a no-nonsense tone. "And don't forget the butter."

They had just about finished eating as much of the awful food as they could manage when the waiter returned with a basket of sliced soft white sandwich bread. It was passed along quickly as everyone took a slice, hoping to gain enough sustenance to survive until breakfast.

"Can I interest you in dessert or coffee?" inquired the waiter, pencil poised to take their orders.

"None for me," said Lucy, rising to go to the restroom. If the dinner was anything to go by, the coffee was sure to be thin and lukewarm, she thought as she groped her way down the poorly lit stairway. The door to the ladies' room was missing the letter *L* but when she entered, it was brightly lit, which was unfortunate considering the state of the facilities. She wrinkled her nose at the unpleasant smell and cautiously pushed open the stall door, expecting to find a filthy situation. The toilet was passably clean, however, and she was sit-

ting on it when she heard the outer door open and recognized Jennifer's and Caroline's voices.

She leaned forward, straining to hear what they
were saying, but only caught a few words: "Autumn . . .
who does she . . . like it was her idea . . ."

Lucy zipped up her jeans, flushed the toilet, and
pushed open the door, catching a glimpse of the two
girls with their heads together. Realizing they weren't
alone, they suddenly stopped talking and Caroline
rushed past her into the single stall.

"I didn't mean to startle you," said Lucy, leaning over
the grubby sink and turning on the rusty faucet to wash
her hands.

Jennifer was brushing her long blond hair, absorbed
by her own reflection in the cracked mirror. "No problem," she said. Her voice was cool and assured, and it
struck Lucy that she hadn't heard her use that tone before now, and certainly not when she was talking to Autumn.

Lucy found a clean spot on the roller towel—a relic
of the past that she hadn't seen in years—and dried her
hands. "See you later," she said, leaving the room. As
she made her way up the dusty stairs with the broken
rubber treads, she had the uncomfortable feeling that
something wasn't quite right but attributed it to her digestion.

"We'll be lucky if we don't come down with food poi-
soning," she told Sue as she added her twenty-pound
note to the pile in the center of the table.

Sue shoved her mostly untouched plate away and
glanced at the stuffed bull's head. "We should have
risked mad cow disease."

Chapter Eight

When the morning sun brightened the gap in the flowered curtains the next morning, Lucy was surprised to find she had slept through the night and felt fine. Jet lag was apparently a thing of the past. It was only six, though, and Sue was still asleep, so Lucy pulled a sweater over her pajamas and tiptoed out of the room, intending to get a cup of coffee from the machine in the lounge. Some of the rooms didn't have bathrooms, and there were shared facilities off the stair landing. She paused in one on the way downstairs, pleased that she didn't have to disturb Sue by using the loo in their room.

The lounge was deserted at this early hour. The couches and easy chairs, upholstered in varying shades of red, were somewhat rumpled and still bearing the imprints of last night's occupants. Lucy prepared her coffee and took it over to the computer, enjoying a few sips while she waited for the PC to warm up and let her log on. In a few minutes, she'd finished her coffee and was scrolling through her e-mail, deleting all the junk mail. She wrote a funny account of the horrible Ye Olde English Roast Beef restaurant to Bill and sent it and was about to log off when a message from Elizabeth popped up.

What on earth was the girl doing, writing e-mails at two in the morning? Lucy shook her head in dismay as she opened the message, which was written entirely in capital letters. Elizabeth was clearly upset.

MOM I HAD THAT MEETING WITH THE DEAN AND SHE'S REALLY A STUPID WOMAN WHO DOESN'T KNOW ANYTHING ABOUT OUR SCHOOL TRADITIONS. THE ENTIRE SENIOR CLASS ALWAYS HAS A CANDLELIGHT PROCESSION DOWN NEWBURY STREET TO THE PUBLIC GARDEN THE NIGHT BEFORE GRADUATION. THEN WE ALL STAND AROUND THE LAKE THERE WITH CANDLES AND SING THE ALMA MATER. WE'VE BEEN DOING IT FOR OVER A HUNDRED YEARS AND NOW THIS AWFUL WOMAN SAYS WE CAN'T DO IT. HONESTLY I'D LIKE TO KILL HER!!!

Lucy got up and fixed herself another cup of coffee while trying to think how to reply. Sipping thoughtfully, she stood for a minute in front of the windows, looking out at the empty street and the neat row houses on the opposite side. She had such high hopes for Elizabeth. She hoped the girl wasn't going to sabotage herself before she got started in life.

Dear Elizabeth,
I understand that you're upset about the changes the dean has proposed, but you need to remember that the world has changed quite a lot in the past hundred years. I'm sure the dean is concerned about the

students' safety as well as liability issues. The school
would be responsible if there was an accident and
somebody got burned.
I hope you were polite during your meeting. Perhaps
you should consider apologizing and trying to work
out a compromise of some sort.
You need to keep your RA job—we can't afford the
additional expense if you lose it.
Stay in touch.
Love,
Mom

Lucy reread the message a few times, then clicked
SEND, at the same time sending up a little wish that it
would all work out. She picked up her half-full cup of
coffee and made a fresh one for Sue, then started up
the stairs to their room.

Sue was just waking up when Lucy opened the door.
"You're an angel," she said when Lucy set the coffee on
her nightstand. After she'd had a few swallows, she
stretched her arms over her head. "So what are we
doing today?"

"The Victoria and Albert Museum," said Lucy, grabbing her towel and heading for the shower.

"The Victoria and Albert Museum is the world's
largest with over seven miles of galleries," said Quentin.
The group was seated together in one end of a carriage
on the Piccadilly Line, and he was standing above them,
hanging on to a pole as he delivered a brief introduc-
tory lecture. "It was the vision of Prince Albert to create
a collection that would be available to all people to in-

spire and inform them. Some of the highlights include the Raphael Room, the British Galleries, and the Islamic and Indian Galleries."

Sue was studying her guidebook. "It's also quite near Harrods."

Quentin sighed. "Yes, it is."

"We'll give it a quick look," said Sue, speaking to her friends and keeping her voice low, as if plotting a conspiracy. "Then we'll go shopping. Harrods is the world's most famous, most fabulous department store."

Her fellow conspirators weren't convinced. "I want to see the Great Bed of Ware," protested Pam.

"I want to see it all," said Rachel.

Lucy noticed Sue's expression darkening—she liked to get her way. "There's that exhibit of hats you were talking about," she reminded her friend.

"Okay." Sue was amenable. "I'll look at the hats while you all do the boring stuff."

Lucy felt rather overwhelmed when they arrived at the museum and paused under the enormous Dale Chihuly glass sculpture that looked like a nest of snakes. She unfolded a floor plan and studied it, trying to decide where to begin.

"I think we should start with the British Galleries," suggested Pam, looking over her shoulder.

"I imagine that's where they keep the Great Bed of Ware," said Rachel, amused.

"And Grinling Gibbons's cravat—it's a necktie entirely carved of wood. I saw it in a magazine." Pam was bouncing on her toes, as excited as a kid at an amusement park.

"Doesn't sound very comfortable to me," observed Sue. "I'll stick to hats."

"I always get lost in museums," confessed Lucy. "We better have a meeting place, just in case. Let's meet in the café at one."

Sue liked that idea. "Then we can decide if you want to continue here at the museum or go on to Harrods where they have the really good stuff—and you can buy it."

"Don't hesitate to let us know what you'd like to do," cracked Rachel. "Just speak up."

"You'll see. I'm right," predicted Sue, marching off to buy a ticket for the special exhibition.

Lucy and the others headed for the British Galleries, but when Lucy paused to study a display of Victorian tableware, she lost track of Pam and Rachel. A few twists and turns took her to a roomful of antique medical instruments, and she soon found herself both fascinated and appalled by treatments once considered effective, such as purging and bloodletting. Shockingly, some of the crudest apparatuses, like surgical saws and obstetrical forceps, were still in use today.

Lucy was staring at a jar of leeches preserved in formaldehyde when Ann Smith joined her. "Disgusting, aren't they?" observed Ann.

"They sure are," agreed Lucy, wondering that Ann had managed to separate herself from her husband and daughter.

The mystery was soon solved. "Have you seen Tom and Caroline? I seem to have lost them."

"It's easy to do here," said Lucy. "I lost my friends, too. Shall we stick together?"

Ann was eager to accept her offer. "I'd appreciate it. I get a little panicky when I'm alone."

"I guess we all do," said Lucy, who didn't really think

that at all. It seemed to her that she rarely had a moment to herself, and she liked being alone now and then.

Ann's gaze had fallen on a glass case containing a glittering display of saws and scalpels, and she seemed to physically shrink. "Actually, I think I've seen enough here."

Lucy was agreeable. "Me too. This exhibit is enough to make you appreciate modern medicine."

"I suppose." Ann wasn't looking at either side as they passed through the gallery but kept her eyes lowered, studying the floor tiles.

"They say George Washington's doctors actually killed him by bleeding him too much." Lucy was just making conversation and didn't expect the reaction she got.

Ann whirled around. Her thin body was quivering beneath the worn beige sweater and shapeless brown pants that were too big for her, and red circles had appeared on her cheeks. "Everybody talks about the miracles of modern medicine and says how Americans have the best medical system in the world, but it's not true," she declared, sounding like she'd just bitten into a very sour lemon. "Believe me, they can't save everyone, and they don't even try if you don't have the money to pay. And medical insurance—that's a joke! They take your money, all right, but when you try to file a claim, they find ways to disqualify you."

"It's terrible, I know," said Lucy, who knew all about the problems with medical insurance. Bill was self-employed, and their premium had recently passed their mortgage to become their largest monthly expense. She grudgingly wrote the check every month, but she had no illusions that even the best health insurance policy could guarantee to cure everyone. "Dr. Cope did his best but he couldn't save George Temple."

"Temple! Is that who you think I'm talking about?"

Ann was agitated, quivering with emotion, but exactly what emotion? Lucy wasn't sure what was upsetting her. She kept her voice calm, fearful of agitating her further. "What's the trouble?" she asked. "Can I help?"

Ann laughed, a sudden, harsh explosion of sound. "Help! If only." A sob escaped from between her lips and she pressed them together. "Nobody could help my baby. My baby boy."

"I'm so sorry." Lucy suddenly understood. The Smiths had lost a child. No wonder they clung so tightly to Caroline. She felt a huge surge of sympathy for Ann, knowing that her greatest fear was losing one of her children.

"He died when he was one."

Lucy thought of her grandson Patrick, who would soon have his first birthday. She thought of his soft, fair hair and his chubby wrists and dimpled cheeks, and she knew she couldn't bear to lose him. "That's terrible," she said.

Ann had grabbed Lucy's arm, and her grip tightened. "It was my fault."

"These things happen." Lucy was beginning to worry that Ann might go completely to pieces and looked around the empty gallery, hoping to see Tom and Caroline coming in search of her. Where were they? Where was everybody? Thousands of people come to the V&A every day. How come none of them were coming to this exhibit? Ann needed help—that much was obvious—and Lucy didn't know what to do.

"It didn't have to happen." Ann's eyes were open but

she wasn't seeing Lucy. She was in a trance. The words kept coming, as if once started on this story she couldn't stop. "It was the brakes. We knew they were going, but money, there was never enough money back then, so we kept putting it off. It was always next week—we'd get it done next week. And then it was too late. Caroline was in the hospital for a month. I was there even longer, until the insurance money ran out and they sent me home. That was when they told me that little Bobby was gone. They'd been afraid to tell me before."

Ann was now leaning on Lucy for support, and Lucy felt as if Ann might collapse at any moment, taking them both down.

"When I got home, there was nothing left of Bobby except a little stone in the cemetery. Tom had even cleaned out his room. He said he thought it would be easier for me."

Lucy felt as if her heart were being ripped from her chest as she led Ann to a bench in the stairwell. "Why don't you sit for a minute?" she suggested, lowering the woman onto the seat as if she were a fragile old lady. Then she seated herself beside Ann and took her hand, patting it. That's how they were when Tom and Caroline came up the steps, reminding Lucy of the cavalry in an old Western movie. Like the folks inside the circle of wagons, she felt a huge sense of relief.

"What's happened?" asked Tom, rushing to his wife's side. Behind him, Caroline was breathing heavily from the exertion of getting her extra weight up the stairs.

"Ann was upset by this medical exhibit," said Lucy, standing up. She couldn't wait to get away. "I have to meet my friends in the café," she said, apologizing for her abrupt departure.

* * *

Lucy found her friends seated at a table in part of the café that was decorated in what she now knew, thanks to her brief foray into the British Galleries, as the Arts and Crafts style. Stained glass, colorful tiles, and heavy wood paneling created a cozy nook in the huge, bustling café, where you fetched your food from various serving stations. The girls had already bought cups of tea and were waiting for her before getting their food. Sue wanted only a small salad, so she stayed at the table to save their seats while they got in line at one of the busy cafeteria counters.

"What happened to you?" asked Rachel as they waited to place their orders.

"I don't know. I was looking at some silver and then I couldn't find you, and then I got sidetracked by Ann Smith." Lucy didn't want to say more until she'd sorted out her own emotions, which were still in turmoil. She felt badly for Ann, of course, but she also resented the way Ann had burdened her with such an unhappy story.

"I hope you didn't miss the Great Bed of Ware." Pam was studying the list of menu choices above the counter.

"I think I did. How great was it?"

Pam smiled. "Pretty great. You could fit the whole family in that bed."

"Including grandma, the dog, and a chicken or twelve," added Rachel.

"Which they probably did," said Lucy, appreciating her friends' humor.

"What can I get you?" asked the server, a chubby-cheeked woman.

"Cottage pie." After the unfortunate dinner at Ye Olde English Roast Beef, Lucy had decided the best strategy was to eat heartily when food was available and affordable, and looked good.

Pam and Rachel agreed. "Make that three," said Pam. "And a small salad."

"What exactly keeps Sue going?" asked Pam as they carried their heavily loaded trays back to their table. "What does she run on?"

Lucy shrugged. "Don't ask me. It's nothing but black coffee, salad, and wine, but she has plenty of energy. I can't keep up with her."

"I worry about her." Rachel shook her head. "It's not healthy."

"She's never sick," observed Pam.

"She looks great." The three stopped, simultaneously dropping their jaws, spotting Sue in conversation with a handsome man dressed in a beautifully tailored suit. He had one hand on the back of a chair and was leaning forward, practically dripping charm all over the table.

The three exchanged glances and marched forward in unison. "Here's your salad," said Lucy, placing it in front of Sue.

"These are my friends," said Sue with a graceful wave of her well-tended hand. "Pam, Rachel, and Lucy, this is Perry." She paused, savoring the moment. "He's an earl."

"Nice to meet you." Lucy felt a bit like the upstairs maid, standing there holding her tray. "Are we supposed to curtsy or something?"

"Not a bit. All that's rather gone out of style these days." There was a touch of gray at his temples, his eyes were blue, and his smile revealed a mess of crooked teeth. His gaze returned to Sue. "If you're interested in my collection, just ring me."

Then he was gone and the girls were plunking themselves down at the table, giggling like middle schoolers.

"And what exactly does the earl collect?" inquired Pam. "Etchings?"

Sue was shaking her head. "I married too young. If I'd only known this day would come, I would have saved myself." She speared a piece of lettuce with her fork. "And we have so much in common. I like castles and he has a castle. I like hats and he collects hats, with an emphasis on hats with feathers," she said, provoking gales of laughter.

"I guess he's safe enough, then," observed Rachel drily.

"It's good to know we don't need to worry about protecting your virtue," added Pam.

"I wouldn't be so sure," said Lucy. "He seemed awfully interested."

"No," sighed Sue. "He's after my feather fascinator." Seeing their blank looks, Sue continued. "You know, the little hat I wore at Lizzy Muse's wedding. There was one quite like it in the show, and apparently Camilla wore one at her wedding to Prince Charles. Perry says it was divine, and he tried to buy it but Camilla won't sell. Sentimental reasons, he says." She chewed slowly. "I might sell him mine."

Pam was buttering a roll. "She's obviously lost her mind."

Lucy nodded. "There's only one thing that will bring her back."

"Retail therapy," suggested Rachel.

Sue gave a shaky little sigh. "I do think it's my only hope."

When they joined the stream of people pushing into Harrods—Lucy was quickly learning that people from many other countries do not necessarily have the same sense of personal space that Americans do—they passed glass cases displaying all sorts of luxury items: sunglasses costing hundreds of pounds, handbags costing thousands, watches costing tens of thousands. It was a bit overwhelming until you realized that nobody was buying. This was a temple to consumerism, and the high-priced goods were designed to awe the tourists who streamed past, nudging each other and whispering the astronomical prices.

You would have thought they were in church, thought Lucy with disapproval. "Let's start with the famous food hall."

"I've heard it's amazing," agreed Rachel.

"I did not come to Harrods to go to the supermarket," protested Sue. "I want to see the designer clothes."

"And I want to use the luxury loo," said Pam. "We need a plan."

"I have one," said Sue, consulting her guidebook. "They have a tearoom. Let's meet there at four-thirty."

The four then split up, Pam and Sue taking an elevator up and Lucy and Rachel taking one down to the cavernous food hall.

Seeing the white tile walls with their mosaics picturing foodstuffs and the refrigerated cases containing every sort of meat, Lucy felt she was in familiar surroundings. She shopped for groceries every week, and Harrods food hall wasn't that much different from the IGA in Tinker's Cove. Except, of course, that it was bigger and had a greater variety of products, and the prices were much higher.

"Imagine," said Rachel. "Thirty-two pounds for a hunk of meat."

Lucy was not about to be discouraged. She oohed in delight when she found quail eggs for sale, she admired the glistening fresh fish, and she exclaimed over the fresh-baked bread and rolls. Unable to resist the temptation to buy, she purchased four apples and four oranges in the produce section and was delighted when the clerk wrapped them in one of the highly desirable green plastic carry bags with the Harrods name in gold.

Rachel wanted to get some books for Miss Tilley, so they found an escalator and ascended, rising past a statue of a young man and woman with their arms stretched toward a soaring seagull. Lucy studied it, realizing with shock that the figures were representations of Princess Diana and her boyfriend, Dodi Fayed. Reaching the landing, she saw there was a book in which visitors could inscribe their names, just like the guestbooks provided at the funeral home back in Tinker's Cove. But this wasn't a funeral home; it was a department store and hardly seemed a suitable place for a memorial.

Stunned, she turned to Rachel. "Isn't this the tackiest thing you've ever seen?"

Rachel gave a little half smile, "The man who owns Harrods is Dodi's father. It's his way of making sure his son isn't forgotten."

Lucy stepped off the escalator and through the archway leading to the book department, among others. "It seems an odd way to do it."

"People grieve differently, but I don't think anybody ever gets over the loss of a child, even if that child is grown."

Lucy reached for the spot on her arm where Ann

Smith had gripped it, noticing it was a little tender. She thought of her four children and of Toby's wife, Molly, and their son Patrick, hoping they were all healthy and happy, and she knew that if she were to lose one of them, she would grieve until the day she died.

Chapter Nine

While Rachel was looking for English mysteries to bring back to Miss Tilley, Lucy wandered into the toy department where she looked for a birthday present for Patrick. When she found a little stuffed Paddington Bear to go along with the first book in the series, she bought it, getting another Harrods bag in the bargain. Then they wandered through the housewares, deploring the fact that crockery, no matter how adorable, was an impractical souvenir, being both heavy and liable to break. At four-thirty, they went to the tearoom as planned, only to discover Sue and Pam standing in front of a door with a CLOSED sign.

"It's undergoing renovations," said Sue. "This store has more than thirty restaurants and they have to close the tearoom."

Pam was indignant. "How many days have we been here? Three? Four? And we haven't had afternoon tea yet. What's happened to England?"

"We can go to the pub or the Asian grill or the pizza palace," suggested Rachel. "What about the coffee bar?"

Sue was pouting. "I want tea. I'm in England and I want tea."

"I have an idea," said Lucy. "Meet me at the Tube station in half an hour."

"Let's meet at six," said Sue, who had found some interesting information in her guidebook. "There are lots more stores around here. Harvey Nichols. Habitat. Burberry. If we can't have tea, we might as well shop."

"We can't afford those places," protested Pam.

"But you can always dream," said Sue, marching off with Pam and Rachel following in her wake.

Lucy found a very tired trio drooping on a bench when she arrived at the Tube station a few minutes after six, laden with more Harrods bags.

Sue looked at the bulging green bags suspiciously. "This isn't like you, Lucy. What have you been buying?"

"Food," said Lucy. "Good, wholesome food. Cheese and fruit and salads and bread and even some nice tea—I figured we could get hot water from that weird machine in the lounge. Oh, and I got a couple bottles of wine, too. We'll eat in tonight."

"Good idea." Pam was rising to her feet as the train slid into the station. "I'm too tired to go out."

Rachel secured her purse under her arm as she boarded the train. "And I'm sick of paying too much money for really bad food."

"Did you say tea?" asked Sue, perking up.

"Yes, dear. I found your favorite Lapsang souchong."

"You really are a pal," observed Sue, sinking into the seat a handsome man in a tan trench coat promptly vacated for her.

* * *

Back at the hotel, they all crowded into Lucy and Sue's room where Lucy spread out the food on her bed, picnic style. Sue poured the wine into bathroom tumblers. Lucy tugged her swollen feet out of her shoes and tucked a pillow behind her aching back, reclining against the headboard.

Rachel and Pam brought in pillows and a chair from their room, and soon they were all comfortably settled.

"So what did you think of Harrods?" Lucy asked Sue. "Was it everything you dreamed of?"

Sue was spreading some pâté on a bit of bread. "And more. Especially when it came to prices. I didn't buy anything. I just couldn't do it."

"Even I broke down and bought this," declared Pam, holding up a gaudy flower-printed tote bag with the Harrods logo prominently embroidered beneath the handles in gold thread.

Lucy gulped. "For you?"

"That's not your style at all," observed Sue.

"No. Not for me. It's a gift for Phyllis."

Phyllis, the receptionist at the *Pennysaver*, was known for her flamboyant taste. "She'll love it," said Lucy.

"I got a good deal on books," said Rachel, digging into a container of bean salad with a plastic fork. "If you bought two, you got a third free—and I know Miss T hasn't read them."

Lucy's keen detective mind recalled seeing Sue with a small bag. "You did buy something, though," she said, looking at her friend accusingly. "What is it?"

"I'm guilty as charged," admitted Sue. "I found a lovely camisole in Harvey Nichols." She held up the wisp of lace for the girls to admire. "It was expensive but I think it was a good value."

The other three exchanged doubtful glances. High fashion in Tinker's Cove usually meant something warm and woolly.

"Really! It was less expensive than it might have been, because I found it in the lingerie department. And I can wear it lots of ways: underwear, nightwear, even under a suit to dress it up for evening."

Lucy was dipping into the salad, trying to imagine a situation in which she might wear something like the camisole and failing. "I bought a Paddington Bear for Patrick," she said. Thinking of her chubby little grandson reminded her of Ann Smith's terrible loss, and she felt a bit guilty for the way she had fled from the distraught woman.

"What do you think of the tour so far?" asked Pam, holding out her glass for a refill. "The people, I mean."

Sue was pouring the wine. "Quentin's got a thing for Lucy, that's for sure."

Lucy held out her glass, too. "He's got a thing for anything female. Didn't you notice him flirting with Autumn?"

"That girl is trouble," said Pam.

"She definitely has some serious issues," observed Rachel. "And so does Jennifer. I think she's anorexic."

"Her grandfather keeps a close eye on her," said Lucy.

"And Laura Barfield sure keeps tabs on her son," said Pam. "Poor Will—he's desperate to escape."

"I wonder what happened to his father," mused Lucy. "I wouldn't want to raise a son without a husband."

"Maybe he just didn't come on the trip," speculated Sue. "The Smiths are certainly a tight little family unit. I can't imagine Sidra ever clinging to Sid and me the way Caroline sticks to her parents."

Lucy put down her glass. "I ran into Ann in this gruesome exhibit of surgical tools. She'd gotten separated from Tom and Caroline and was frantic over it. She told me she had a little boy who died in an auto accident when he was a baby. She was pretty upset."

"Why was she telling you that?" asked Sue.

"I don't know, really. My sympathetic face?" Lucy tried to make light of it but couldn't quite carry it off. "It was pretty strange. I mean, it must have happened at least eighteen years ago. She said Caroline was a baby when it happened."

"You'd think she'd be over it by now," said Sue.

Rachel ran her finger around the rim of her glass. "The loss of a child stays with you forever. It changes your personality, your outlook on life, your relationships. It's like an emotional earthquake. Nothing is the same afterward."

Lucy thought of the statue of Diana and Dodi, soaring heavenward along with a seagull and decided it was an attempt, perhaps a futile attempt, to recast their terrible fate into something more acceptable. She supposed a lot of people would rather think of them as happy spirits than recall the sordid details of that crash in a filthy Paris tunnel.

Falling silent, they heard a soft knock on the door. When Sue opened it, she found Emma Temple standing there, holding a white blouse.

"Oh, I'm sorry to barge in like this," she said, retreating.

"No, no. Come in," invited Lucy. "What can we do for you?"

"I'm looking for a needle and thread. A button is coming loose on this blouse and I want to wear it tomorrow."

Pam, always as prepared as a good scout, popped up. "I've got a sewing kit in my room. I'll be right back."

"Oh, don't go to any trouble . . ."

"It's no trouble—it's right next door. Have some wine while I get it."

"Yes, do," said Lucy, noticing that Emma's eyes were lingering over the picnic spread out on the bed. "And some food. We've got plenty."

Emma swallowed. "Are you sure?"

"Absolutely," said Rachel. "We can't eat it all, and we have no way of keeping it."

"I'm starving," admitted Emma. "I simply couldn't face Ye Olde English Roast Beef again."

"Dive in—I hope you don't mind fingers. We're a bit short on cutlery." Lucy eased herself off the bed carefully so as not to spill anything and went into the bathroom for another glass. Emerging, she held it aloft. "Some chardonnay?"

"Actually, I'd prefer water." Emma was spreading some pâté on a hunk of baguette.

Sue was on her feet, too. "I was just going downstairs to get some hot water for tea. Would you like some?"

"Tea would be heaven," Emma said. "I've had a really tiring day."

She did look exhausted, thought Lucy. Emma had pulled her hair back into a sloppy ponytail, and her makeup had worn off to reveal pale, colorless lips and dark circles under her eyes. Beneath that glossy professional surface, she was really only a very young, vulnerable girl. "Were you able to make all the, um, arrangements?" she asked.

"Yes." Emma flashed a quick smile of thanks to Pam when she returned with a little plastic case containing threaded needles. "These are great. I don't know if I could see to thread a needle, my eyes are that tired," she said, choosing the white one. "I can't wait to take out my contacts."

"Let me do that," said Lucy, taking the blouse. "I'll sew while you eat."

In a matter of minutes, she had stitched the loose button back in place and bitten off the thread.

"That was fast," said Emma as Sue returned with five paper cups of tea precariously balanced on a guidebook she was using as a makeshift tray.

"I made some for everybody, to save another trip downstairs," she explained between gasps for breath. "Or another climb upstairs."

"Do we have dessert?" asked Rachel, glancing at a small white box tied with string.

"Cookies!" exclaimed Lucy, lifting the lid. "Scottish shortbread."

"Perfect!" declared Rachel, choosing a petticoat tail and taking a bite. "I can't believe Ye Olde English Roast Beef is the only restaurant in London. There must be better places."

"This is my first trip to London," said Emma, sipping her tea. "I have to say it's been a bit of a disappointment. I'm glad I'm going home tomorrow."

"London's great," declared Sue. "I think your perception may be colored by your sad mission. You haven't had time to shop or see the sights or go to the theater."

Rachel nodded in agreement. "It's always hard to lose a parent."

Emma shook her head. "Honestly, he was like a stranger to me."

Rachel was having none of that; she knew all about the tricks the mind could play. "Sometimes being estranged makes it even harder."

Emma sniffed. "Unresolved issues?"

"Exactly." Rachel was reaching for another cookie.

"Frankly, I think I'm suffering more from jet lag than grief." She sighed. "Plus the frustration of dealing with very polite but very obstinate bureaucrats."

They all laughed and Lucy took advantage of the moment to pose a question that had been bothering her. "Is the coroner still satisfied that anaphylactic shock was the cause of death?"

Emma's big blue eyes widened in surprise. "Why, yes. Isn't that what happened? Some of you were right there, weren't you?"

"Right there," said Sue. "Just across the aisle."

Emma's face softened. "That must have been terrible for you."

Sue was philosophical. "They gave us free drinks."

Lucy was shocked at Sue's rudeness, fearing Emma would be insulted. But instead, she tilted her head back and laughed. "That's exactly what my mother said when she heard. She said that if the airline gave everyone free drinks because he died, it would be the nicest thing he ever did."

No one quite knew how to react—except Sue. "That must have been one really nasty divorce."

Emma nodded. "I think so. It all happened when I was quite small. I don't remember anything about it. It's always been just Mom and me, but that's the way it was for a lot of kids in my school. Some had stepparents they hated, so I figured I was pretty lucky to have Mom all to myself. We always got along fine; we're a lot alike. And Mom made a good living as a court reporter.

That's how I got interested in the law—sometimes she'd bring me along if it was an interesting case."

Sue drained her teacup. "So there was no picture of Dad on the mantel?"

"No Dad at all." Emma grinned. "Really, I could have been the product of an immaculate conception. No Dad, no men. Mom wasn't interested in dating. One time I asked her about it, and she said once was enough and that was all I could get out of her."

Rachel tapped her lip with a finger. "Did she discourage you from dating?"

"Not in so many words, but she did keep me pretty busy. School was a top priority, and there were lots of dance and music lessons, soccer, Girl Scouts. She always said it was important for me to be able to support myself and not to expect some Prince Charming to rescue me."

Lucy approved. "That's good advice. That's what I tell my girls."

Rachel was thoughtful. "But weren't you curious about your father?"

"Yeah," agreed Pam. "Didn't you want to know if heart disease or cancer or hemophilia ran in his family?"

Emma laughed. "I think I'm a little too young to worry about that stuff, but it's a good point. I know he had allergies, that's for sure, but I don't seem to have any." She paused. "Maybe now that he's gone, Mom will be more willing to talk about him. I definitely would like to know more about him."

Pam was fingering the sewing case. "For what it's worth, I can tell you he was well liked at Winchester College. I never heard anyone say a bad word about him. He always got high marks on the student evaluations every year, even the underground one the students do.

They said his classes were interesting, and he took an interest in the students. And he was popular with the faculty, too. I teach a yoga class, evening school, you know, and he was a regular. He was very good, very flexible." Pam's expression was thoughtful as she trolled for memories. "He had a nice attitude, serious but not too serious. I'll miss him."

Emma impulsively wrapped an arm around Pam's shoulder and hugged her. "Thank you. That means a lot to me." She got to her feet. "I really need to turn in. I've got to be at Heathrow at five tomorrow morning. Thanks for everything."

"You're welcome," said Pam. "Have a safe trip."

"Safe home," said Lucy, beginning to clear away the food wrappers in hopes that the others would take the hint. She was tired and talked out; she wanted to sleep. But when she'd brushed her teeth and slid between the sheets, she found her mind was a whirl of conflicting images. George Temple had seemed like a nice enough person; that's certainly how Pam had seen him, but not his wife. Why had she cut him out of her life so completely? What had he done?

Chapter Ten

There was definitely a different atmosphere in the breakfast room Wednesday morning. Lucy noticed it as soon as she and Sue entered. Instead of the usual hushed silence, there was a lively buzz of conversation. When she seated herself and glanced about, she noticed that everyone from the tour was there, except Quentin and, of course, Emma, who had had to catch an early flight back to the United States. This was a definite departure from the usual order of things—Autumn, Will, and Jennifer had taken to skipping breakfast the last couple of mornings, presumably so they could sleep in as long as possible. But today all three were gathered at a table, chirping away as bright as birds.

"Am I hallucinating or is something different?" asked Lucy as the waitress brought their pot of coffee and filled their cups.

Sue was lifting her cup. "I guess they're excited about going to Brighton."

Lucy took a sip of coffee and considered. The itinerary for the day was a bus trip to the famous seaside town, where they would tour the Royal Pavilion. Lucy knew a bit about the town from reading English mysteries: It featured a honky-tonk pier as well as the Pavilion, which was an architectural marvel built as a private pleasure palace by some prince. "I don't think that's it," she said. "It's like some big cloud has lifted." She lowered her voice. "Do you think it's because Emma's gone?"

"Could be, but I think it's more likely they're excited about the roller coaster." Sue was refilling her cup. "I can't say I share their enthusiasm. It sounds hideous: a fusty old historical building and an amusement park. It's not really my sort of thing."

"There's shopping, too." Lucy had checked her guidebook. "Adorable boutiques in an area known as the Lanes."

Sue perked up, causing Lucy to wonder if it was the caffeine or the possibility of more shopping. Pam and Lucy joined them, and the waitress announced today's breakfast was egg, bacon, and sausage.

"Oh, my, that's a lot of protein," said Pam.

"Fat, you mean," said Sue. "Just toast for me."

Lucy was ready for a change. "I'll have the egg and sausage, but no bacon."

"Bran cereal for me," said Rachel.

"I'm going for the whole kit and caboodle," declared Pam. "It looks like we have a busy day ahead of us." She drank some coffee. "They say Brighton is known for its fish-and-chips shops."

"And the candy—Brighton rock." Lucy was watching as Quentin made his entrance, pausing in the doorway before joining the three students at their table. Will and Jennifer reacted as Lucy expected, straightening up and giving him polite smiles. He was a professor after all, and they were hoping to earn a couple of credits on this trip. Autumn, however, kept her elbows on the table and gave him a slow smile, as if they shared a secret.

Quentin didn't sit down, however, but picked up a spoon and tapped his glass, causing conversation to cease.

"Just a quick announcement. We will depart by minibus, or minicoach as they call it here, at precisely nine o'clock, so don't be late." He waved a warning finger, which Autumn seemed to find hilarious. He raised an eyebrow in her direction and continued. "Also, on a more serious note, I'm sure you know that Emma Temple has left our little group and is now returning to the States. As far as I know, the family is not planning a funeral service, but President Chapman has asked me to inform you that the college will be holding a memorial service on April third, the Friday after we return. She—and I join her in this—hope you will all be able to attend."

The silence that followed this somber announcement was broken by a loud guffaw, and everyone turned to see Tom Smith clapping a hand over his mouth. His wife, Ann, was glaring at him and he quickly apologized. "Sorry. I know that was terribly inappropriate. I was thinking of something amusing that happened yesterday."

Ann did her best to smile, as if she was also recalling the incident. "Yes, we saw the most proper British gentleman on the Tube yesterday, you know the type, in a suit and tie and even an umbrella and a bowler hat, and he had a big piece of newspaper stuck to his shoe!"

She and Tom shared a rather forced laugh, but all they got from the others was a scattering of fleeting smiles. Their story struck Lucy as false; when she left the family at the museum, they hardly seemed to be in a mood to notice such a sight, much less find the least bit of humor in it. But maybe she was wrong, she admitted to herself as the waitress set down a plate loaded with the usual egg and two plump sausages. If she'd learned anything in this life, it was that people often behaved strangely and in ways you didn't expect.

"How's the sausage?" asked Rachel, digging into her bran flakes. "It doesn't look like our sausage."

Indeed it didn't. It was a richer brown color and plumper. Lucy cut a piece, finding it firmer than she expected, and popped it into her mouth. "Not as fatty-tasting and with a hint of spice, nutmeg maybe." She chewed. "It's good. Different, but good."

Sue was pushing her chair away from the table and rising. "I don't know about you guys, but I need to get myself organized for the day," she said, glancing at the sunlight streaming through the window set high in the basement wall. "Don't forget your sunblock!"

"Sunblock?" mused Pam when she'd gone. "Who brings sunblock to England?"

"Sue." Lucy was polishing off her second sausage. "Only Sue."

As always, traffic was heavy and the minicoach progressed with stops and starts through London. The sun made it stuffy in the bus, and Lucy nodded off, waking to find they had reached open countryside and were passing rolling fields divided by hedgerows. This was the England she'd seen so often in movies, generally with a red-coated party of hunters on horseback racing after a pack of baying hounds. Foxhunting had been outlawed, however, so today the hunters were only in her imagination and the horses were grazing peacefully in lush green fields.

She watched the passing scene, noticing how the sky became brighter and the landscape seemed to open up, somehow seeming airier, as they passed a road sign indicating the turn to Brighton. Soon they were winding their way through narrow streets, past shops and houses, until they arrived at the bus drop-off by the Brighton Pier. There they disembarked and gathered on the sidewalk as Quentin fussed about, keeping his troops in order.

"It's a short walk to the Pavilion, which we will tour as a group, and then I will dismiss you to spend the rest of the day as you wish. The bus will pick us up here at this spot at five-thirty." He raised his finger in a gesture that was becoming familiar. "I suggest you look around and familiarize yourself with the area so there will be no confusion when it's time to leave." He waited a moment as they all gazed around, then led them on to the Royal Pavilion.

"We're not in Tinker's Cove anymore," observed Sue as they followed along with the rest of the group, and Lucy knew exactly what she meant. Brighton and Tinker's Cove were both resort towns, perched on the shore, but they had little in common. Tinker's Cove was at heart a country town, with one traffic light. Only a few streets even had sidewalks, which tended to be winding, ramshackle affairs made of various materials—asphalt here, concrete there, and, now and then, a slab of granite. The shops and houses were built of wood with clapboard or cedar shingles for siding. They tended to be one or two stories tall, with peaked roofs.

Some dated from the eighteenth and nineteenth centuries, while others were more recent, generally ranches and a few McMansions.

Brighton, on the other hand, was a busy city, and they were walking on a smooth concrete sidewalk past bus stops and traffic lights. There was a constant hum of traffic rounding the rotary in front of the pier and lots of motorcycles. The buildings, uniformly tall and square, were made of white stone. If it weren't for the brightness and the tangy seaside air, Lucy would have thought she was back in London.

Rounding a corner, they got their first view of the Royal Pavilion, also built of white stone but certainly not foursquare like the others: This fantasy had sprung tall turrets and bulging domes that gave it a fairy-tale atmosphere. Unlike the Tower, there were no walls enclosing this royal domicile, only an iron fence that gave passersby a clear view of the garden. It was sizable, but not enormous, and neither was the Royal Pavilion itself. Lucy thought it had a suburban air to it, as opposed to the heavily fortified Tower of London and the expansive complex at Hampton Court.

Quentin was eager to explain the building's significance, gathering them all in the front entrance. "This was a party house built by the prince regent, a place where he could gather with his friends without the formality of the royal court. He considered himself a bit of a connoisseur of the arts and chose the very new and exciting style that was taking nineteenth-century England by storm: Orientalism. But remember, this is an English adaptation of Oriental style, taken from drawings and written descriptions since few architects and artists had actually been to China or Japan."

Once inside, they were given audioguides that led them along a prescribed circuit. In the enormous dining room, they all stared in awe at the massive table, set for thirty people, and the amazing chandelier. "I really must remodel," quipped Sue, gazing at the glittering fantasia that combined English crystal with Asian dragons.

The group drifted apart as members followed the audioguides at their own pace, stopping to linger as various items caught their interest. Lucy noticed that Autumn's major interest seemed to be sticking as close as possible to Will and wondered if she were making a play for him or perhaps trying to make Quentin jealous. Jennifer tagged along with them but was obviously the odd one out.

"It was okay," said Pam when they emerged into the gift shop, "but it seems like it would take a lot of dusting."

"Like you dust!" scoffed Sue.

Rachel jumped to her defense. "I've seen Pam dust. Once when I stopped by at her house, she answered the door holding a feather duster."

"Ah." Lucy knew that appearances could be deceiving. "You saw her with a duster, but did you actually see her use it?"

Pam quickly changed the subject. "I don't know about you guys, but I'm ready for some fish and chips. When we got off the bus, I saw a place advertising 'world famous fish and chips.' "

Harry Ramsden's was located on a corner opposite the Brighton Pier and was clean and spacious inside. Lucy was a bit disappointed when she was presented with a laminated menu instead of a chalkboard, and the fish and chips were served on a plate instead of wrapped in a sheet of newspaper, but there were consolations.

"They serve wine!" exclaimed Sue, ordering a dry white.

Pam was excited about something else. "And the fish comes with mushy peas! I've always wanted to try them."

When their meals were served, they discovered that she was right. Each portion of battered fried fish and French fries was accompanied by a little round bowl full of astonishingly bright green mush.

Lucy poked her peas suspiciously with her fork. "I never saw peas this color. They look radioactive."

"They're almost glowing," agreed Rachel.

Pam was not to be deterred. She dug in eagerly and lifted a big forkful to her mouth, but her expression of delighted anticipation soon turned to disappointment. "They taste like baby food."

Lucy wasn't tempted by the peas but found the fish delicious.

Sue sprinkled her fries liberally with malt vinegar and nibbled on one, sipping her wine. "So much better than fries with ketchup—and fewer calories."

"Chips," corrected Lucy, remembering those mysteries she loved so much. "They call them chips here. And potato chips are crisps."

"Whatever." Sue waved a graceful hand and ordered another glass of wine.

When they left the restaurant, they discovered the sun had gone and clouds had moved in. The air was cold and heavy with moisture that clung to their faces, chilling them.

"Just like home," said Lucy, shrugging into her jacket.

"It's good for the complexion." Sue studied her map, then pointed a finger. "The Lanes are thataway."

Retracing their steps toward the Royal Pavilion, they entered a narrow alley between two substantial white stone buildings and found themselves in a maze of tiny streets that twisted this way and that. It was like stumbling into a medieval village; the narrow streets were filled with groups of chattering shoppers wandering from store to store.

"What if there was a fire!" Rachel seemed to be sniffing for smoke. "A fire truck could never get in here!"

"They must have special apparatuses," declared Sue. "Look! Cath Kidston!"

"What is Cath Kidston?" asked Pam.

"You will love it." Sue grabbed Pam's hand and pulled her toward the store.

They all loved Cath Kidston, which offered household linens printed with colorful vintage designs. There were items for children—bibs and bedding and clothing, covered with bunnies and kittens for girls and fifties-style cowboys for boys. Kitchenware was abloom with flowers of all sorts, but most especially roses, in gorgeous pastel colors.

Lucy could have bought out the shop but contented herself with a cowboy bib for Patrick, and Rachel limited herself to a packet of printed tissues. Pam, on the other hand, emerged with an enormous shopping bag bulging with tablecloths and napkins and dish towels and a seriously depleted wallet.

Only Sue had resisted. "Not my style. Too flowery." Noticing Pam's disappointment, she quickly added, "But I understand the appeal. Very cute."

Continuing on, they found a jewelry store that was having a closeout sale, offering everything at 90 percent off. They quickly joined the eager throng pawing through the bins and boxes. After a few minutes, Lucy concluded the stuff wasn't to her liking, and she was uncomfortable in such tight quarters. She went back outside to get a bit of air and noticed an antique shop across the way.

Unable to resist, she opened the door, setting a little bell to jangling. It reminded her of a similar bell on the door at the *Pennysaver* office, and she felt immediately at home. The storekeeper was sitting at a desk off to one side and looked up from the newspaper she was reading, giving her a welcoming nod. "Looking for anything in particular?"

Lucy shook her head. "Just browsing."

Much to her surprise, the little shop seemed to go on and on. She wandered through room after room, past shelves of china and old toys, tarnished silver tea sets, battered and rusty tins that once contained Lyle's Golden Syrup and Horlicks powder. She paused to flip through a box of old prints and gazed longingly at an antique "Souvenir of Brighton" plate priced at thirty-five pounds. That was something like fifty dollars. Could she bargain for a better price? She was just reaching for the plate to examine it more closely when she heard a familiar voice.

"Lucy!"

She turned her head and saw Quentin, a book open in his hand, standing in front of a shelf packed with more old books in faded covers.

"Anything interesting?" she asked.

"Nothing as interesting as you," he said, making eye

contact. "How did you manage to get away from the Three Musketeers?"

She laughed. "They're looking at jewelry. There's a big sale across the way."

He replaced the book. "And you don't like jewelry?"

"I like antiques more." Lucy picked up the plate. "And it was awfully crowded in there."

He lifted his head in surprise. "You suffer from claustrophobia?"

Lucy studied the plate. Search as she might, she couldn't find any cracks. "A little bit."

"Why don't we head for the Pier, then, and get some fresh air?"

Lucy was wondering if the plate was perhaps a bit too perfect. Could it be a fake? "Sounds good," she said, replacing the plate.

Quentin took her elbow. "Do you need to check with your friends?"

Lucy shook her head. "They know I can take care of myself."

The clouds thinned when they left the store and began weaving their way through the crowded lanes, and for a moment or two there was enough sunshine to create shadows. Lucy could see her silhouette and Quentin's, stretching before them on the wide sidewalk as they walked along the busy main road to the pier. From this angle, it seemed a flimsy structure, perched on stilts and extending some distance into the blue-gray water.

"It doesn't look very safe." Looking along the shore, Lucy could see the remains of an earlier pier that had collapsed, leaving ragged and dangerous-looking beams poking out of the gray waves.

Quentin slipped his arm around Lucy's waist. "The British are very safety conscious. Mind the gap and all that. I'm sure it's inspected regularly."

They passed under the metal archway welcoming them to the pier and walked along the boardwalk, passing shacks that sold food and candy. Lucy wasn't interested in them; she wanted to walk along the white-painted railing and take in the view. They paused for a moment, a chilly breeze ruffling their hair, looking along the beach where families were gathered in little clusters along the water. A busy road ran behind the beach, lined with substantial white hotels.

"It's a whole different attitude," said Lucy, thinking of the shingle-style Queen Victoria Inn in Tinker's Cove where guests lingered in rocking chairs to enjoy the view. "They don't have porches."

"No wonder," said Quentin, drawing her closer as the sun again disappeared and a light drizzle began to fall. "It's freezing here."

Lucy pulled away, wrapping her arms around herself. Her interest was caught by a pair of elderly women, dressed as if for church in suits and heels, walking arm in arm along the pier. "Look at them, they're wearing their best bib and tucker."

Quentin touched her chin. "That's what I love about you, Lucy. *Bib and tucker.* You really have a way with words."

Lucy took a step backward, uncomfortable with the direction this was going and resumed walking. "People here do seem to dress more formally than we do in America. I haven't seen anybody in a tracksuit."

Quentin fell into step beside her. "I got into a conversation with a woman at Hampton Court. We were sitting on the same bench, in the garden. She was asking about our itinerary, and when I told her we were going to Brighton, she began to reminisce about childhood family excursions. She said everyone dressed up to go to the seaside; they wore their best clothes—the men even wore suits. They'd sit there on the shingle—that's what they call the beach—and spread out a picnic. If it was hot, the men would take off their shoes and socks and roll up their trousers to wade in the water. If it was sunny, they'd knot their handkerchiefs to make little hats to protect their heads." He paused, holding the door for her as they entered an enormous enclosed arcade filled with ringing and buzzing games. "It was a different world."

The arcade was crowded with people who had been driven inside by the weather, and Lucy was jostled by a group of laughing teens. "It's a bit—"

"I know." Quentin took her elbow. "Claustrophobic. But I see light ahead."

They made their way past the pinball machines and barkers and emerged onto the far end of the pier near the merry-go-round. Even in this weather they could hear screams from thrill seekers on the roller coaster. A refreshment area offered shelter from the weather behind a wall of glass, and that's where Lucy spotted her two ladies, each enjoying a glass of beer.

"That place seems respectable enough." Quentin's smile was teasing.

"I am a married lady and a mother of four," Lucy reminded him. "I have my reputation to consider."

Quentin opened the door for her. "And how is the family?"

Lucy's thoughts immediately turned to Elizabeth. "My oldest daughter—she's an RA at Chamberlain College—is in trouble with the new dean."

Quentin was holding a chair for her. "I know from experience that deans, especially new ones, can be very annoying."

Lucy laughed and sat down. Quentin took the opposite chair, and she studied his face. It was a nice face, she decided, and you couldn't see the bald spot from this angle. He had laugh lines spreading from his eyes, his smile was easy, and he had a good sense of humor. Lucy had to admit she was finding it hard to resist him.

Chapter Eleven

❧

"**W**inchester seems to take better care of its students than Chamberlain," she said, smiling.

He furrowed his brow. "Why do you think that?"

"Well, Autumn and Jennifer told me they're in a support group to help freshmen adjust to college life."

Quentin laughed. "Is that what they call it?"

Lucy gave him a sideways look. "Isn't that what it is?"

"Not quite." Quentin raised a hand, signaling the waiter. "It's more of a last-ditch effort by the college to avoid expelling them."

Lucy thought this over as the waiter approached to take their order.

"A pint of bitter for me," said Quentin.

Lucy had spotted an advertising poster that caught her interest. "What's shandy?"

"It's a mix of lemonade and beer." Seeing her doubtful expression, he continued. "It's quite good. Ladies enjoy it."

"In for a penny, in for a pound—I'll try it," said Lucy, causing Quentin to grin. "I've got a million of them." She paused, gazing out at the flat gray expanse of water. "So what exactly is this program?"

"It's an intensive group therapy session for students who are considered high risk. I don't know the exact circumstances that led to their enrollment in the program, but"—he leaned across the table—"I have heard the campus scuttlebutt."

"Ah!" Lucy jabbed a finger in the air. "That's one for you: scuttlebutt."

Quentin waited a moment for the waiter to place their drinks on the table, then raised his thumbprint mug in a toast. Lucy raised her glass, too, and tapped his. "Here's to kindred spirits," he said.

That seemed harmless enough, thought Lucy. "Kindred spirits." She took a cautious sip of her drink and found it exactly as described, fizzy and lemony, with a beerish tang. It was good. "So what's the scuttlebutt on these kids?"

"I don't know if there's any truth to these stories or not—you know what a college campus is like. It's a small, enclosed community and people talk about each other."

"Just like Tinker's Cove," said Lucy.

"Exactly. Sometimes these rumors are true and sometimes they're not. You have to take them with a grain of salt. But I do happen to know for a fact that Autumn did assault her roommate, because the girl came to me to complain covered with scratches and a black eye."

"Oh my," said Lucy, reaching for her glass.

"Yeah." Quentin nodded. "The upshot of that was they both got single rooms and Autumn got sent to the group."

"What about Jennifer?"

"I don't actually know but I'm guessing anorexia and anxiety. I think she has real mental health issues."

"It's too bad. She's such a pretty little thing. She ought to be enjoying her youth."

Quentin was thoughtful. "The longer I've been teaching, the more I've come to understand that very few kids do enjoy their youth. It's something we look back on with nostalgia, thinking only that we had a full head of hair or a flat stomach and forgetting how miserable we really were."

"You have a point. But what about Will? He's a handsome kid and seems to be having a pretty good time."

"Too good." Quentin had drained his pint and was signaling for another. "He's a real party boy. He not only got himself put on academic probation because of his grades but he also got arrested for drunk driving. And there's a nasty rumor about a monkey—I don't know the details. He's this close"—Quentin almost pressed his thumb and forefinger together—"to getting kicked out."

"No wonder his mother doesn't want to let him out of her sight," said Lucy.

"He's been doing better." Quentin paused as the waiter delivered the fresh pint and took away the empty one. "And then there's Caroline. Kids on campus call her the Tuber."

"That's cruel." Lucy suspected that one of the attractions of teaching was that it allowed Quentin to indulge an unpleasant streak of immaturity.

"You're right. We don't really know what she's like. The poor girl is obviously taking some powerful psychotropic drugs. She may look like a zombie, but they seem to be getting her through the days."

Quentin's explanation made a lot of sense to Lucy. No wonder Caroline seemed so subdued, and her parents' clinging concern suddenly made sense.

"It's a shame that all four signed up for this trip," continued Quentin, shifting his gaze away from her and studying the coaster under his beer.

"How so?"

He raised his eyes to meet hers. "Once the word got out that they were coming, nobody else wanted to sign up. George almost had to cancel the whole thing. Then Pam got you guys to come and that gave him a dozen—just enough people to make it worthwhile." He nodded. "These trips usually attract about thirty or forty people."

Lucy was stunned. "You mean we're responsible? That poor George would have been home in Tinker's Cove and most probably wouldn't have had an allergy attack or if he did would have gotten treatment in time?"

Quentin's warm hand covered hers. "Don't be silly. When your time's up, it's up."

Lucy snatched her hand away. "Not at all. The rescue squad is terrific. We get grateful letters all the time at the *Pennysaver*. They could have saved him."

"If they'd been called in time, but George was stubborn. He wouldn't have allowed it. And believe me, he died doing what he loved. If he'd had his choice, I'm sure he would rather have died exactly the way he did, en route to his beloved England."

Lucy didn't agree. She remembered the terrified, frantic expression on George's face when he reached out to her for help on the plane. He was fighting for every breath; he was fighting for his life. Lucy also had had another thought, one that troubled her for some time. She thought of the awkward silences whenever his name was mentioned, the inappropriate bursts of laughter, and the palpable sense of relief she'd noticed in the breakfast room after Emma's departure.

"You know, for somebody who went to so much trouble for others, George doesn't seem to have been very popular with the folks on this tour. There seems a real absence of, well, I don't know, compassion, for lack of a better word. Have you noticed?"

"Can't say I have," he said, draining his mug and pushing his chair back. "Let's see what's at the end of the pier."

Lucy was agreeable. The pub was musty from its humid location on the pier, and she was ready for some fresh air. "Good idea."

She was thoughtful as they went outside and wandered past the merry-go-round and other attractions. The rattling roller coaster took up the entire end of the pier, so there was no view of the sea, but there was plenty of activity to interest a people-watcher like Lucy: moms comforting cranky babies, boyfriends teasing girlfriends and attempting to lure them onto the thrill rides, dads with toddlers perched on their shoulders, a couple of old duffers contentedly puffing away on stinky cigars that were probably forbidden at home.

Watching all these people enjoying themselves, Lucy pondered Quentin's assertion that George had died the way "he would have wanted." She'd often heard similar phrases in the course of her work as a reporter interviewing family members for obituaries. "Well, Mom is probably happier now she's with Dad," a daughter would say, and Lucy would remember a merry widow who enjoyed her volunteer job at the historical society and her weekly bridge game. Or "His suffering is over—he never did get used to that titanium hip," and Lucy would remember the enthusiastic bowler she'd interviewed for a story on the senior bowling league.

It was natural enough, she supposed. People looked for comfort when confronted with the inevitability of

death; they were looking for a bright side. Some people
even believed in heaven and an afterlife of perfect hap-
piness, whatever that was. Personally, Lucy found the
promises of heavenly reunions somewhat unnerving—
would she encounter her mother before or after the
Alzheimer's took over? If before, she would have to en-
dure an eternity of carping criticism; if after, a sweeter,
confused stranger.

"You're miles away," said Quentin as they propped
their arms on the railing and gazed at the choppy gray
water. The wind had picked up and had blown a lock of
hair across her face. He gently smoothed it away and
leaned toward her, and she suddenly realized he was
going to kiss her.

"I guess we should head back," she said, pulling away
and turning to go, but the way past the merry-go-round
was suddenly blocked by a crew of EMTs rushing toward
the roller coaster. Behind them the crowd surged forward, eager to see what all the fuss was about. As the
crowd pressed around her, Lucy was jostled and Quentin positioned himself protectively, wrapping an arm
around her shoulder. For once Lucy didn't resist, but
strained onto her tiptoes, trying to see what was happening.

The rescue crew, carrying cases of equipment and
pushing a wheeled stretcher, had disappeared into an
area beneath the roller coaster that was blocked from
public access.

"Bet it's a jumper," said a woman with frizzy, bleached
blond hair.

"A jumper?" Lucy leaned over the railing and spotted one of the rescuers descending a ladder fixed to
one of the supporting pilings beneath the pier. Leaning
a bit farther, she saw, or thought she saw, a face beneath

the surface of the water and perhaps a glimpse of a shoulder.

Then, as she watched, a rescue swimmer in a wet suit lowered himself from a ladder into the water and began swimming toward the spot where she'd seen the face, and another rescuer quickly followed. When he was in the water, others on the pier began lowering a metal basket equipped with floats on either side. Lucy could only imagine how cold the water must be, even with the wet suits, and was struck by the rescuers' selfless efforts to save the jumper.

It was hushed on the pier as the people along the railing strained to watch and pass along the rescuers' progress to the others. " 'E's got 'er now!" declared someone with a Cockney accent, and Lucy saw the swimmer had seized the jumper in the familiar cross-chest hold she'd learned herself in a Red Cross lifesaving class when she was a teen. "They're puttin' 'er in the basket," announced the Cockney. "Oops, bit of a slip there."

The crowd gasped as the limp, plump body rolled out of the basket, only to be seized once again by the rescuers. This time they were successful, and the crew atop the pier began raising the basket, straining against its weight. As soon as the victim was hoisted onto the pier, one of the EMTs immediately began CPR. The two rescuers who'd gone into the water were wrapped in blankets and given hot drinks; they joined the crowd watching the EMTs attempt to revive the girl. Lucy stared at a pair of plump, hairless white legs. One chubby foot was bare, the other covered with an ugly white running shoe. A chunky, clumsy shoe that somehow seemed familiar.

She reached for Quentin's sleeve. "Could that be Caroline?"

His cheeks, rosy from the alcohol, suddenly drained of color. "Ohmigod."

"She's comin' 'round." The word spread through the crowd as Quentin began pushing his way forward.

"Hey, there!" protested one woman. "We were here first!"

For a moment Lucy thought of the crowds that had once flocked to Tower Hill to witness the gruesome public executions that took place there, and she stepped back against the railing. What was she doing here? Why had she joined this group of ghouls?

"I think I may know the victim," said Quentin. "Please let me through."

The ghouls were suddenly transformed into caring, concerned citizens. "Let 'im through," they were saying, stepping aside. " 'E says 'e knows 'er."

Stepping forward, Lucy grabbed the back of Quentin's jacket and followed him through the crowd until they were directly behind the EMTs gathered around the victim. Quentin tapped one on the shoulder, and when he turned around, Lucy got a good look at the girl's face. It was round and somewhat bloated with strands of wet brownish red hair clinging to her forehead, but it was unmistakably Caroline Smith.

"I have information about the victim," said Quentin.

"Come with me," said a policeman, pulling out a notebook. While Quentin supplied Caroline's particulars, Lucy watched as an oxygen mask was slipped over her face and the crew of rescuers lifted the wire basket onto a gurney and began wheeling it through the crowd. Quentin followed, answering the officer's questions as he went, and Lucy tagged along, occasionally supplying a bit of information.

An ambulance was waiting when they emerged from

the enclosed arcade, and Caroline was quickly bundled inside.

"I'll have to go with her." Quentin didn't look happy about it. "You must find her parents and tell them what happened."

"Where are you taking her? They'll want to go to the hospital."

"Brighton General, ma'am." The EMT closed one of the rear doors.

"But how will you get back to London?"

"I don't know. The train . . ." Quentin paused, realizing the EMT was waiting impatiently for him to get into the ambulance. "I've gotta go. You can tell the others what's happened, get them back to the hotel."

Then he was inside and the second door slammed shut. The ambulance took off, siren wailing and lights flashing. Lucy stood watching it leave and wondering how she was ever going to find Tom and Ann in this crowded holiday town. Where would they be? Were they frantically looking for Caroline? Or had they agreed to go their separate ways, planning to meet later? She had no idea.

Lucy retraced her steps along the pier, realizing it gave her a good vantage point from which to search the beach. She went from one side to the other, standing at the railing and looking down at the handful of people scattered on the pebbly beach. They were mostly walkers, hardy types, striding along the water's edge to take the air, but some were huddled in little groups with blankets held over their heads to ward off the drizzle. She tried to remember what the Smiths were wearing and failed completely. No, she reminded herself, they were traveling and were probably wearing the same jackets they'd worn to the museum. She concentrated hard, trying to remember how they'd looked in the stairwell at the V&A.

Ann had been in brown, she remembered. Brown pants and a beige sweater. No good, she must have worn a jacket of some sort today. But what about Tom? Leather? A black leather jacket? Yes. So she should keep her eyes peeled for a stocky man in a black leather jacket and a beigy brownish woman.

Lucy turned around and scanned the passing crowd. Lots of leather jackets, lots of beigy women. This was not working, she decided. There was nothing to do except to keep walking and hope she spotted them, or perhaps someone else from the tour who might have seen them. She decided to take a systematic approach and began by hiking along the wide sidewalk that bordered the beach, first heading to the left and then coming back to cover the area on the other side of the pier.

The crowd was thick, especially where portions of the sidewalk were allotted to motorcycle parking. It was a little clearer on the bike path, but there she ran the danger of being run over by a biker. She hiked on, uphill, until she reached a little covered pavilion with a couple of benches, where she sat to catch her breath and watch the passing crowd. After a few minutes, she began to feel guilty about sitting there while the Smiths were unaware of their daughter's plight, and she got up and began walking back toward the pier. She scanned each face but didn't recognize Tom and Ann.

At least she was going downhill, and the crowd on the other side of the pier, past the aquarium, was thinner. The aquarium, she realized, might have caught the Smiths' interest, so she lingered for a while by the entrance, watching the people who came and went. When she noticed a woman paying for her admission with a charge card, she had a sudden brainstorm. When they'd finished their transaction, she went up to the ticket window.

"This is a bit unusual," she began, speaking to a middle-aged woman with a pixie haircut. "But I'm here with a tour group from America, and one of our members just went off the pier."

The woman nodded, her expresson sympathetic. "They do it all the time. It's the number-one location for suicides in the UK."

"Really?" Lucy was shocked. "Are they often successful?"

"They can usually save the daytime ones, but the nighttime . . ." She shook her head. "The currents are something terrible here." She leaned forward. "Did they save your friend?"

"Yes. I think so." Lucy realized she'd digressed. "But I'm trying to find her family, her parents. They're on the tour, too."

"And you wondered if they'd come in here?" The woman shook her head. "I don't know that I'd remember them, even if I knew what they looked like. A lot of people come here. Beats me. It's just a bunch o' fish."

"I was thinking they might've charged their tickets," said Lucy.

"Good idea!" The woman produced a thick packet of charge slips. "What's their name?"

"Smith," said Lucy. "Ann and Tom Smith."

"Couldn't be more common if they'd made it up, could it?" The woman was flipping through the slips. "Smith, Gerald, no; Smith, Patricia, no; Smithson, William, no." Suddenly she stopped. "Here you go, luv. Thomas Smith. Two adults."

"Are they still inside? Can you tell?"

"Maybe. They went in about an hour ago."

That seemed about right, Lucy realized. They'd probably split up, Mom and Dad going to the aquarium and Caroline, seizing the moment, for whatever reason, to end her life. Lucy reached for her wallet, but the woman waved her hand. "Go on in that door, the one marked 'exit.' Work your way through backward—and good luck, dearie."

Lucy smiled her thanks and went to wait by the exit for somebody to come out so she could grab the door and dart inside, which she was shortly able to do. Once inside, it was dark and dank and a bit smelly. Tanks of blue and green water containing various forms of sea life glowed in the walls. Lucy waited a few minutes for her eyes to adjust to the darkness, then began searching for Tom and Ann. She found them in front of a tank containing an octopus.

"Hi!" she said, approaching them and wondering how to begin. Probably the most direct way would be best, she decided. "I've got some bad news for you."

Ann seemed to sway on her feet, and Tom grabbed her elbow to steady her. Behind them the startled octopus scooted into its rocky shelter. "Is it Caroline?" he asked.

"I'm afraid so. They just pulled her out of the water."

Ann slumped against her husband, her eyes closed. "Is she . . . ?"

"She's alive," said Lucy. "They took her to the hospital. Quentin went in the ambulance with her."

Tom's face hardened. "What was he—?"

Lucy quickly defended him. "He was with me—we just happened to be there. It was very fortunate."

Ann was clinging to her husband's arm. "We have to go to her."

"Yes, I think your best bet is a taxi." Lucy was escorting them to the exit. "She's at Brighton General."

"Thank you, thank you for finding us," said Ann as they made their way through the swinging doors and out into the darkening afternoon. Lucy gave the woman in the ticket booth a wave as they crossed the crowded sidewalk to the curb where a couple of taxis were waiting. She opened the door and held it for them, waiting until they were settled and then telling the driver to take them to the hospital.

Then she raised her arm in a parting wave and watched the taxi pull out into traffic, taking them to an uncertain future.

Completely drained, she sighed, then spotted Harry Ramsden's across the way. Maybe they'd give her a cup of tea.

Chapter Twelve

The lunchtime crowd had long since dispersed, and only a handful of people were seated at tables inside the fish and chips restaurant, most of them with pots of tea. When a server told her she could sit where she pleased, Lucy chose a table for two near the window, where she could keep an eye out for her friends. As soon as she sat down, she felt enormously tired, as if she'd run a marathon, and her hands began to shake.

"What can I get you, luv?" The server was a spry fellow in his sixties with a military haircut.

"Just tea, please."

"Filthy weather out there, ain't it? Sure you wouldn't like a bit of sweet? We've got sticky toffee pudding and spotted dick—fruit crumble, too."

Lucy hadn't the faintest idea what he was talking about.

"They come with your choice of custard cream or vanilla ice cream."

The very thought of anything with custard made her feel queasy. "I'll stick to tea," she said.

"Very well."

He left and she stared out the window, watching the people hurrying by, heads lowered against the drizzle and clutching the collars of their lightweight spring jackets. They'd been tricked by the sunny morning weather, which hadn't lived up to its promise. Now the day had turned gray and cold, with drizzle and showers, just the way it often did in Maine.

"It's too bad, really. All them folks hoping for a nice holiday by the seaside." The server put a pot of tea and a cup and saucer in front of her, along with a pitcher of milk and a china box containing packets of sugar and sweetener. "I heard there was a bit of a fuss on the pier."

"There was. They had to pull a young woman out of the water."

"A jumper?"

Lucy considered. "That's a good question." She remembered teasing Pam, or maybe it was Sue, that just because she was holding a duster didn't mean she actually used it. Everybody seemed to assume that since Caroline was fished out of the ocean that she must have jumped voluntarily, but that wasn't necessarily the case. Maybe she hadn't jumped; maybe she'd been pushed, although it did seem unlikely due to the sturdy, chest-high railing.

"I saw the ambulance. They took right off, so she must've been breathing." He lifted the pot and filled Lucy's cup. "They don't rush with the goners."

"I hope she'll be all right," said Lucy, wrapping her hands around the warm cup. "I heard this happens quite a bit."

The server's tanned, wrinkled face was solemn. "Too often, if you ask me. England's changed, you know. Used to be everybody kept a stiff upper lip, keep calm and carry on, that sort of thing. When Princess Diana died, that all changed." He put the pot down. "I liked the old way better."

Using both hands, Lucy lifted the cup to her lips and took a sip. Despite her efforts to control the trembling, the sharp-eyed waiter noticed. "Don't tell me you know the jumper?"

The cup clattered in the saucer as Lucy set it down. "I do."

"Dear me. That's dreadful." He glanced out the window. "A friend of yours?"

"Not exactly. I'm here with a group from an American college. She's a student there."

"A young person." He clucked his tongue. "That's a shame."

Lucy nodded. What sort of mind-set prompted a healthy young person to jump off a pier that was thirty or forty feet above the water? Why had her future seemed so bleak?

The waiter tapped his tray. "Tea's on the house," he said before turning to greet a new customer.

Lucy stirred some sugar into her cup and drained it, then refilled it from the pot. She was feeling better; the trembling had stopped and she was even wondering what spotted dick could possibly be when she saw a familiar face on the opposite side of the street, waiting at the crosswalk for the light to change. It was Autumn and she wasn't alone. Will was standing beside her. They didn't seem like a couple, however. Autumn was scowling, shaking her head, and Will was bent over her, talking to her, trying to convince her of something. At least that's what it looked like. And they seemed to be coming from the pier—where else could they have been in this foul weather? Unless they'd been in the aquarium, which Lucy didn't think was likely. The arcade seemed more their style. Lucy wondered how long they'd been there. Had they been on the pier when Caroline jumped?

The sky was darkening and Lucy checked her watch, realizing with a start that it was almost five and she needed to get over to the bus drop-off to meet the minivan. She hurried out of the restaurant and dashed across the street, but when she rounded the corner, she was surprised to discover the group had already gathered, waiting. It was a much smaller group, of course, without Quentin and the Smiths—only Lucy's three friends, Dr. Cope and Jennifer, Laura Barfield, Will and Autumn.

"Where were you?" demanded Sue when Lucy was within shouting distance. Her tone was accusatory, and Lucy felt guilty, realizing she shouldn't have spent so much time with Quentin. She'd enjoyed herself but perhaps she'd led him on without meaning to.

She was saved from answering when the minivan pulled up and they all hurried to get on board, complaining about the way the weather had turned so cold. When everyone was seated, Lucy delivered her little speech.

"I'm sorry to tell you there's been an accident—Caroline Smith was taken to the hospital by ambulance. Her parents are with her and so is Professor Rea. He asked me to see that we all get back to the hotel tonight." Lucy took a head count but wasn't at all sure she'd got it right. "I think we're all here. Is anybody missing except for the Smiths and Professor Rea?"

Nobody was paying attention; they were all buzzing about the accident.

Rachel came to her rescue. "Speak now or forever hold your peace," she said, pronouncing their names and counting them up on her fingers. "I make nine.

With the missing four, that's thirteen. We're all here," she told the driver, who began pulling out into traffic.

"Thirteen!" Lucy slid into her seat next to Sue. "I hadn't realized."

"It's unlucky." Pam nodded seriously. "No wonder we've had so much trouble. First poor Professor Temple and now Caroline. What happened? Was it an accident? The traffic here is terrible."

The group was silent—everyone was listening—but Lucy wasn't sure how much to tell. Then again, she decided, it was a public event. It had all taken place in the clear light of day. There was no question of confidentiality here, no request to keep the incident off the record. On the other hand, she could only tell what she knew for sure. "Rescuers pulled Caroline out of the water beneath the pier and rushed her to the hospital. That's all I know."

Jennifer's face was paler than usual. "Did she jump?"

"I really don't know how she got into the water. I didn't see that part."

Laura leaned forward, her expression anxious. "Will she be all right?"

"I don't know that either. They were giving her oxygen when they put her in the ambulance."

"There may well be considerable trauma, internal injuries, broken bones," advised Dr. Cope. "It depends on how she hit the water. From a certain height, the impact can be the same as hitting concrete."

They were all silent. Lucy glanced over her shoulder, looking for Will and Autumn. They were seated together in the very back. Autumn was bobbing slightly, listening to her iPod, and Will was staring out the window, scratching at his chin.

"Look, even here," said Sue, pointing out the window as they passed the Gap and McDonald's.

A little bit of home, thought Lucy. She should have been pleased, reassured, even, but she only felt depressed.

"Caroline didn't seem like a very happy girl." Laura Barfield's tone was thoughtful. "But I'm sure she didn't mean to kill herself. This was probably one of those cries for help."

Across the aisle, Rachel caught Lucy's eye. "I think so, too," she said. "This may be a turning point for her. She may get the care she needs."

"She was lucky." Dr. Cope put his arm around Jennifer's shoulder and pulled her close to him. "I've seen a number of suicides in my time, and the ones who survive always say the same thing—that as soon as they jumped or pulled the trigger or shoved the chair out from under their feet, they realized they'd made a terrible mistake. They wanted to live after all."

They were in the countryside again, and the clouds had parted to let the last rays of sunshine bathe the green fields in golden light. Here and there, flocks of sheep were scattered like cotton balls spilled on a green carpet; many of the ewes had little lambs resting beside them. It was like something out of a Cath Kidston print or a Kate Greenaway illustration, and Lucy hoped the little lambs were being raised for wool and not the dinner table.

As if reading her thoughts, Sue covered her hand with her own. "Wool, sweetheart, they're going to give bags and bags for the master and the maid. . . ."

Lucy managed a little smile, spotting a kid with a backpack wheeling his bike up a steep drive toward a thatched cottage, the windows blazing red from the setting sun. "And one for the little boy who lives *up* the lane."

Dinner that night was better. Rachel had spoken with the chambermaid and learned there were a number of restaurants on nearby Charlotte Street, and since they'd had a hearty fish and chips lunch, they opted for pizza and salads at Pizza Express, along with big glasses of red wine. Back at the hotel, Lucy went straight to the lounge to check her e-mail, but there was no word from Elizabeth. Bill, however, had calculated the amount they would owe if she lost her resident advisor position: It was nearly five thousand dollars.

"Better watch your spending!" he advised, and Lucy wasn't sure if he was joking or not. She was signing off, a lengthy process on this cranky old computer, when Autumn came in and switched on the TV. Lucy's interest was caught by an outrageous performer with peroxide hair in a shiny violet suit, and she watched, amazed, as he welcomed an American country music star to the show. Fascinated, she joined Autumn on one of the battered red sofas.

"Isn't that Dewey Pike?" she asked. The singer, who was wearing a red, white, and blue shirt; cowboy boots; and a ten-gallon hat, clearly hadn't known what he was in for when he agreed to do the show. The host, Graham Norton, got right down to business, asking Dewey if he was gay or straight.

Autumn was in stitches. "This guy's all about guns and pickup trucks and the flag—look what he's wearing—and Graham Norton wants to eat him up!"

Dewey, however, was more sophisticated than he looked. He winked at Norton, said he was open to new experiences, and offered to sing a song. Norton was happy to oblige, setting the singer in front of a shimmering curtain for his performance. Dewey was well into his hit song about a woman who done him wrong when the glittery silver curtain opened to reveal Norton, dressed in drag, swooning and shimmying behind him. The live studio audience went wild. Dewey caught on and began singing to Norton, ending by wrapping him in his arms and planting a big kiss as they went to commercial.

"That guy was way cooler than I expected," said Autumn.

"He's in show biz." Lucy shrugged. "That superpatriot persona is probably just an act. For all we know, he's a registered Democrat."

"No. He campaigned for McCain."

Lucy hadn't expected Autumn to be so well informed, but she wasn't about to talk politics. The subject had become so divisive lately. Instead she changed the subject. "Are you enjoying the tour?" she asked.

"Yeah. England's a lot more modern than I expected."

Lucy wondered if Autumn had expected the England of costume dramas, then revised her thinking. By old-fashioned, Autumn probably meant Guy Ritchie films.

"Is this your first trip out of the U.S.?"

"Yeah." Autumn snorted. "The people I was living with, my foster parents, they were mostly interested in getting that check from the state every month. They weren't exactly into education and enrichment. It was more about keeping gas in the car and Kraft mac 'n' cheese on the table."

"But you got into college, right?"

"No thanks to them. The guidance counselor helped me out, made me apply and told me about scholarships and loans." Seeing that the show was over and the news was next, Autumn clicked the remote and turned off the TV. "The Rotary Club gave me money for this trip, in case you were wondering. Professor Rea wrote them a letter."

Lucy wasn't surprised by her defensive attitude; it was understandable for a kid who'd been through the foster care system and had to fight for everything. "I have a daughter in college, so I know how expensive it is." She scowled. "She's fighting with the dean and may lose her RA job and the free room and board."

"That job sucks. I hate my RA. She's always snooping around, looking for drugs and stuff."

Lucy had a sudden insight. "That may be the problem. I can't imagine Elizabeth doing that. She couldn't care less."

"Where does she go to school?"

"Chamberlain College in Boston."

"I'd like to go somewhere like that. I might transfer. Tinker's Cove is dead."

Lucy nodded in agreement. The little town was quiet, especially in winter. "I guess it's pretty claustrophobic. Everybody knows everybody at a small school like Winchester." She paused. "Did you have any classes with Caroline?"

"No." Autumn clicked the TV back on and began watching a margarine commercial with great interest.

"I heard she wasn't very popular."

Autumn ignored her, flipping to another channel and a dog food commercial.

"I'm just wondering because of what happened today. Do you think she was suicidal? I'm just asking because you were both in that support group. Did she ever say anything about life not being worth it, anything like that?"

Autumn was watching a news segment about a sewage treatment plant in Manchester with great apparent interest. "She was, you know, weird."

"What do you mean?"

"Uh, look, I don't want to talk about it."

Lucy wondered if Autumn had encountered Caroline on the pier, and if something had happened that might have caused Caroline to take the desperate measure of jumping. Considering the way Autumn had tormented Jennifer at the Tower of London, it seemed at least a remote possibility. "If you know anything about what happened to Caroline, you need to speak up," said Lucy. "She could have died. She might still."

"Look, that's got nothing to do with me!" The rings and studs that dotted Autumn's face seemed to be bristling. "And just for the record, I had nothing to do with that creepy old professor's death either. It was an accident. I didn't mean to knock the medicine thing out of his hand, but it probably wouldn't have made any difference anyway. He was really old."

"Accidents happen," said Lucy, hoping to calm Autumn's temper. She actually thought Autumn and Jennifer had behaved badly on the plane. Their reckless behavior had certainly contributed to Temple's death, even if it hadn't caused it.

"Jennifer had the peanuts, you know." Autumn's tone was self-righteous. "How was she supposed to know he had a peanut allergy?"

Lucy's jaw dropped. Why hadn't she thought of that? Not only had they been dancing around in their seats, but they'd been shaking that bag of trail mix, spreading peanut dust in the air. "You should have known better."

"Well, I know now." Autumn practically spat out the words. "But I didn't know then. We were just excited about the trip and having a good time."

Lucy thought things were getting a little intense. It was time to change the subject. "Did you enjoy Brighton? I saw you and Will leaving the pier. . . ."

"So what?"

Lucy had intended to say what a nice couple they made, but her maneuver backfired.

Autumn turned on her with the ferocity of a feral cat. "I suppose you think we pushed Caroline into the water, too."

Lucy drew back into herself. "Not at all. I didn't think that. I was just making conversation. Everybody seemed to be having a lot of fun on the rides and all."

"I wouldn't call it fun. Roller coasters make me puke. And I couldn't get rid of Will. He was stinking drunk, you know. He was all over me, pawing me. I hate when guys do that. He's so immature."

Lucy was shocked and fascinated by Autumn's sudden change. At first she could hardly get a word out of her, but now the girl was on a roll. It was all pouring out, and Lucy wondered if she was the first person who'd ever listened to her.

"Guys are such creeps. It's like they just assume if you don't wear little pink blouses and pearl earrings that you're some sort of slut, that you'll do anything they want. And they always want it—anywhere, anytime. In the backseat, up against a wall, on a stinky old frat house couch." She paused, considering a new possibility. "I bet that's it, you know. I wouldn't be surprised at all. It's obvious." The stream of words stopped abruptly and she sat primly, lips pressed together.

"What's obvious?"

"Will and Caroline, that's what. He must've lured her to one of those secluded spots there underneath the roller coaster. A guy like Will would think he was doing her a favor, giving a fat girl a big opportunity. And when it turned out she didn't appreciate the wonderful chance to, you know, do whatever with him, he probably got mad, and maybe she tried to fight him off or something and he ended up pushing her into the water." She looked at Lucy. "I can just see it, can't you?"

Unfortunately, Lucy could.

Chapter Thirteen

The breakfast room was once again terribly quiet when Lucy and Sue went down on Thursday morning. They soon discovered the reason: Tom Smith was standing by the kitchen door, requesting trays to take up to his wife and daughter.

Lucy went right up to him. "How is Caroline?"

"She's doing pretty well," he said. There were dark circles under his eyes, and he seemed to have lost about twenty pounds in one night. "She broke her arm and is covered with bruises. She's in a lot of pain, but at the hospital they all said how lucky she was."

"And when did you get back?"

"Around midnight. We hired a town car. It was expensive, but Caroline was in no shape to take the train, and Professor Rea offered to split the cost."

One question was on everyone's mind, but Lucy didn't mention it. She just couldn't bring herself to ask how Caroline managed to end up in the water. Instead she said, "That's good news. We were all worried about her. I hope she makes a speedy recovery."

When she joined Sue at the table, she was met with an accusation. "You waffled."

Lucy nodded. "I know. But how could I? The poor man is obviously shattered."

"And you call yourself a reporter!"

Lucy picked up the coffeepot and filled her cup. "I'm on vacation. If you want to know so badly, you ask him."

Sue shook her head. "No, I was brought up to never ask personal questions."

Hearing that, Lucy was chuckling when Quentin Rea arrived, practically bumping into Tom in the doorway. Tom was carrying the heavy breakfast tray the kitchen had prepared for him.

"Glad you're up and about," said Quentin. "I was wondering if you'll be coming along to Westminster Abbey and the War Rooms?"

Tom didn't answer. He was looking over Quentin's shoulder, into the hallway, at Autumn. The girl no sooner spotted Tom than she whirled around and darted back upstairs.

"I'm coming," said Tom. "Ann insisted. She knows how much I was looking forward to seeing Churchill's command center. She's going to stay here with Caroline."

"I'll see if the hotel can provide them with some lunch," said Quentin.

"That would be great," said Tom, heading down the hall.

Lucy turned her attention to the waitress, who had arrived to take their order. "This morning it's eggs, bacon, and beans," she said.

"No beans for me," said Lucy. She couldn't help wondering if Caroline was tucking into the complete breakfast or if in her fragile emotional state she was daintily nibbling a bit of toast. If her past behavior was anything to go by, she was going for the beans.

"I don't buy it," she said to Sue as Pam and Rachel joined them. "I just don't see Caroline as the suicidal type."

Westminster Abbey was a gorgeous remnant from the Middle Ages, surrounded by soulless modern buildings made of glass and steel. There was no expansive lawn here, no encircling wall. Only a small patch of grass and some sidewalk protected the Abbey from the noisy traffic on Victoria Street, where buses and taxis streamed past Big Ben on their way to Westminster Bridge and busy Waterloo station on the other side of the Thames. Across the street, plastic orange barricades and a large police presence awaited the protesters who regularly filled Parliament Square.

It was all hustle and bustle and honking horns and diesel engines outside, but inside the Abbey it was quiet as death. Tourists spoke in hushed voices as they wandered among the tombs of the royal and great, closely observed by robed clergy and volunteers sporting official badges on their dark clothing. A priest climbed the pulpit every now and then to remind all those present that this was a house of worship and to invite them to participate in a moment of silence and prayer.

Lucy and the girls were gathered together at the front of the nave near the Tomb of the Unknown Soldier, heads bowed along with everyone else, when they heard Will's voice ring out, echoing in the huge vaulted space. "Dr. Livingstone, I presume?" he cracked, then laughed. Nearby, one of the volunteers rolled her eyes.

Lucy wondered how many times a day she heard the same bad joke.

Nevertheless, when the moment of silence ended, Lucy headed straight for the plaque marking Livingstone's resting place. BROUGHT BY FAITHFUL HANDS OVER LAND AND SEA HERE RESTS DAVID LIVINGSTONE, MISSIONARY, TRAVELER, PHILANTHROPIST. FOR 30 YEARS HIS LIFE WAS SPENT IN AN UNWEARIED EFFORT TO EVANGELIZE THE NATIVE RACES, TO EXPLORE THE UNDISCOVERED SECRETS, TO ABOLISH THE DESOLATING SLAVE TRADE OF CENTRAL AFRICA.

"I didn't know that," said Rachel. "I thought he was just an explorer."

"Me either." Lucy raised her eyes to look at the massive stone walls of the nave, rising high above her and blocking out the sun. "Poor man, if he'd had his druthers, I bet he would have preferred to be buried in Africa."

"He was a national hero," said Quentin, joining them. "It's a great honor to be buried here. They wouldn't let Byron in, you know. He was considered immoral—he set a bad example by falling in love with his half sister Augusta."

"Unlike the Unknown Soldier, who went off to fight for God and country." Pam paused, fingering the peace symbol charm she'd clipped to her handbag. "I guess the Germans worship a different God from the English."

"If we've learned anything on this trip, it's that God is an Englishman." Quentin caught Lucy's eye and smiled at her. "There's lots more to see. Follow me." Falling into step behind him, they crossed the nave to the south transept, stopping in front of a number of plaques bearing writers' names. "This is the Poets' Corner."

Standing together in a little group, their eyes wandered from one carved name to another: Dickens, Tennyson, Auden, Browning.

"Where's Elizabeth Barrett?" asked Sue.

Quentin had the answer. "In Florence."

"That's so sad," said Lucy. "They ought to be together."

"There are some odd pairings," said Quentin. "Elizabeth I and Mary are next to each other. It's true they were half sisters, but they didn't get along."

"That's odd," said Laura, joining them. "Elizabeth had Mary's head cut off, didn't she?" Will was tagging along with his mother but didn't seem to like it much. He was fidgeting, bouncing on the balls of his feet, and she gave him a warning look. "Listen to the professor and you might learn something."

"That's a common misconception," said Quentin. "Mary died a natural death from illness. Elizabeth executed Mary, Queen of Scots. Her son brought her body here when he became king. It was kind of a slap in the face to Elizabeth. He even made sure his mother's tomb was much prettier and more fashionable than Elizabeth's."

"Who was Bloody Mary?" Laura was keeping an eye on Will, who had begun to drift away toward a door leading to the cloister.

"Mary Tudor, Elizabeth's half sister." Quentin grimaced. "It was a well-deserved nickname. She executed more than three hundred Protestants, mostly by burning them alive."

"I don't like it here," said Lucy, shuddering. "It's a big old mausoleum." She unfolded the brochure she'd been given with her admission button and noticed a green patch, the College Garden. "I think I'll check out the garden."

"Don't you want to see Elizabeth's tomb?" Quentin seemed disappointed.

"Not really." She left the others, who were following Quentin to the Lady Chapel, and stepped through the same door Will had taken. She found herself in a chilly corridor, open on one side to the cloister. A sign pointed the way to the Chapter House and she followed it, finding herself in a simpler and more serene part of the Abbey. It was an octagon-shaped room, the walls filled with stained-glass windows. There was nothing inside except a few explanatory signs pointing visitors to the faded decorative paintings on the rough stone walls.

Unlike the rest of the Abbey, this room was full of light, and she lingered, studying the windows that had been damaged by German bombers during World War II. Standing there, she was struck by the incongruity of this building supposedly devoted to faith and prayer that was so full of reminders of war and death. She was thinking of soldiers who fought for God and country, kings and queens who executed their rivals, and planes that rained nighttime terror down on innocent people. It was too depressing. She had to find that garden.

But when she finally discovered it, she found a notice on the door advising it was closed for the day. Retracing her steps, she encountered Will and his mother in the cloister. Laura was holding Will's sleeve and speaking earnestly to him, but she stopped abruptly when she spotted Lucy.

"You should have stayed with us," she said. "That's what I was just telling Will. Professor Rea makes it all so interesting. He said Mary and Elizabeth really hated each other but they're buried together, side by side."

"Talk about rolling in your grave—they're probably tearing each others' hair out," said Lucy.

Laura gave a funny little chuckle and slipped her arm firmly through her son's. "Family members should care for each other. Don't you agree?"

Will was looking across the cloister to the other side, where Autumn was leaning against a stone pillar. Dressed in her habitual black, she looked a bit like a witch and every bit as out of place as a genuine witch would be in this Christian shrine.

Lucy turned to Laura, noting her anxious expression. "I think we should all care for one another. We're all on this little overheated planet together, after all. We all have the same needs and hopes. It's time we put our differences aside and work together to make life better for everyone."

"Like Livingstone," said Will, detaching himself from his mother and heading toward Autumn.

Laura watched him go. "I worry about that boy," she said.

Lucy thought she was right to worry but didn't say so. "Come on, let's find the others," she said.

Lucy wasn't in the mood to see the Cabinet War Rooms but went along with the group since the admission fee was included in the tour. She didn't want to dwell on the terrible loss of life caused by World War II but focused instead on the homely details of Churchill's simple living quarters: the kettle on the old-fashioned stove, the dining table and chairs that were just like those she remembered seeing as a child in her great-aunt Mary's house in Ludlow, Massachusetts.

As they trooped through the underground rooms, Lucy noticed that Autumn and Will kept their distance from Tom Smith, who pointedly ignored them. He was a big Churchill fan and expressed his enthusiasm in the museum devoted to his life. "He fought in the Boer War, you know," declared Tom. "He wasn't just a politician; he was a real soldier. He'd seen combat himself—he knew what it was all about."

"He was an artist, too," said Rachel, pausing before a landscape painting of green fields.

"And they say he was a real family man," added Laura with a glance at Will.

He and Autumn were whispering together in a corner.

"He adored his wife, Clementine." Sue was staring critically at a photo of a rather plump, middle-aged woman. "You'd think she would have done more with herself."

"He loved her the way she was. They were married for more than fifty years," observed Pam.

"If it wasn't for the old bulldog, Hitler might've won the war," said Tom. "The Blitz took a terrible toll on London."

"And the Allies did even worse to Dresden and Berlin, but you don't hear about that," said Pam, who was a staunch member of the Mothers March for Peace. "And we're the ones who dropped the atom bomb on Japan."

"It had to be done," said Dr. Cope. "The war would have dragged on much longer and many more lives would have been lost."

"Churchill was right about Hitler," said Tom. "He

knew from the beginning that appeasement wouldn't work."

Lucy was growing impatient with all this talk. "Hitler got his in the end," she said. "I'm ready for lunch."

"Hitler committed suicide—he took his own life," said Dr. Cope. "He never faced a war crimes tribunal. He was never punished for the terrible things he did. By committing suicide, he denied the survivors even the small satisfaction of seeing him disgraced and punished."

Tom Smith agreed. "The Italians strung up Mussolini. They tore him apart. Literally. They realized he'd led them astray and they took it out on Il Duce. The Germans never did. They collaborated; they followed orders. They're just as guilty as Hitler because they didn't stop him."

"Tom Cruise tried," said Sue, and everyone turned to look at her. "In that movie, I mean. German officers plotted to kill Hitler but the bomb misfired and they were all rounded up and killed."

"They were betrayed," said Dr. Cope, addressing the group in a serious tone that struck Lucy as sounding more like a warning than a casual observation.

"Something's going on," she said, unwrapping the sandwich she'd bought in a Pret A Manger shop. She was sitting on a bench along with her three friends in St. James's Park, watching the ducks and pelicans gathered at the edge of the lake, looking for handouts. It was a sunny afternoon and the friends had decided it was much too nice a day to spend in the Tate Britain museum, which was where the rest of the group had gone.

"What do you mean?" asked Sue, who was sipping a bottle of iced tea.

"There's some kind of tension. Don't you feel it?"

"Not really," said Pam, ripping open a bag of salt-and-vinegar crisps. "It's a tour. There's bound to be personality clashes."

"Pam's right," said Rachel, biting into her egg and cress sandwich. "Whenever you put a random group of people together, there's bound to be conflict. Dr. Cope is serious and intellectual; he has a scientific bent. Tom Smith is more of a man's man. I bet he's a big sports fan, too. Poor Laura is trying to keep tabs on Will. . . ."

"Autumn says he's got a drinking problem," said Lucy, wondering if that was why Laura was so worried about her son.

"Or maybe just an immaturity problem," said Pam.

"Poor Quentin's really got his hands full," said Rachel.

Sue grinned wickedly, glancing at Lucy. "He'd like to get his hands on you, that's for sure. You should have seen the way he watched you when you left us in the Abbey."

"Yeah, Lucy, what were you two doing in Brighton?" asked Pam.

They were all looking at her, and Lucy felt she had to defend herself. "Nothing. We didn't do anything. We had a drink, that was all." She smoothed her paper napkin. "He's barking up the wrong tree if he's after me. I'm another Clementine Churchill, loyal to a fault."

"Just as long as you don't start looking like her," muttered Sue, sending them all into gales of laughter.

Chapter Fourteen

The group was scheduled to see *The Mousetrap* on Thursday night, but the choice didn't sit well with Rachel.

"Why do we have to see an old chestnut like that?" she asked as the four friends waited in the lounge for the rest of the group. "London's known for wonderful, cutting-edge theater and we're stuck with this old thing."

"I agree," said Quentin, rising from his seat at the computer and joining them. "But George apparently felt that no trip to London was complete without seeing it. And it's certainly a safe choice with nothing to offend anyone."

He gave a slight tilt of his head to the doorway, where the Smith family had just appeared. Tom and Ann were on either side of Caroline, whose arm was in a blue sling. She seemed more stolid and robotic than ever. Lucy figured her glassy eyes and listlessness were due to medication, but apart from that and the broken arm, she seemed none the worse for her dunking.

There were plenty of free seats in the lounge, but only the saggy old couch provided seating for three. Lucy was wondering why Tom Smith was staring at her in that pointed manner and, receiving a sharp jab in the ribs from Rachel, realized he wanted them to give up their seats.

Lucy thought it was ridiculous, but she got up and moved to an equally saggy armchair on the opposite side of the room. Sue, she saw, was rolling her eyes at the maneuver.

Rachel, true to her nature, was full of sympathy. "It's great to have you back with the group," she told Caroline. "How are you feeling?"

Caroline was slow to answer. "Okay, I guess."

Rachel received this news with a delighted smile. "That's wonderful. I'm sure you'll enjoy the show."

Her efforts to engage Caroline in conversation were not received well by her parents, however. Tom was glaring at her beneath bristly eyebrows, and Ann was nervously stroking Caroline's hand, as if this harmless bit of small talk might trigger an emotional breakdown.

Ann's anxiety increased when Will and his mother arrived; she practically leaped out of her seat when Will demanded to know if they'd have to stand for "God Save the Queen."

"I think that stopped when World War II ended," said Quentin. "But the theaters do have bars. That hasn't changed."

"Really," sighed Laura. "Must they have alcohol available at every event?"

"I thought England would be stuffy," said Autumn, "but it's great. They drink, they smoke, and they swear."

Quentin's face lit up. "So the UK's okay with you?"

"It's bloody marvelous," declared Autumn, practically sending the Smiths into paroxysms of propriety. Tom humphed and Ann straightened her back and pursed her lips in disapproval.

Dr. Cope, however, chuckled as he settled himself in the last available chair. "I was here in the sixties," he said as Jennifer perched on the arm of his chair. "Studying, you know. I tell you, it was difficult to keep my mind on the intricacies of the endocrine system with all those birds popping about in miniskirts. It was a great time to be in London."

"Were you a mod or a rocker?" asked Sue with a naughty grin.

Dr. Cope sighed. "Neither, I'm afraid. I was a grind."

"You made the right choice," said Quentin, assuming a professorial air. "The mods and rockers are gone but the endocrine system is eternal." He stood up. "I think we're all here, so we can get this show on the road—pun intended! We can walk together over to the Goodge Street station. It's just two stops to Leicester Square."

"I've arranged for a taxi," said Tom with a nod to his daughter.

Ann was quick to defend her daughter. "It's not anything to do with Caroline," she declared. "I don't like the noise and the smell of the Underground."

"Of course," said Quentin diplomatically. "We'll see you at the theater, then."

When they emerged from the theater into the narrow neon-lit street, which was slick from an evening shower, Sue insisted they stop at a nearby pub for a drink. "Otherwise, I'm sure I couldn't be trusted not to reveal the surprise ending of the play."

She was referring to the fact that everyone in the audience had been asked not to reveal the killer's identity, thereby spoiling the surprise for future audiences.

"After twenty-three thousand performances, I suspect the secret is out," said Rachel.

"Were you surprised, Lucy?" asked Pam. "You're the reporter, after all. Did you suspect the, well"—she dropped her voice to a whisper—"the *you-know-who* wasn't what he seemed to be?"

The three turned to look at her and Lucy blushed. "That play was written by a master—there were a lot of red herrings."

"She didn't guess!" crowed Sue.

Lucy turned the tables on her friend. "Did you?"

Sue didn't answer; she was busy pushing her way into the crowded pub.

The crowd was mostly in the front, near the bar; they discovered plenty of free tables in the rear. They were gathered around one, sipping white wine and nibbling assorted flavors of crisps, when they spotted Dr. Cope standing awkwardly with a pint of beer in his hand. Pam waved him over and he joined them, followed by his granddaughter Jennifer and Will Barfield.

"Where's your mother?" Lucy blurted it out without thinking.

"Laura was tired and went back to the hotel with the Smiths," said Dr. Cope.

Will didn't seem to be missing his mother at all. He was busy whispering in Jennifer's ear and had draped his arm along the top of the banquette where it rested behind her. Dr. Cope noticed, his face hardening in displeasure, but he didn't say anything. Instead, he turned to Rachel. "Did you enjoy the play?"

"I didn't expect to, but I did," she said. "I guess there's a reason why it's lasted all these years."

"You can't argue with success," declared Quentin, arriving with Autumn and pulling up chairs for both of them. "Do you know why it's called *The Mousetrap*?"

Nobody did.

Quentin wasn't shy about telling them. "It's based on a short story called 'Three Blind Mice,' which doesn't quite have the snap of *The Mousetrap*. Pun intended!"

At this, Autumn groaned, but Quentin continued. "*The Mousetrap* is the name of the play in *Hamlet*, which is designed "to catch the conscience of the king."

"From what I've seen, none of these kings, or the queens either, had much in the way of consciences," said Lucy, draining her glass.

"It's a funny thing about consciences," said Dr. Cope. "Some people have them and some seem not to have them at all. They just carry on without a care, conveniently ignoring the damage they've done."

Lucy suspected he was directing this to Will, issuing a warning to be careful of Jennifer's emotions. If so, he had missed his target—Will's arm was now draped across the girl's shoulders.

Pam was trying a prawn-flavored crisp. "But Maureen Lynn—the abuser in the play—she went to prison. She paid for her crime. I don't see why you-know-who had to kill her."

"Some crimes can't be forgiven," said Dr. Cope.

"Two wrongs don't make a right," insisted Pam. "And you-know-who wrecked his own life—now he'll get sent to jail."

"Or even hanged," said Quentin. "The death penalty was in force when the play was written."

"I expect he felt so strongly about taking his revenge that he was willing to face the consequences," said Dr. Cope, placidly twirling his empty glass.

"My husband, Bob, he's a lawyer," said Rachel. "Bob

says the law really has nothing to do with moral truth. It's a system. It's better than nothing, but it doesn't allow for every situation. Sometimes there are mitigating circumstances, like abused women who kill their abusers, situations like that."

"That's exactly the point Agatha Christie makes in *Murder on the Orient Express*," said Pam. "I love that book, because justice—real justice—triumphs in the end. Poirot solves the case but decides the twelve have acted as a jury. The dead man deserved what he got, and Poirot decides they shouldn't be punished."

Dr. Cope had turned rather pale, and Lucy turned to see Will was nuzzling Jennifer's neck.

But it was Autumn who spoke up, her voice charged with emotion. "Anything can happen in books—authors make things end the way they want." Her voice dropped. "Something like that could never happen in real life."

"Point taken," said Quentin, popping up. "I need to get drinks for myself and Autumn. Can I get you all another round?"

No one had any objection and he soon returned carrying a tray loaded with drinks. Conversation flowed as everyone had a good time, freed from Laura's sense of propriety and the Smiths' dampening influence. Lucy found her thoughts wandering, recalling Christie's intricate plot in which twelve seemingly unrelated travelers come together on the Orient Express to execute a kidnapper.

Her mind was awhirl as she stared into her glass, watching how the surface of the wine reflected the light from the wall sconce behind her, refracting differently as she moved the goblet. Was it the same with this tour?

Had this odd group of travelers come together to exact revenge by killing George Temple?

It was possible, she realized, if they'd known about his allergies. Thinking back to the events at the airport, she could see a clever set of circumstances that could have been designed to trigger and exacerbate an attack. First there was the trouble at security, when officers found something in Temple's pocket that required them to question him, perhaps even search him. Something that he claimed he hadn't known about. What was it?

When he returned to the group at the gate, he was already exhibiting symptoms. Ann Smith had rushed to his aid as he sat, struggling to catch his breath, by wrapping her pashmina around him. But this effort to soothe and relax Temple had backfired; his breathing only got worse.

That situation had accelerated when Laura Barfield frantically announced her son Will was missing, just as the boarding process began. She was practically hysterical, pleading with Temple to make the airline delay the flight, something that he had no power to do. Her panic was contagious; everyone in the group was upset by the time Will arrived, nonchalantly explaining he'd been in the bookshop and had lost track of the time.

And then, of course, there was the business with Jennifer and Autumn that Lucy had witnessed. It could have been a series of accidents—that's what it had seemed like at the time—but what if the girls had behaved deliberately? What if they'd known about Temple's peanut allergy and made sure to shake the trail mix, releasing the peanut dust into the air? And what if Autumn had purposely knocked the inhaler out of his hand?

But there Lucy felt she'd gone too far. These two young girls had their own problems; it hardly seemed likely they would plot to kill a respected teacher. Why would they do such a thing? And if this was indeed some sort of macabre plot, Dr. Cope would have had to be involved, and Lucy had seen him use the EpiPen with her own eyes. And furthermore, she'd seen his serious expression when he announced that Temple was dead. She was convinced the doctor was not one who took death lightly.

She looked across the table at Dr. Cope, noticing his usually severe expression had brightened with the appearance of two red patches on his cheeks. He was clearly enjoying himself—and the pub's best bitter. He'd even forgotten to keep an eye on Jennifer, who was kissing Will.

Back at the hotel, Sue was brushing her teeth and Lucy was turning down her bed when Pam knocked gently on their door. "Can I come in? I need a Band-Aid." She held up her finger, which was wrapped in a wad of toilet paper.

"How did that happen?" Lucy was examining the cut.

"I dropped a bathroom glass and cut myself when I was picking up the pieces." She shook her head. "I can't believe I didn't bring any—I always have a couple in my purse."

"No problem, I've got some." Lucy pulled a ziplock bag out of her handbag and produced a little plastic first-aid kit. "I've even got antibiotic cream."

Pam was dabbing at her finger with the toilet paper. The bleeding had slowed, and after a few dabs, Lucy was able to apply the ointment and stick on a Band-Aid.

"She's a real Nurse Nancy." Sue had popped out of the bathroom and was watching the operation with interest.

"More like Nancy Drew." Pam was tossing the bloody bit of paper into the wastebasket. "Did you see her at the pub? That suspicious mind of hers was in overdrive."

"We should never have allowed her to see a mystery. She really can't handle them." Sue sat on her bed. "Well, are you going to tell us or not?"

"It wasn't *The Mousetrap*," said Lucy. "I'm thinking more of *Murder on the Orient Express*."

Pam and Sue exchanged glances. "You think they—meaning everybody on the tour except us four—plotted together to kill George Temple?" demanded Sue.

"That's the craziest thing I ever heard." Pam was studying her finger. "Everybody at Winchester loved him."

"I agree with Herr Doktor Professor Shtillings." Sue had adopted a phony German accent. "It is crazy. She has these recurring episodes in which she sees murderers everywhere. It's a form of paranoia."

"Or maybe schizophrenia," added Pam with a sharp nod.

"There is only one cure that I know of," continued Sue.

"Und vat is dat?" Pam was enjoying herself.

"Shopping! She must go to Topshop, and the sooner the better."

"I agree, Herr Doctor." Pam was yawning, heading for the door. "Until tomorrow, then."

"Wait a minute." Lucy was tapping her chin. "In *Murder on the Orient Express,* and *The Mousetrap*, too, the murder, the act of retribution, takes place long after the original crime, right?"

"Oh, Doktor, it is vurse, far vurse, than I thought." Pam was shaking her head.

"It's the vurst!" exclaimed Sue, laughing hysterically. "It's the bratvurst!"

Lucy was laughing, too. "Cut it out. I'm serious. The George Temple you knew at Winchester was a nice guy, but maybe he wasn't always a nice guy. Maybe he has a past. Maybe he did something unforgivable. Dr. Cope was sort of talking like that, wasn't he? About people not having consciences, not caring that they'd wrecked other people's lives?"

"He was just speaking generally," protested Sue. "Making small talk. We'd just seen a murder mystery."

"I know," admitted Lucy. "But I've got this feeling. I just can't shake it."

Pam held up a finger. "Dis is progress, Doktor. She admits she may be delusional."

"It's a first step," agreed Sue.

"Okay, if I'm delusional, prove it," challenged Lucy.

Pam sighed. "And how am I supposed to do that?"

"Ask Ted to do a bit of research. He's the chief reporter at the *Pennysaver*. . . ."

"Editor and publisher to you," said Pam.

"He loves reporting most of all," said Lucy. "He'll enjoy doing a little digging. It will keep him out of trouble until you get home."

"Okay," said Pam, "but in the meantime, you must agree to treatment."

"If you insist," agreed Lucy. "But I'm afraid I may have maxed out my credit cards."

Chapter Fifteen

When Lucy awoke on Friday morning, she found Sue's bed was empty. Reaching for her watch, she realized with a shock that it was close to nine o'clock. How had this happened? She never slept this late. Folding back the covers and swinging her legs out of bed, she yawned and scratched her head, trying to remember the day's itinerary. It came to her as she stood in the bathroom, studying her puffy face in the mirror over the sink: Windsor Castle. They were supposed to go to Windsor, and the bus was leaving at nine o'clock. Hurrying over to the window, she was just in time to see it pulling away from the curb and driving down the street.

She was throwing some clothes on, intending to find out what was going on, when Sue arrived with a cup of coffee for her. "I hope you don't mind. I made an executive decision."

Lucy took the cup. "What about Windsor?"

"It's just another musty old castle," said Sue with a shrug. "And you were sleeping so soundly, snoring away. . . ."

"I don't snore."

Sue cocked an eyebrow. "Sweetie, I hate to break it to you, but you do. Just a little bit, now and then. It's actually more of a ladylike little snuffle. Positively mouse-like."

Lucy took a swallow of coffee. "This mouse wanted to see Windsor Castle."

"Mother knows best, dear. Trust me on this. Time is running out and we haven't had time for any serious shopping."

"What do you call Harrods? That was pretty serious shopping."

Sue shook her head. "I happen to know that all you've bought are those sad little odds and ends from Portobello and a toy bear. What about the girls? Aren't you going to get anything for them? And Bill? What about him? He deserves something for keeping the home fires burning and all that."

"There are shops in Windsor," protested Lucy.

"No, dear. We all talked it over and decided you definitely need a break from the group and your wicked suspicions. And some of us want a decent breakfast."

That was the last straw. Lucy realized she'd missed breakfast. "No eggs and bacon?"

Sue patted her on the shoulder. "We're going to go out and get some nice fruit and yogurt and get you back on the right track." She spoke in a soothing voice, as one might to a fretful invalid. "And if you're good, maybe a bit of wholemeal toast with jam."

Lucy knew when she was beat. "All right, Mother."

"Now finish your coffee and get dressed like a good girl. We're meeting downstairs in fifteen minutes."

Pam was sitting at the computer terminal in the corner when Lucy arrived in the lounge a half hour later.

"It's about time you got here," said Sue, who was flipping through a magazine.

"What is the matter with this thing?" muttered Pam.

Rachel put down the guidebook she was reading and went over to her. "What's the problem?"

"I've got this attachment, and I want to print it, but it won't cooperate."

"Let me try," suggested Rachel, reaching for the mouse. She clicked a few times, then shook her head. "It's got a virus scan going or something. It's too busy to bother with your attachment."

"How long will it take?" asked Sue.

"I don't know. It says it will complete waiting tasks when the scan is complete. We might as well go. Your attachment will be here when we get back."

Pam considered. "I don't want people reading my e-mail."

"Don't be silly," said Sue, impatient to get going. "Who's going to be interested in your boring e-mail?"

"Just close it out and do it later," said Lucy. "I'm starving."

"Good idea, Lucy." Pam clicked the little X in the corner of the screen and hopped up. "There's a Starbucks in that bookshop across the way—let's go there and get some decent coffee."

Lucy felt a lot better after she'd eaten, and she had to admit her friends were right about Starbucks, which was a big improvement over the watery orange juice, weak coffee, and greasy eggs the hotel provided.

"I kinda missed the bacon," she teased as they emerged from the Underground at Oxford Circus.

Sue ignored her, as her gaze was focused on the Topshop sign as if she'd finally found the Holy Grail. "There it is." She sighed in rapture before leading the charge across busy Oxford Street.

Once inside, Lucy found the loud rock music and jumbled displays disorienting.

"This is the perfect place to find something for Sara and Zoe," said Pam, joining Sue in energetically flipping through racks of colorful shirts.

Lucy moved a few hangers in a halfhearted way, then turned to Rachel, who looked uncomfortable. "Let's find the ladies' loo," she suggested, and Rachel agreed.

"Too much coffee this morning," she said as they stepped onto the escalator for the descent to the lower level.

"Too much music," said Lucy.

Much to their surprise, when they emerged from the ladies' room, they found a café where they could sit in comfort and gather their thoughts.

"There are a lot of other shops around here," said Rachel. "Maybe we could meet them later."

"I saw Marks and Spencer," said Lucy. "Bill needs some underwear."

"My guidebook says Marks and Sparks, that's its nickname, is the place for underwear."

"We better go find them and figure out where to meet."

The store had become crowded, filled with chattering girls darting from one rack to another, like distracted honeybees in a flower garden. There was no sign of Sue, but they did find Pam pawing through a bin of colorful scarves.

"Can you believe it? Twenty pounds for this!" She held up a garish black and yellow striped number. "Sue said this place had great bargains but I haven't found any."

"We're going on to Marks and Spencer," said Rachel. "Want to come?"

"No, I want to find Liberty. It's around here somewhere."

"Okay, let's say we all meet back here, out front, in an hour. Okay?"

"Sounds good to me," said Pam, digging down and pulling up a polka-dot scarf, which she held up. "What do you think?"

Lucy and Rachel both shook their heads no.

When the four friends met at the appointed place, only a quarter of an hour late, they all had something to show for their time. Rachel had found some colorful glass and brass knobs on sale at Liberty, and Pam had discovered a shop selling natural cosmetics where she splurged on skin lotion and bath bombs. Lucy had found briefs at Marks and Spencer for Bill, and faux Burberry scarves that she bought from a street vendor who was selling them for about five dollars each. Back in Tinker's Cove, nobody would know the difference.

Sue wasn't impressed. "Oh, Lucy, anyone can see that's not really a Burberry scarf."

Lucy studied the pink plaid strip of acrylic fabric. "I don't care. I think they're pretty and I got one in every color." She pulled out a gray and black one. "This one's for Toby."

Sue examined it. "You know, that's not bad. It's this season's color." She came to a quick decision. "Where'd you get it?"

"Over there." Lucy pointed across the street, where the vendor had set up a portable table displaying his wares.

"Let's go." Sue was leading the way with the others following in her wake. Lucy and Rachel were just behind her, crossing the street as the light began to blink. Pam, who'd dropped her bag and stopped to scoop it up, was running after them and just made it to the crowded pedestrian island in the middle of the street before buses and taxis began surging past. She was perched at the very edge of the island, barely on it. One moment she was there and the next she'd fallen backward, into the path of a cab that was speeding to catch the green light. The driver swerved and avoided her, passing with a blare of the horn.

"Oh my goodness," said a gentleman, stooping to help Pam get on her feet and back onto the curbed island. "You must be American—Americans always forget to look right."

"No, no," insisted Pam, shaking her head as her friends gathered around her. "I wasn't crossing. I was on the island. I was pushed off."

"Did you see who did it?" asked Lucy.

"I didn't. I was looking at the light, waiting for it to turn and keeping an eye on you guys so I wouldn't get separated from you. Then, all of a sudden, I felt a jab from my left side and over I went."

"She's right—I saw him," said a tiny Indian woman dressed in a red sari topped with a Western-style jacket.

"What did he look like?" asked Lucy

"Young and tall." She considered a moment. "I don't think he did it on purpose. These islands get so crowded. I think it was an accident."

"Yes, I'm sure that's what it was," said Pam. "It was an accident."

But as they crossed the other half of the road, Lucy wondered. The woman's description of a tall young man could fit Will. Of course, it could also fit a lot of people, but Autumn had speculated that Will had pushed Caroline off the pier. Trailing along behind the others, Lucy thought it was one heck of a coincidence. Or was it? It would be easy to find out if Will went along with the group to Windsor or if he'd taken off on his own. She was thinking about that when she caught up with the others, who were waiting outside a pub.

"Pam's twisted her ankle," said Sue, "so we thought we'd grab some lunch in here and see if she recovers."

"Fine with me," said Lucy as they filed into the mahogany and red plush interior. She perched on a banquette with Pam while Sue and Rachel went to the bar to get drinks and order their food.

"Salads all round," announced Sue, returning with a glass of white wine in each hand.

"The menu's pretty limited," added Rachel, who also had a wineglass in each hand."

"It's just nice to sit," said Lucy. "How's the ankle?"

"Fine, as long as I don't put any weight on it." Pam sighed. "I hate to spoil your day."

Lucy was pawing through her bag looking for the little tin of painkillers she always carried. She finally produced it after a prolonged search, finding it lurking beneath a business card.

"Take two," she told Pam, passing over the tin and giving the card a quick glance. It was a bit crumpled but still quite legible; it was the card the Scotland Yard detective had given her after interviewing her on the plane.

She debated whether to discuss her discovery with the girls for a moment, then decided not. There'd been too much discussion; it was time to put her suspicions to the test. If he thought she was on to something, he'd talk to her. If not, she'd forget the whole thing. Anyway, the chance that he would actually be at his desk and answer his phone was exceedingly slim. She could live with that, but she had to try. Without a word to the others, she got up and went over to the pay phone that hung on the wall, dropped in some coins, and dialed.

"Neal here." The voice was firm and brusque, businesslike, to the point.

"I'm Lucy Stone. You questioned me about George Temple, the man who died on the plane from America. . . . You gave me your card, in case I thought of anything more."

"Umm, right." Neal didn't sound very interested. "This was . . . when?"

"Just about a week ago," said Lucy, a bit annoyed. How many people died on flights en route to the UK? You'd think he would remember.

"Uh, sorry. I was multitasking. Now what's this about?"

"George Temple. The man who died on the airplane. I may have some new information."

"Go on."

"I think he was murdered."

"Well I guess you better come round, then, and tell me about it. I'm here until six o'clock."

Lucy didn't need any encouragement. "I'll be there in about an hour," she said.

"What was that all about?" inquired Sue, putting down her fork. She'd been poking halfheartedly at a blob of tuna salad that was nestled in a bed of iceberg lettuce along with some pineapple chunks and a scoop of mayonnaise.

"What's this?" The same dish was waiting for Lucy.

"It's the pub version of a salad," said Pam, who was cutting up her lettuce chunks with a knife and fork. "It's not bad."

"It's full of calories," said Sue. "The tuna is loaded with mayo."

"And they give you extra, in case you need a bit more to clog up your arteries for good," said Rachel.

"Between those greasy breakfasts and lunches like this, it's a miracle they don't all drop dead in the streets," said Lucy, spearing a pineapple chunk.

"You haven't told us who you were calling," reminded Sue.

"Don't laugh," warned Lucy. "I called that Scotland Yard detective. I found his card in my purse."

Sue gave her a look. "Just to chat?"

"Oh, come on." Lucy felt defensive. "You've got to admit there've been an awful lot of so-called accidents on this trip. I don't think the average tour to London includes a sudden death in the air, a leap off the Brighton pier, and a near-miss auto accident."

Pam nodded. "And there's the atmosphere—like everybody's hiding something."

Lucy leaned forward. "You've felt it, too?"

"Not really," admitted Pam, "but you keep talking about it and I'm beginning to think you're right." She gave a sharp nod. "I was definitely pushed into traffic. I'm absolutely certain about that."

"Want to come to Scotland Yard with me?"

"If we take a taxi—I don't think I can manage the Tube with my ankle."

"While you do that, Sue and I can go to the Natural

History Museum," suggested Rachel. "I've been wanting to go."

Sue looked at her as if she were crazy. "Don't be silly, darling. There's a marvelous gallery around here, just a street or two over, that's an absolute can't-miss. It's got fashion—"

Rachel's good nature was being stretched. "Fashion isn't really my thing. . . ."

"You can say that again." Sue was looking at her empty glass, considering whether to have another. "Just joking, sweetie. No, the reason this gallery is so special is that it has nature stuff, too. Skulls and twigs and things."

Rachel knew when she was beat. "If you say so."

Lucy couldn't help it—she was excited when the taxi pulled up in front of the revolving New Scotland Yard sign she'd seen in so many British crime dramas on TV. And here she was, actually at Scotland Yard, to assist on a case. But first, she had to help Pam out of the cab and pay the fare. After that, there was quite a bit of security to negotiate and miles of corridors, which Pam insisted were fine but which Lucy knew must be terribly painful for her. It was a great relief when they finally reached Inspector John Neal's office.

The office was very small, painted green, but very neat, and it had a wonderful view of the Thames. Neal, who had hung his suit jacket on a coat tree and had rolled up his shirtsleeves and loosened his necktie, immediately noticed Pam's swollen ankle and leaped from behind his desk to hold a chair for her. She expelled a huge sigh as she settled herself. Lucy, sitting beside her, noticed and felt guilty for dragging her along on what was probably a wild-goose chase.

"Soo, Mrs. Stone, you say you have new information about George Temple's death, which the medical examiner and the coroner have determined to be the result of an asthma attack."

Lucy spoke slowly and carefully. "I think the attack was caused by the tour members. I think they did things on purpose that would cause him to have a reaction."

Neal didn't seem convinced. "Really? How so?"

Lucy ticked off the events at the airport, the peanut granola, and the incident with his inhaler. Seeing that she wasn't making much of an impression, she made a reckless accusation. "Even the EpiPen could have been faked," she added.

Pam was shaking her head. "I don't think Dr. Cope is involved, but I do think something weird is going on. Caroline Smith was pushed off the pier, and I was knocked into traffic today, twisting my ankle."

"Foreigners always forget to look right," said Neal, leaning back in his chair. He'd formed a little tent with his fingers and seemed to be enjoying himself.

"I was pushed," insisted Pam. "It was not a matter of not looking in the right direction."

Neal smiled. "And have you been having a nice time in London? Seeing the sights?"

Lucy didn't like the direction this was taking. "London's fine; it's the group that's worrisome," she said.

"I fear that is often the case when an oddly assorted group of people travel together. Tensions often arise." He paused. "I wonder, have you been to the theater?"

Pam and Lucy nodded.

"I mention it, because the incidents you've described

to me almost seem like the plot of a play. You didn't perhaps see a thriller?"

"We saw *The Mousetrap*." Lucy felt as if she were signing a confession.

"Aha." Neal nodded. "Case solved. I think we can put your suspicions down to less than congenial company and overwrought imaginations." He stood. "I'll be happy to call a cab for you, and I think we can rustle up a wheelchair to get you back downstairs."

Pam was touched by his consideration. "Thank you so much."

Lucy less so. "Thanks for your time," she grumbled.

Back at the hotel, Lucy and Pam stopped in the lounge and had a cup of tea to fortify themselves for the climb upstairs. Pam insisted she could manage by taking each stair with her good leg and hanging on to the railing for support. Lucy was doubtful.

"Maybe we can get you a room on a lower floor," she suggested, heading over to the computer where she planned to check her e-mail. A stack of papers on the printer caught her eye, and she glanced at them, finding they were from Ted.

"Here's your e-mail," she said, taking the pages over to Pam.

"Oh, good, this is that story about Tim's project in New Orleans," she said, flipping through the papers. "Oh, and Ted says he'll get on that George Temple research for you when he has a minute."

"Tell him thanks for me," said Lucy, closing out her e-mail account. No word from Elizabeth. Oh, well, she decided. No news was good news. At least she hoped it was.

Chapter Sixteen

"Don't you think there was something positively sinister about that place?" asked Sue, holding the hotel door for her friends who were returning from dinner at a highly recommended French restaurant.

"The food was awfully good," said Rachel.

"And it was the closest one—I was glad not to have to walk very far," said Pam.

"But those waiters . . ." Lucy shuddered. "I didn't like the way they stood around, watching. It was weird."

"Like in a movie, when they're focusing on supposedly everyday activities to build the tension." Sue gave a knowing nod.

"Maybe it was just everyday stuff," said Pam. "I think you're overreacting. It's just that we were early and they didn't have much to do. The place was just starting to hop when we were ready to leave."

Sue yawned. "I don't know about you guys, but I'm beat. I think I'll go on up to bed."

"Me too," said Rachel, starting up the stairs and leaving Lucy and Pam in the foyer.

"I'm not tired yet. I slept in this morning," said Lucy. "Besides, I'd like to check my e-mail again."

"I'm not ready to face the climb," said Pam. "Let's see what's doing in the lounge."

When they entered, they found a card table had been set up and Laura Barfield, Ann Smith, and Dr. Cope were all playing Scrabble. Pam immediately hobbled over.

"Do you mind if I join? I love Scrabble," she said.

"I don't mind at all. You're quite welcome," said Ann.

"But you'll be at a disadvantage," warned Dr. Cope, studying his tiles. "We've already racked up quite a few points."

"Not a problem." Pam was lowering herself into the fourth chair. "I don't care about winning—I just like to play."

Not a problem at all, thought Lucy, seating herself at the computer. If she were a betting person, she'd put her money on Pam, even with a late start. She was an absolute fiend at Scrabble, never missing an opportunity for a triple-word score, preferably one with an *X*.

"Did you all enjoy Windsor?" Pam was busy arranging her tiles on the little wooden rack.

"It's a bit of a factory—they move you right along," said Ann, putting down some tiles. "There. *Ambiguity.* And a double-word score."

"Very nice," said Dr. Cope. "Afraid all I can come up with is yak."

"Did you get a look at Eton?" inquired Lucy, waiting for the computer to connect and authorize.

"*Student,*" crowed Laura, laying down the letters. "Thanks, Lucy."

"No, the weather was foul and the hike up the hill to the castle entrance was rather strenuous, so we ended up having a long lunch at a nearby pub." Dr. Cope looked at Pam. "It doesn't seem to me we've left you much room to maneuver."

Lucy had opened her account but once again found no message from Elizabeth. Bill, however, had sent a long, rambling note about Zoe's big track meet against the rival Gilead Giants and Sara's problems with her history term paper. She was busy writing back with congratulations for Zoe and helpful hints for Sara when there was a sudden upset at the Scrabble table and the board went flying, scattering wooden tiles every which way.

"Oh my goodness! I didn't mean to do that!" Laura was on her knees, gathering up the little wooden squares.

"Let me help." Dr. Cope dropped to the floor to help. "We better find them all."

Ann was also stooping and picking up the game pieces. "We don't want to spoil the game."

"I wish I could help," said Pam. "But I'm on the disabled list."

Dr. Cope looked up at her. "What's the problem?"

"I twisted my ankle. I expect it will be better tomorrow."

"Better let me take a look at it."

Pam smiled as he hobbled across the floor on his knees. "Sorry—I'm already married."

"If you would just lift your pants leg," he said, smiling at her joke as he took her ankle in his hand. "It's definitely swollen. Does this hurt?"

"Aah," protested Pam.

"Doesn't seem too serious to me. Try to stay off it as much as you can. Ibuprofen will help with the pain and reduce inflammation."

"Thank you, Doctor," said Pam. "Shall we try another game?"

Ann was already back at the table, flipping the tiles so the letters faced down.

"I think I'm done for the night," said Laura, dropping a handful of tiles on the table and dashing for the arched doorway.

Lucy, who was rising from her seat at the computer and relocating to the sofa, watched her sudden departure and caught a glimpse of Will taking the stairs two at a time, with his mother hurrying after him. A moment later, Jennifer wandered into the lounge with her usual uncertain attitude and seated herself on the sofa.

"Do you mind if I sit here?" she asked, tugging at a lock of hair.

"Not at all," said Lucy. "There's room for two." She paused, reaching for a magazine. She opened it and began turning the pages. "Did you enjoy Windsor?"

"The castle is like a fairy tale," said Jennifer. "I'd like to live there." She blushed. "I guess every girl wants to be a princess."

At the card table, Ann Smith, Pam, and Dr. Cope were choosing their letters and arranging them on their racks for a fresh game.

"A princess in a castle needs a gallant champion," said Pam. "Any prospects?"

Jennifer laughed. "Not a one."

"Not even Will?" asked Lucy, keeping her eyes on the magazine.

"He didn't come. He wanted to see some dungeon thing here in London."

Lucy's and Pam's eyes met as Dr. Cope slapped down all of his tiles on the board.

"Look at that: *dragons*." He chuckled as he filled his rack again. "Will the Dragon Slayer."

Jennifer was looking uncomfortable, so Lucy decided to change the subject. "Are you looking forward to getting back to school?" she asked.

"I've really been enjoying the trip, but now that we're nearing the end, I have to admit I've been thinking about all the work that's waiting for me back at school. Finals are coming up soon."

"My daughter's going to graduate in a few weeks," said Lucy, "if she manages to stay out of trouble."

"Where does she go?"

"Chamberlain, in Boston. She's an RA. At least she was. She hasn't been getting along with the new dean, and I wouldn't be surprised if she lost her position."

Jennifer turned to her. "Are you angry with her?"

Lucy considered the question as tiles clicked in the background. "A little bit, I guess, but this sort of thing is nothing new. Elizabeth's always been a challenging kid."

"She's lucky to have such understanding parents. At school it seems kids are always at odds and fighting with their parents. Nobody at school ever says anything nice about their parents. They resent them."

Lucy didn't have any trouble imagining this. "What about you? Do you say bad things about your family?"

Jennifer shook her head. "No. Gramps and I are real close." She turned her head and winked at him, and he winked back. "My father died when I was a baby, and Mom and I moved in with Gramps. He's been super."

"It's been a pleasure, my dear." He was watching Pam put down her tiles and groaned. "You are a devil," he said, toting up her score. "Eighty-seven. How do you do it?"

"Practice. I play a lot with my husband. He's a newspaper editor."

"Humph." Dr. Cope was studying the letters on his rack. "I call that an unfair advantage."

Ann's usually worried expression seemed to deepen. "What newspaper?"

"Tinker's Cove," said Pam automatically, replacing the tiles she'd used.

Lucy yawned and stood up, deciding to give her e-mail one more try before heading up to bed. "Cross your fingers for me—I'm giving Elizabeth one more chance before I turn in for the night."

"Consider them crossed," said Pam, busy rearranging the letters on her rack.

The computer was much faster this time, and Lucy got right into her e-mail account. There was no news from Elizabeth, but there was one from Ted. Opening it, she found he'd done the research about George Temple that Pam had requested.

I had to go back quite a few years, all the way back to the savings and loan crisis in the nineties. He lost his job as a bank president. He was basically fired by the board of directors and went into business for himself as an investment advisor. The fact that he'd been fired was kept secret, and quite a lot of bank customers signed on with him, but he wasn't any better with investments than he was with banking. When the investments he recommended started losing value, he began falsifying the statements and inevitably began using good money to cover bad. The business turned into a Ponzi scheme. It all came apart in 1991 when a client began to suspect something was fishy and complained to the state. An investigation followed, and a lot of people who thought they were prudent investors learned they were broke, and Temple was convicted of fraud. He had a sympathetic judge—a lot of eminent types testified on his behalf, saying he never meant to hurt anyone, that he was just trying to keep things afloat until the market recovered—and he went to jail for a couple of years.

When he got out, he went back to school and got a master's degree in history, cum laude, no less. Those same friends who testified on his behalf helped again and found him the job at Winchester College, where he seems to have been a great success. I called the college president, who says his death is a great loss to the school; Temple was even being considered for a professorship, something she said was long overdue. She also said a memorial service is planned for next week. If I learn anything more, I'll pass it along. Meanwhile, Lucy, the work is piling up on your desk!

Lucy grimaced, picturing the stack of papers that she would face when she returned, and hit the PRINT button. Instead of obediently printing the page for her, the printer began beeping, alerting her to a paper jam. When she cleared it and tossed the offending paper into the nearby wastebasket she noticed a couple of sheets that looked familiar. Bending down to retrieve them she realized they were copies of the same attachment from Ted that she was printing. Ted must have sent the information to Pam as well, and Pam's copy had printed earlier that day when the virus scan was complete. Which meant, thought Lucy, that somebody else had found it.

"I guess I'll say good night," she said to the room in general as she bundled the papers together.

Pam gave an ostentatious yawn. "You know, I think I'll head upstairs, too. All this thinking has plum worn me out." She added her tiles to the others spread out on the table. "It was fun. I hope we can do it again."

"Absolutely," said Dr. Cope. "You've certainly raised the level of the game."

"Sleep well," said Ann.

Lucy and Pam climbed the stairs in silence, except for the occasional groan from Pam, until they reached the top floor. There, she caught Lucy's arm. "A funny thing happened during the game."

Lucy was interested. "Really?"

Pam gave her a knowing look. "Remember when the board spilled?"

"Yeah."

"Laura knocked it on purpose."

"Why? Is she a sore loser?"

"I think it was the word I put down. The minute she saw it, she went all white."

"Interesting. What was the word?"

Pam paused for emphasis. *"Murder."*

"That is very interesting," said Lucy. "And there was another interesting thing. Did you notice? Will didn't go to Windsor. He stayed in London today."

"I noticed that, too." Pam shrugged. "But why would he want to knock me into the street?"

"Remember your attachment from Ted, the one you couldn't get? Well here it is," said Lucy, handing the papers to Pam. "It came through on the printer. I found it in the trash—somebody didn't want you to see it."

"You really think there was some sort of conspiracy to kill George?"

"Tell me what you think after you read it. It's pretty interesting stuff."

"See you in the morning." Pam was already reading as she limped across the hall to her room.

Opening the door to the room she shared with Sue, Lucy found the lights were on but Sue had fallen asleep with an open magazine spread out on her chest. Her mouth was open, and in the harsh light of the bedside lamp, she looked much older than she did in daytime, when her face was carefully made up. Even Sue, thought Lucy as she carefully lifted the magazine off her chest and turned off the light, was beginning to show her age.

They all were, she mused as she brushed her teeth and washed her face and carefully applied her drugstore night cream. Then, tucking herself into bed, she reached for the mystery she was reading. She found it difficult to concentrate on the story, however, as her thoughts returned over and over to George Temple's death.

Perhaps Inspector Neal was right and she did have an overactive imagination, but she had learned to trust her instincts, and they were telling her that something was odd about this tour. People were jumpy; their reactions didn't seem quite normal. There was Tom Smith's inappropriate guffaw when Quentin announced the memorial service for Temple, and there was Laura Barfield's startled reaction when Pam used the word *murder* in the Scrabble game. And these were just small incidents. Lucy's mind began to whirl, remembering Autumn's warning to Jennifer in the Whispering Gallery at St. Paul's and the way she'd teased her with the ravens at the Tower of London. And, of course, there was Caroline's tumble off the Brighton Pier. Autumn had been quick to suggest Will had something to do with it, but did he? And had he spent the day playing some fantasy game, or had he read the e-mail and decided to follow Pam instead? And if he did indeed push Pam into traffic, was he issuing a warning or intending to kill her?

Lucy didn't know the answers to any of these questions. She closed her book, turned off the light, and rolled over, intending to go to sleep. She closed her eyes but couldn't stop the film that was running in her mind. It was the faces of the tour members, one after another, all expressing sorrow, anger, anxiety. If someone had asked her to sum up the group in a word, it would be *tense*. They were all nervous and jumpy; it was in the air and it was contagious. It kept you awake at night, she decided, flopping on her back and opening her eyes to stare at the ceiling.

She had learned one thing, though, that might explain everything. George Temple had a history. Before he was the esteemed instructor at Winchester College, he'd been involved in financial misconduct. He'd even gone to jail. He'd been punished. Lucy yawned. And it had all taken place a long time ago. It was history, a footnote in the cycle of booms, bubbles, and recessions. That's what Lucy was thinking of, bubbles and dollar signs, when she finally drifted off to sleep.

Chapter Seventeen

Friday morning, the group departed on the minibus for Bath, which Quentin made a point of announcing was properly pronounced *Baaath*.

"Bath is rich in historic and literary associations," he began from his perch in the front of the minibus. "The original Roman baths for which the city is named are well preserved and offer a fascinating glimpse into ancient times. But for many of us, including myself, it is the city's association with Jane Austen that most fascinates. Those of you who have read *Persuasion* and *Northanger Abbey* know that she used the city as a setting for part of the action. The famous Pump Room is still in business serving tea."

"Tea!" Sue gave Lucy and Pam a little nod. "We'll finally get our afternoon tea."

"And on the way we'll stop at Salisbury Cathedral. It has the tallest spire in England," he said, pausing when Autumn and Will groaned in protest.

"I know, we have seen a lot of churches, but this one has quite a nice lunchroom where we can get something to eat, and it has one of the four existing copies of the Magna Carta. And on the way home, we're going to pause at Stonehenge. I'm hoping to time it so we can see the sunset there."

For once Will seemed interested in the itinerary. "They did human sacrifices there, right?"

"Perhaps," admitted Quentin. "No one knows for sure what the circle was used for." His eyebrows rose. "That's what makes it so fascinating, for me at least: the mystery."

"I believe it has something to do with the solstice—a calendar of sorts," suggested Dr. Cope.

Lucy was listening, watching the street scene as the minibus wove its way through the city. People were walking along purposefully, probably on their way to work. She had enjoyed the trip—she loved being in a different country—but she was eager to get home. She missed Bill and the kids, she was worried about Elizabeth, and she missed her job. Back in Tinker's Cove, she was sure of herself. She knew her roles as wife and mother and reporter. Here, it was different. She couldn't escape the feeling that something was very odd about this group of tourists, but she wasn't comfortable crossing the line and investigating them. It wasn't her business to pry into their lives—or was it? If there had been a conspiracy to murder Temple, wasn't it her duty to expose it? After all, murder wasn't only a crime against the victim; it was a crime against society as a whole.

"I read the attachment." Pam had cupped her hand around Lucy's ear and was whispering.

"What do you think about it?"

"Well, it was a long time ago." Pam's voice was low. "People change. He was tried and punished. As far as I'm concerned, he paid his debt to society."

Lucy nodded. "We've all done bad things."

"And it's not like he killed somebody or anything," continued Pam. "It was only money. White-collar crime."

From the window, she saw a couple of men walking along on the sidewalk, togged out in dark suits and carrying briefcases and umbrellas. They looked terribly respectable, irreproachable even, headed no doubt for jobs in the City, as London's financial district was known. "Not exactly a home invasion," said Lucy, thinking of a violent episode that had recently taken place in a neighboring town.

"Or a serial killer." Pam shifted in her seat and flexed her ankle. "My ankle is much better today," she added. "But I am glad for the minibus. And it's nice to get out of the city and see some more of the countryside."

Lucy agreed. One of the things that had surprised her most about England was the large amount of unspoiled countryside. She loved seeing the rolling green fields dotted with sheep or cows and sometimes horses. There was much more than in Maine, where family farms were going the way of the dodo, replaced either by strip malls or gradually overtaken by trees and reverting to forest.

Of course, in England they still had open markets where small farmers could sell their produce. In Maine, farmer's markets were just beginning to sprout, and there was nothing like Portobello, where the stalls with meat and eggs and vegetables were mixed right in with the used clothing and antiques. She settled back in her seat, intending to enjoy the ride, but her thoughts kept straying from the pastoral scenes outside to the group inside the minibus.

Only money. That's what Pam had said, but that was an oversimplification. It was never "only money" or "only my house—thank heaven we're all still alive." After the shock of the hurricane or tornado or fire wore off, there you were with nothing but the clothes on your back. She and Bill had struggled financially when he gave up Wall Street to become a restoration carpenter in Tinker's Cove, and she remembered the hard choices they'd had to make. Groceries instead of a new winter coat, heating oil instead of Christmas presents, and paying Doc Ryder five or ten dollars a month against the balance he patiently carried for years before they finally got caught up.

They had been fortunate. A generous check from Bill's parents had helped them through that terrible first winter, and Bill's business gradually became successful. Not that they hadn't had lean years since, but they'd always managed. They even had a tidy sum put away for the kids' college expenses and maybe, some-day, if anything was left, retirement. So even though she wasn't exactly pleased that Elizabeth might lose her RA position, it wasn't the end of the world. She had money to pay the additional expenses.

But what if she didn't? What if the college refused to grant credit for Elizabeth's course work because she owed money? They could even withhold her degree! What would happen then? Instead of starting on a satis-fying career, Elizabeth might have to take a low-level survival job. Instead of hanging out with upwardly mo-bile young professionals, she might start dating some loser drug addict type. Lucy could picture it, a tragic spiral downward into poverty, drug addiction, perhaps even crime. She knew she was being a bit melodra-matic, but the sad truth was that she had seen too many local kids bottom out on drugs.

"What are you thinking about?" demanded Pam. "You look like you're about to cry."

"Nothing." Lucy laughed. "My imagination was running away with me."

"Look at that house with its thatched roof. Isn't it adorable?"

It was, and so was the town of Salisbury, where tiny old houses lined the twisting, ancient streets. The cathedral, in contrast, was located inside a spacious walled "close," which included a large, grassy lawn and scattered houses for clergy and their families. Lucy thought the church was amazing, especially when you considered it was built over 750 years ago.

Lucy knew a bit about construction and the difficulties Bill encountered in his work, but she was awestruck at the labor and skill of the builders who had constructed the massive cathedral with its soaring spire using only the simplest of techniques. Merely hoisting the stones up to the top of that fantastic spire without the use of a modern crane seemed an incredible feat.

Inside, she discovered that this church was not simply a monument to the past but also had kept pace with changing times. A distinctly modern baptismal font was the first thing she noticed; it had been installed for the cathedral's 750th anniversary to mixed reviews. Quentin sneeringly called it a "saucer," but Lucy rather liked its simple shape and moving water. Wandering farther into the huge interior, she found a kindergarten class set up on child-sized chairs and tables in one of the side aisles, working on a project with crayons and paper.

The children were dressed in navy blue school uniforms. Most seemed to have blond hair and rosy cheeks. They were completely comfortable in the impressive structure, chattering away with each other as they exchanged crayons and displayed their work.

Quentin led them to the transept, where they stood beneath the spire and pointed out how the weight of the tower had bowed the supporting pillars. "Don't worry," he advised them. "If you look through those windows, you can see the bracing that was added to support the spire."

Lucy looked and she supposed it was all safe enough; it had stood for three-quarters of a millennium, but she knew that Bill wouldn't approve of anything that wasn't straight and true.

Advising the group that Bath was still some distance away, Quentin suggested they take a quick look at the Magna Carta and then purchase sandwiches and drinks in the café to eat on the bus. Only a few members of the group followed Quentin into the dimly lit display room, where the ancient charter was displayed in a lighted case.

"Kind of an anticlimax," said Dr. Cope. "It's just a piece of parchment."

"A piece of parchment that changed history," said Quentin. "It was the beginning of democracy; the nobles forced the king to share power."

"So instead of one white male running the show, you got a bunch," said Rachel. "I'm not sure that's a big improvement."

Quentin was standing close to Lucy; she could feel his breath on her neck. She would have liked to move away, but the gallery was small and they were crowded together in front of the Magna Carta. "What do you think, Lucy?" he asked in a teasing voice. "Are you a feminist like Rachel?"

"I guess I'm a humanist," said Lucy, seeing a gap and

moving toward the door, ready to find some lunch. "A hungry humanist."

Other visitors had the same idea, as the little café was crowded. Lucy and Will approached the cashier at the same time, and he stepped back with a graceful sweep of his arm and a courtly bow. "After you, m'lady."

Lucy smiled despite herself. "Thank you, m'lord," she said, putting down her food on the counter and fumbling for her wallet. The kid was so full of life and so charming it was easy to sweep aside her suspicions about him. But, of course, she reminded herself as she accepted the change from her ten-pound note, charm was one of the characteristics associated with sociopaths. She resolved to keep an eye on him as they explored Bath. She certainly didn't want a repeat accident, one that might have more dire consequences than a twisted ankle.

Back on the bus, Lucy sipped her tea and chewed her ploughman's cheese and pickle sandwich. "These sandwiches are so good," said Lucy. "I don't know why we can't have sandwiches like these at home."

"There's a rule, I think," said Pam. "Packaged sandwiches must be soggy and horrible." She was unscrewing the cap on her bottle of apple juice. "I couldn't help noticing that Quentin was standing awfully close to you."

"It was crowded." Lucy took another bite of sandwich.

"Not that crowded." Pam was unwrapping her sandwich.

"I thought he'd given up on me and was going after Autumn and Jennifer, but now he seems to be back after me. I like him; he's fun. I had a good time hanging out with him in Brighton. But I'm a married woman. Happily married. I'm not interested in any extracurricular activities." She took another bite of sandwich. "What's his reputation on campus?"

"Oh, everybody knows he's a lech." Pam had smoothed out the cellophane wrapper and had set the sandwich on it, in her lap. She picked up one half and took a bite. "He's kind of a legend in that department. They say some years he works his way through all the girls in the freshman class."

Lucy was skeptical. "That seems like an exaggeration."

"I'm sure it is, but the truth is that his reputation has hurt him. He's been passed over several times for a professorship. The word is the college wants to be able to fire him in case there's a scandal." She took a sip of juice. "It makes sense. It's almost impossible to get rid of a professor. I guess that's why they were considering Temple to take old Crighton's chair when he retires."

"It's too bad," said Lucy, draining her tea and crumpling the cellophane into a ball. "He's a gifted teacher."

Pam chuckled. "From what I hear, that's not all he's gifted at."

"Well, as tempting as you make him sound, I'm sticking with Bill."

"Smart move."

The bus dropped them off in front of Bath Abbey, which Quentin informed them was definitely worth a look. "The Roman baths are just yonder," he said, pointing the way. "Follow me."

A few minutes later, he'd distributed admission tickets and told everyone to be back at the Abbey at four o'clock; until then, they were on their own, free to explore the city.

"I couldn't help noticing there seems to be a lot of

shops," said Sue. "And we'll have time for an early tea in the Pump Room."

"We need to stay together." Lucy didn't want a repeat of yesterday.

"And we need to remember that Pam may not be up to much walking." Rachel had given Pam her arm for the walk across the uneven cobblestones of the square.

"Don't worry about me—I'll be fine." Pam was waving her ticket to the baths. "I've always wanted to see this. I remember seeing pictures in *National Geographic*, and now I'm here."

Once inside, they discovered the baths were larger and more complex than they'd imagined. They listened to audioguides that explained different aspects as they made their way down ramps and across uneven, time-worn paving stones, past displays picturing ancient Roman life, the sweat room, and the East Bath. Finally they found themselves standing in an open courtyard with a large rectangular pool in the center filled with bright green water.

"Yuck!" declared Sue. "You couldn't pay me to dip my toe in that."

Lucy was about to say something about the water's high mineral content when she noticed Pam wasn't with them. "Where's Pam?" she asked in a panicked voice.

"I thought she was with you," said Sue, turning to Rachel.

"We were together—she was hanging on to my arm—but then she said the paving was so uneven she'd do better on her own." Rachel reproached herself. "I got so caught up in the audioguide . . ."

"Never mind." Lucy was already retracing her path through the ruins. "We have to find her."

Lucy had to dodge past a group of German tourists who were blocking her way, pointing out the various statues that stood atop the arcade that enclosed the pool. Then she was weaving her way through the East Baths, cursing the stagy dramatic lighting that kept the corners in darkness while making the tank of water glow. Farther on, she darted into the sweat rooms, a massive space that was also dramatically lit to highlight the rows of square pillars that had once supported the floor. Standing on the walkway, Lucy peered down at the mazelike area, where numerous shadows offered plenty of places to conceal a body.

A body! What was she thinking? This was a crowded tourist attraction; it was hardly the place you'd expect an assault to take place. Except that it wasn't very crowded today, and there was that weird lighting that created contrasting patches of light and dark. For a public place, it sure had a lot of nooks and crannies, spaces tucked behind displays of stone carvings, ancient coins, and other artifacts.

"Any sign of her?" Rachel and Sue had caught up with Lucy in the sweat room.

Lucy shook her head.

"Come on, let's finish the tour. Maybe she went on ahead of us," said Sue.

"With that bad ankle?" Lucy was wondering if it would be possible to slip off the observation deck and explore the far corners of the sweat room.

"Maybe. She might have stuck to the ramps and walkways."

"Or she might have fallen behind and been attacked," said Lucy. "What if she's down there somewhere, bleeding or concussed? And how come there are no security guards here? What kind of place is this?"

Sue was holding her arm. "I have a feeling you'll find out if you venture off this viewing platform. I'll bet you fifty pounds they've got closed-circuit surveillance cameras."

"And if anything happened to Pam, they would have seen it," said Rachel. "Come on. We've checked back here and now we have to continue on."

"Okay," grumbled Lucy, following her friends back past the large open pool and on to the Sacred Spring, where water gushed from an underground source. The Germans Lucy had so rudely brushed past were there, listening to their audioguides and blocking the exit. This time, she could tell from their expressions that she wasn't going to get past them.

It seemed to take them forever to listen to the recording, and then they had to discuss what they'd heard; at least that's what Lucy thought they were doing. Maybe they were talking about rude Americans. She didn't understand German, and she was beginning to think she didn't much like these particular German people either. Then one very large-hipped lady turned, and Lucy was able to slip past, into the hall outside the restrooms and gift shop. And there, sitting on a bench, was Pam.

"What took you guys so long?" she asked.

Chapter Eighteen

"Well, actually, we were looking for you." Lucy sounded rather annoyed. "That's what took so long."

"It's my fault," admitted Pam. "I got separated from you guys. I figured this was the best place to catch up with you." She tilted her head toward the door of the ladies' room.

"Good thinking. In fact, I think I'll . . ."

"Go ahead. I'm not moving," said Pam, catching sight of Sue and Rachel emerging from the exhibit and giving them a wave.

When they'd all used the facilities and gathered again in the lobby outside the gift shop, Sue suggested they go on to the Pump Room. "Our ticket to the baths entitles us to a free glass of Bath water. . . ."

"My mother told me not to drink the bathwater," quipped Pam.

Sue gave her a look. "And we can have tea. A real afternoon tea."

"I'm not really very hungry," protested Lucy.

"This may be our only chance," warned Sue. "We can't go back home without having a real English tea."

"If you say so." Rachel shrugged. "I could use a reviving cup of tea, and I guess I could nibble on a scone."

"Perhaps we could share one," suggested Pam. "Just to get a taste."

But after working their way through the gift shop and emerging outside the Pump Room, they found themselves blocked once again by the German tourists—and a long line of others.

Sue scowled. "Where did they all come from?"

"All over. It's a famous tourist attraction." Rachel was pulling out her guidebook. "There's lots to see: the Royal Crescent, Regency architecture, a covered market, the guild hall. . . ."

"And the shops." Sue was brightening.

"I'm not really up for a lot of walking," said Pam. "But you all should go ahead. I'll go sit in the Abbey and read my book."

Lucy wasn't about to leave Pam on her own. "I'll go with you," she said. "I love old churches."

Sue gave her a quizzical look. "You do?"

Lucy nodded. "I never knew, until I got here. I like the way they, uh, smell."

"If you say so." Rachel was doubtful. "Come on, Sue. I see a National Trust gift shop across the way."

"You know where to find us," said Lucy, watching them depart.

"You don't have to do this, Lucy," protested Pam. "I'm fine on my own, and I feel guilty keeping you from seeing the city."

"Don't be silly." Lucy took her arm. "Bath Abbey is the Lantern of the West, and I don't want to miss it."

Inside, the Lantern of the West definitely had that musty old church smell and seemed a bit shabby. At least that's what Lucy thought after she installed Pam in a pew and began to look around. Maybe, she decided, it was simply that those famous windows let in more light than the smaller windows in the other churches they'd seen. And that light revealed the effects of age, just like a sunny day coming after a rainy spell illuminated unnoticed dust and cobwebs in the house. Or maybe it was the fact that history hadn't treated the Abbey well: It had been stripped when Henry VIII dissolved the monasteries and left to fall into disrepair. Various restoration projects had been undertaken through the years, but it was once again damaged by German bombs in World War II.

Still, it was a beautiful and active church, as the brochure describing its architectural features took pains to point out. Lucy was walking along the side aisles, studying the enormous windows and the graceful vaulted ceiling, when she noticed Laura Barfield, bent in prayer. She didn't wish to disturb her and continued on her way, but Laura called out to her.

"Lucy! Are you on your own?"

"My friends wanted to shop, but I'm out of money," she said. "And besides, Pam can't do much walking because of her ankle. She's sitting in the back."

"It's a beautiful place to spend a quiet hour."

"They call it Perpendicular Gothic," said Lucy.

"Whatever they call it, it's good for the soul." Laura cocked her head. "Are you a person of faith?"

"Not really." Lucy slipped into the pew beside Laura; maybe she could turn the conversation toward Will. Most mothers were eager to talk about their kids. "How about you? Are you a churchgoing family?"

"Not so much the family, but I am." She raised her eyes to the intricately decorated ceiling high above them. "Church is the only place I find peace."

Lucy was all sympathy. "Tell me about it. My daughter, she's in college, is driving me crazy. And I've got two more at home. They say boys are tough to raise, but I think girls are worse."

"Oh, I'm not troubled about Will. Boys will be boys—that's what my husband says. He'll sow his wild oats and settle down."

This attitude surprised Lucy. From what Quentin had told her, the college considered him to be at risk; that's why he was in the special support program. She had expected Laura to be eager to discuss her son's problems, but now it didn't seem she thought he had any. Lucy wasn't quite sure how to continue when Laura solved the problem for her.

"No," she said with a sad smile, "it's not Will that troubles me. It's my mother."

"Mothers and daughters," said Lucy cautiously, feeling her way. "It's a special relationship."

"I adored my mother."

Lucy was pretty sure her daughters didn't adore her, especially Elizabeth. But they seemed to get along most of the time, which was a big improvement over the relationship she had with her own mother. Lucy had been a Daddy's girl, and her mother hadn't appreciated her daughter's claim on her husband's affection. "My mother died some years ago," was the best Lucy could come up with. "Alzheimer's."

Laura turned to her, her eyes brimming with tears. "Mine, too. It was awful. Early onset."

"Hard for the family," said Lucy, remembering her mother wandering around a posh assisted-living facility in a happy haze, imagining herself the lady of the manor. "My mother didn't know what she was missing."

"I didn't want to put her away—I tried to care for Mom at home."

"That would be difficult."

"It was impossible, especially after I got pregnant with Will. I had to put her in a, you know, one of those places." This was a wound that hadn't healed; tears were trickling down Laura's cheeks.

"You shouldn't blame yourself. I found that my mother was much happier at Wonderstrand Manor than she would have been with me. They had special programs, wonderful meals. And she was safe there. They kept the doors locked so the residents couldn't wander off." Lucy hadn't thought about this in a long time and found her resentments had lessened; she was remembering her mother fondly. She smiled. "She loved the sing-alongs, all those old songs like "How Much Is that Doggie in the Window?" and "Wunderbar."

"That place sounds wonderful." Laura had placed her hand on Lucy's arm. "We couldn't afford anything like that. We had to depend on Medicare."

"But even so . . ." protested Lucy.

"No. This was almost twenty years ago. Things were different then. This was a Medicare mill. The patients were kept strapped in their beds; they got minimal care. It was terrible."

"I'm so sorry." Lucy knew her father had provided well for her mother; there had even been a modest inheritance left for her after her mother's sudden death from a stroke.

"The worst part is that Mom had money." Laura's chin vibrated. "She should have been in a place like Wonderful Manor, whatever it was called. But Dad trusted an old friend with his investments. . . ." Laura stopped suddenly. "It was that savings and loan crisis. Maybe you remember?"

Lucy remembered. "My father believed in T-bills."

"Smart man."

Now Lucy felt tears pricking her eyes. She'd never really had a chance to say good-bye to her father, never had a chance to tell him how much she loved him. He'd survived a massive heart attack and was convalescing when he suddenly developed pneumonia. Her mother had been caring for him at home. She'd discouraged Lucy even from visiting and had disregarded his symptoms. Lucy had often felt she should have insisted on visiting; she should have realized her mother was already suffering from Alzheimer's, which she'd tried to hide.

"We have to remember that hindsight is twenty-twenty," she told Laura. "Of course we should have and could have, if we'd only known, but we didn't. We have to forgive ourselves."

Laura's eyes were huge and she cast them upward. "That's what I pray for, all the time: forgiveness. But I don't think He does forgive me."

Lucy was no theologian, but she had attended church enough to pick up the general gist. "Of course He does."

Laura shook her head. "No. I saw my mother's body—the undertaker showed me. He was so upset, said he'd never seen anything like it. Bruises and bedsores and marks from the restraints, her skin rubbed raw. She looked as if she'd been tortured."

"Did you report the nursing home to the authorities?"

Laura's eyes widened. "I was so ashamed—I didn't say a word." She sobbed. "But I can't forget. I'm haunted. Whenever I close my eyes, that's what I see."

Lucy was beginning to feel out of her depth. She furrowed her brow and patted Laura's hand. "Maybe you should talk this over with a professional."

"That's what my husband says. He keeps saying how lucky we are, how Will has grown up to be so fine and he goes to a great college and we have a nice house and no money worries. He says I should get over it and enjoy life."

"That's easier said than done—but he does have a point. You can't change the past, only the future."

Laura brushed away her tears with the backs of her hands and then clasped Lucy's hands with both of hers. "Oh, Lucy, thank you. You've made me feel so much better."

"I'm glad I could help," said Lucy, standing up and looking back toward the pew where Pam was sitting, absorbed in her book.

"Really," insisted Laura. "I think you have a calling. Have you considered the ministry?"

Lucy was chuckling, about to admit the thought had never crossed her mind, when she jumped, hearing a sudden enormous crash. Her first thought was for Pam, but Pam was fine, looking about curiously for the source of the noise. Turning the other way, she saw Will in the center aisle, bending down to replace a kneeling stool.

"That boy is so clumsy," said Laura, giggling as her son advanced down the aisle toward them.

"Aren't they all?" said Lucy, deciding to head back to Pam.

"But don't you want to see the museum?" asked Laura.

"Thanks, but I need to get back to my friend."

"Oh, well, now that Will's here, I can go with him. He loves old things and museums. Isn't that right, Will?"

"Sure, Mom."

Will was smiling agreeably enough, but Lucy wasn't

convinced. Her experience had taught her that teens could be less than honest when they were engaged in achieving their own ends. They pleaded for permission to spend the night at a friend's house, declaring that "of course her parents are going to be home," and you got a call from the cops at one in the morning advising you to pick up your kid at the police station because neighbors had called complaining of a drunken party. Or you found a charge on your cable bill for an adult movie that your teenage son swore must be a mistake because he'd never do anything like that. Never. Not ever. And fools that we are, thought Lucy, watching Laura and Will going off together, parents want to believe their children are telling the truth.

"What was that all about?" asked Pam when Lucy joined her on her pew. "It looked intense."

"You can say that again. She's guilt-stricken over her mother's death. She feels she didn't do enough for her."

Pam sighed. "I guess we all feel that way when our parents pass on."

"Not like this. Laura really feels guilty. She needs help."

"I hope she gets it," said Pam, a mischievous glint in her eye. "You know, I believe I spotted an ice-cream place in the plaza outside."

"I believe you're right," said Lucy.

"And I think I could just about manage to hobble over there."

"Well, let's go," said Lucy, taking her arm. "I've had it with churches."

"You said you loved them."

"I've changed my mind," said Lucy, stepping through the door and taking a deep breath of fresh air.

Chapter Nineteen

After finishing their ice-cream cones, Lucy and Pam made their way back to the pickup point in front of the Abbey. They were the first ones there and perched themselves on some concrete bollards to wait for the others to gather.

Predictably, Dr. Cope and Jennifer were the first to arrive. Dr. Cope greeted them with his usual courtesy. "Did you enjoy Bath? I'd have to say this has been my favorite day of the tour. The Roman baths were really something to see. And to think, the Romans appreciated the healthful benefits of regular bathing and had the engineers to create these baths thousands of years before modern man."

Jennifer smiled. "I read somewhere that Queen Elizabeth—the first, that is—took a bath once a month."

"Whether she needed it or not," added Pam, smiling. "And I imagine she did."

"They say the Native Americans in Maine could smell the European ships from shore and were pretty disgusted by the new arrivals' poor hygiene," volunteered Lucy.

"I've heard that, too," said Quentin, sidling up to

Jennifer. "Indoor plumbing is one of civilization's finest achievements." His gaze drifted over her figure, lingering at her bust. "Which do you prefer: a shower or a bath?"

Dr. Cope gave him a stony look and wrapped a protective arm around his granddaughter's shoulders. "That's rather personal, isn't it?"

Quentin shrugged, regarding Jennifer with a certain sparkle in his eye. "I just wondered, because the hotel has only showers. I'm looking forward to a nice long soak when I get home."

"Me too," said Lucy. "And I'm awfully glad the water in Tinker's Cove isn't bright green."

"Point taken," laughed Quentin. "Did any of you sample the water in the Pump Room?"

Jennifer wrinkled her nose. "It was disgusting. I couldn't finish the glass."

"A pity." Dr. Cope's tone was serious. "They say it's full of healthful minerals."

"We tried it." Ann Smith joined the group, along with her husband and daughter. "I wouldn't recommend it."

"Absolutely foul," agreed Tom.

"But the food was very good." Caroline actually smiled, seeming relaxed and comfortable for the first time since the incident in Brighton. "That Devonshire cream stuff is awfully good."

"The prices were ridiculous, however," said Ann.

"It was a treat—nothing wrong with a treat now and then," replied Tom.

Listening, Lucy thought this was a conversation the Smiths repeated from time to time, with Ann arguing for restraint while Tom pushed for small extravagances. She suspected there was absolutely nothing he wouldn't do for Caroline, who reminded her a bit of a baby cow-bird. The mother cowbird was a heedless creature who laid her eggs in another bird's nest, replacing the nat-ural parents' eggs with her own. When the baby cow-birds hatched, they were usually much larger than the surrogate parents, who struggled to keep up with the growing chicks' enormous appetites.

Across the street, Lucy spotted Sue and Rachel, both toting a couple of shopping bags.

"Golly gee, I was worried we were late and had missed the bus." Sue was a bit out of breath. "The shop-ping was fabulous."

"The Jane Austen house was lovely," added Rachel.

"It was a fake," protested Sue. "They admitted she never actually lived there."

"It was typical of the period." Rachel smiled. "I think I may have been a Regency lady in a previous life."

"More likely a scullery maid," said Lucy, catching Quentin's eye. "We all think we'd be lords and ladies, but the truth is our ancestors were probably peasants. I'm sure mine were."

"Not me," insisted Rachel. "I'm sure I was to the manor born." She opened her shopping bag and showed off a mug with the words *Her Ladyship* painted on it. "See? It was waiting for me at the National Trust gift shop. And I got one that says 'His Lordship' for Bob."

Lucy rolled her eyes and glanced at Sue. "Actually, I did, too. In fact, I bought tea towels and cocktail glasses as well. For me and Sid. We're officially Lord and Lady Finch."

"I wonder if there's time. . . ." Laura Barfield had ar-rived, looking a bit wan and out of breath. "Where is that shop?"

"Too late," said Quentin. "There's the bus."

"Oh, dear," Laura fretted. "I'm afraid I've lost track of Will."

"I suppose you mean Sir Will," suggested Dr. Cope in a somewhat sarcastic tone.

The sarcasm was lost on Laura, who'd spotted her son rounding the corner of the Abbey, along with Autumn. "He's my prince," she chirped, giving him a wave that he ignored.

"Some prince," muttered Tom Smith, glaring at Will and stepping protectively in front of Caroline.

"Princes aren't perfect," said Jennifer. "Prince Harry seems to get in a lot of trouble."

"He sets a poor example to be sure," said Dr. Cope.

They had all gathered in a little group—only the Smiths were standing apart—waiting expectantly for the minibus to pull up when a huge tour bus slid to a stop in front of them, braking with a loud hiss. The doors opened and a large group began to disembark, chattering noisily and shoving them aside as they maneuvered to snap photos of each other in front of the Abbey.

"Germans," muttered Tom Smith. "This is how they took Poland."

"Shhh," cautioned his wife. "They might hear you. A lot of them speak English, you know."

"I hope they do hear me." Tom lowered his brows. "People are too quick to forgive." He turned to Quentin. "And since I'm mouthing off, how come we're backtracking to Stonehenge? I was talking to the bus driver, just happened to run into him on the plaza there, and he said we're doing things backward."

Quentin nodded, watching as the Germans formed ranks behind their leader and the bus pulled away, allowing the minibus to take its place. "You're right—I juggled things a bit so we'd be able to walk among the stones at Stonehenge. Unless you make arrangements for a special tour, after hours, you can only walk around the perimeter of the henge." He paused as the door opened. "Trust me, this will be much nicer—and we'll be there at sunset."

There was little conversation as the minibus driver retraced the route from Salisbury and on to Stonehenge. It had already been a long day, and Lucy suspected most of the older folks were tired. She sure was, and she was looking forward to getting back home to Bill and the girls and the familiar surroundings of Tinker's Cove. She was surprised to discover that she missed her house: her bed with the pillows that were just right, her roomy rolltop bathtub, even Libby the dog's musty odor that clung to the old sofa in the family room where she liked to nap. But as she gazed out the window at the green fields and rolling hills, she was very glad she'd taken the trip.

They'd certainly got off to a rocky start, with George Temple's death, but now that event, dreadful as it was, seemed like ancient history. So much had happened in the week that it was easy to forget the horrible circumstances of his death, especially since she hadn't really known him. These things happened, she supposed, and even though she had her suspicions, she knew it was her nature to question things. That was why she was a good reporter. But she also knew that she tended to make mountains out of molehills, and the truth was that she didn't really have any hard evidence that Temple had been murdered or that Caroline's fall off the Brighton pier was anything but a sign of that poor girl's disturbed mind. As for Pam's slip off the curb, well, it was probably just that. And Autumn and Jennifer's odd relationship? That could be explained by the fact that they were rivals for Will's affection.

Lucy let out a big sigh and relaxed against her seat. It was time, she decided, to turn her thoughts toward home. She was worried about Elizabeth, she wondered how Bill had managed with the girls, and she really missed little Patrick. It would be great to get home, she decided, noticing the sky, especially in the west, was taking on a pinkish hue.

"We're here!" announced Quentin as the bus turned off the highway into a spacious parking area. The last of the day's buses were lined up at the exit, waiting to depart, and only a few cars were parked at the far end, probably belonging to employees. It looked as though the group was going to have Stonehenge to themselves.

Descending from the minibus, Lucy heard the buzz of steady traffic and was surprised to see the ancient site was quite close to a major highway that carried a heavy load of rush-hour traffic.

"Never mind the traffic," advised Quentin as they followed him toward the ticket booth. "Remember, this is a sacred site, a place of great mystery and spirituality. It was also a place of sacrifice—archaeologists have unearthed the skeleton of a small child, it's skull neatly cleaved in two. Clearly a blood sacrifice."

Laura grew pale. "How terrible!"

Quentin shrugged. "It may have been deformed or mentally deficient. . . ."

"Why, that's even worse," protested Ann. "We must protect the weak."

Quentin's smile was patronizing. "A modern concept, I'm afraid. The ancients were more concerned with basic survival and couldn't afford to waste scant resources on the weak and sick. Everyone had to pull their own weight, even children. If not, they went back to the gods." He paused. "At least that's one theory."

The man at the ticket booth didn't seem terribly thrilled to see them. "Ay, here you are," he said in a voice that sounded like a grumble. "I suppose we might as well get started."

When he stepped outside the booth and stood before them, they saw a man of medium height, dressed in shiny brown polyester slacks and a black sweater with the World Heritage Site logo. His gray hair could use a wash, his brows bristled over his horn rims, and a name tag informed them his name was Dick.

"Follow me," Dick said, leading the way along a winding asphalt path that dipped into a tunnel that ran beneath the roadway. "We've got plans to jazz the place up," he told them. "When you come back—that is, if you come back in a couple of years—you'll find the roadway's been rerouted and we're going to have a fine new visitor center." He stopped abruptly in the middle of the tunnel, beneath a fluorescent light that cast deep shadows on his face. "Mind now, we don't want any nonsense. Don't touch the stones; don't even think about carving your initials on them; don't be a joker and try to push 'em over. Got it?"

They nodded and he resumed the march through the tunnel.

"Awright, then, remember, this 'ere site is a source of inspiration and fascination and a place of worship. There's druids gather 'ere every summer, at Midsummer Eve. 'Course, the builders weren't druids; they were Bronze Age folk, lived here some three thousand years ago. Took it into their 'eads to put up these stones, brought 'em some hunnerd and thirty-five miles from Wales.

"How you ask? Well, we think they floated 'em on barges, came through the Bristol Channel and up the river. That makes the most sense. But we don't really know. And we sure don't know why. The stones line up with the rising of the summer solstice and the setting of the winter solstice, so it probably had something to do with that, but like I said, nobody knows."

He stopped at the tunnel opening. "Well, here you are, wander around to yer 'eart's content. I'll be 'ere if you want to ask about something, but I pretty much told you ever'thing we know. And don't forget to stop in our gift shop on your way out. We keep it open late, especially for groups like you, and we have a fine selection of books and gifts."

Emerging into the dying light of day, Lucy took Pam's arm. "How are you doing? Can you manage here?"

Pam's face glowed in the reddish light of the setting sun; she was standing still, awestruck by the sight of the massive circle of golden stones standing on the green and grassy plain. "This is amazing," she said. "I want to see every bit, even if I have to crawl!"

Personally, Lucy didn't get it. The stones were interesting, all right, but they weren't as tall as she expected; in fact, they were rather stumpy. It did seem a massive undertaking—you had to admire the builders' effort—but without knowing why they went to all that trouble, it seemed a bit pointless.

"What a gorgeous sunset," said Rachel as they made their way toward the stones.

The group had spread out, falling into the groupings they'd adopted over the course of the tour. Quentin was eading the way, followed by Dr. Cope and Jennifer. The miths were a tight group of three. Laura Barfield valked alone, and Will and Autumn had gone off to-;ether ahead of the others. Lucy and her friends were oringing up the rear, walking slowly with Pam until Sue topped abruptly.

"You know, I didn't bring my sweater and it's awfully chilly. I think I'll go back. . . ."

"She just wants to go to the shop," said Pam.

"Well, I haven't got anything for Geoff," she said, naming her son-in-law. "He's a scientist. They've probably got something he'd like. About rocks or astronomy . . ." She wrinkled up her face. "Don't you think?"

Rachel laughed. "It's okay—you're dismissed."

"No demerits?"

Lucy took Sue's hand and patted it. "Obviously, this is not your thing."

"Wide-open spaces, nature . . . ," chimed in Pam.

"Not a price tag in sight," added Rachel.

"It's okay. We'll catch up with you later."

"What a relief," sighed Sue, scurrying back through the tunnel.

"She's a shopaholic," laughed Rachel as they stepped off the path and crossed the grassy space to the stone circle.

Up close, the stones seemed taller to Lucy, and she stood in front of a pair, looking up at the third enormous stone that formed a crude arch above her head. She found herself giggling, remembering a silly movie in which Chevy Chase had toppled the whole thing. But these stones, she realized, weren't going anywhere. They projected an enormous sense of solidity and enclosure. The circle invited believers to gather in this spot; it was a place of communion. She instinctively reached her hands out, expecting to touch Pam and Rachel, but they were gone.

So much for a communion of souls, she thought, somewhat disgruntled. Looking around, she saw the group had largely scattered, each individual pursuing his or her own thoughts and reactions. The Smiths were the exception, circulating among the stones in their own little orbit.

Making her way to the very center of the double circle, Lucy watched as the rosy sky deepened to a deep, blazing red and shafts of light from the sinking sun pierced the openings between the stones. It was an amazing sight, and she stood, awestruck and silent at the spectacle. She'd seen some pretty fabulous sunsets in Maine, of course, but this was different. The place itself, with its strange formation of stones, almost like something a child might build out of stones on the beach, made it different. And maybe, she thought with a flash of insight, that was what Stonehenge was really about. Maybe it was a grand, exaggerated version of that innate desire to build that children had, the same impulse that made children reach for building blocks and LEGOs and Tinkertoys. She was smiling to herself, musing on this thought, when she heard the scream.

The sound hit her like an electric shock and she went rigid, snapping to attention. She turned, straining, listening for a repeat but no sound came. She started to run, dodging around the stones, trying to find the screamer. Was it a joke? Had Will startled one of the girls? Had Quentin gotten a little too amorous?

No. What she heard was a gut-wrenching scream of terror. She'd heard that cry before and knew it must be heeded. It was as impossible to ignore as a baby's cry.

Somebody was in trouble, and every fiber of her being impelled her to do something.

She was breathing heavily now, getting confused as she ran from stone to stone in the steadily dimming light. The sky was violet, and the stones were hulking black shapes casting long shadows. She was beginning to fear she wouldn't be able to find whoever screamed when she caught a flash of white beyond the farthest stone, a single massive pillar that stood alone.

Panting and gasping for breath, she ran as fast as she could across the circle; then, reaching the stone, she stopped and listened. There was nothing, nothing but the brooding black stone. Maybe it was all a mistake; maybe she'd overreacted. She turned, about to return to the lighted tunnel and the gift shop where her friends were probably waiting for her, when she heard a muffled moan.

Without thinking, running on adrenaline, she charged around the stone and found three dark figures. At first, it wasn't clear what was going on. Then her eyes adjusted and she saw Will was holding Pam tight against him, his hand clapped over her mouth. In the fading light, Pam's eyes gleamed, wide with terror, because the third person, Autumn, was waving a knife in front of her nose.

"What's going on?" demanded Lucy.

Autumn lunged toward her, and Lucy, too shocked to move, would have been stabbed except for the sudden arrival of Tom Smith. He barreled in like a rugby player and took Autumn down; the knife went flying and Lucy scrambled to pick it up.

"Enough is enough," declared Tom. "Let her go."

Will stared at him, still holding tight to Pam, who

struggled to free herself. "Are you crazy?" he demanded, glaring at Tom. "We have to get rid of them. They know all about it. I saw the e-mails. Do you really want to go to jail for life?"

"Yeah." Tom pulled himself up to his full five feet six inches and stuck out his barrel chest. "Yeah. I'll go to jail. If somebody has to take the rap, I'm ready. I'll do it. I killed Temple and you know what? I'd do it again!"

Chapter Twenty

Will reluctantly released Pam, and she collapsed into Lucy's arms. Pam was trembling, her teeth chattering, and Lucy held her close. Lucy was cold, too, and still wary. The three could turn on them at any minute, and she was relieved when Quentin came striding toward them.

"It's getting cold and the staff are eager to lock up for the night," he said, apparently so intent on rounding up the group that he ignored the fact that Autumn was sprawled on the ground and Pam was tearfully clinging to Lucy. "Let's go back to the minivan."

"Not so fast," protested Lucy. "Will and Autumn attacked Pam," she said, showing him the knife. "And Tom's confessed to killing Temple. We need to call the authorities. I insist on it."

Lucy didn't get the shocked reaction she expected. "No one was hurt, were they?" asked Quentin, watching as Will bent over Autumn and helped her to her feet. "We'll sort this all out in comfort, in the van. Let's go." He pointed the pair toward the exit and waited for them to take the lead before starting off himself.

Tom fell into step beside Quentin. "Like I said before, I'll take the rap for Temple. It's the only way to end this thing."

"I don't think that will be necessary," said Quentin, slapping him on the back. "But I certainly appreciate the gesture."

Lucy and Pam brought up the rear, saying little. Pam still clung to Lucy, who found herself increasingly furious with Quentin. Her friend had been attacked, and Quentin seemed more concerned with keeping the tour on schedule than doing the right thing and reporting the incident to the authorities. Will and Autumn were out of control and had to be stopped. It was outrageous, and she was determined to get justice for Pam—and Temple, too. Because the more she thought about it, the less she believed Tom Smith's confession. Of the group, he seemed the least likely to be involved, and she suspected his confession was nothing more than a clumsy attempt to protect somebody else. Caroline? His wife? Both were obviously troubled, but neither seemed a likely murder suspect.

Finally reaching the van, Lucy hesitated a moment before climbing aboard the van. What were she and Pam getting into? But the interior lights were on and Sue and Rachel were there, as well as the driver. She looked back over her shoulder, but the windows were already dark in the gift shop and ticket area. The parking lot was now deserted except for the minivan, and she could see the red taillights of the departing employees' cars. Still holding tight to Pam's hand, she clambered up the steps.

"What took you so long?" asked Rachel. "Were you enchanted by the mystery of Stonehenge?"

"Not exactly," muttered Lucy, glaring at Quentin. "I think we're owed an explanation."

The driver cast a questioning look at Quentin. "We're getting late here, sir."

"Yes, yes, we must get going," replied Quentin.

The driver dimmed the lights and the minibus began to move; Quentin seated himself sideways with his legs in the aisle in order to face the group.

"Lucy is right," he said. "There was an altercation involving two Winchester students. . . ."

"*Altercation* isn't the right word," insisted Lucy. "Will and Autumn attacked Pam."

Rachel gasped and Sue reached her hand over the seat to pat Pam on the shoulder.

"This has gone too far," said Dr. Cope. "I—"

Quentin cut him off. "Before you say anything more, let me continue. Obviously there is no excuse whatsoever for violence, but Autumn and Will were acting under the mistaken assumption that Pam was not satisfied that George Temple died of natural causes and had begun an investigation. They were fearful they would be implicated in some way."

"She was asking questions—I saw the e-mails!" declared Will.

Quentin chuckled and shook his head. "One of the things I always warn my students about is their tendency to jump to conclusions. There is no substitute for solid research, and I think Will and Autumn were a bit too impetuous—that is, of course, one of the hallmarks of youth, perhaps complicated in this case by certain emotional and social deficiencies, which the college is working to address in a supportive group setting." He looked at Lucy. "You can be sure this incident will be reported and dealt with by the college, but I'm sure we don't want to expose our young travelers to the vagaries of the British justice system."

Lucy rolled her eyes. "I don't like this, but it's really up to Pam."

"I'm fine with it," said Pam. "But I will hold you to your word. If you don't report them, I will." She paused. "But what about Tom's confession?"

Ann Smith's voice was shaky. "What confession? What did you do, Tom?"

Quentin spoke quickly, before Tom could answer. "This trip has been stressful, and I think Tom was . . . well, I guess you could say he cracked for a minute there, and, well, this is a psychological phenomenon related to stress. It's not all that uncommon actually, where an individual reacts to a traumatic situation by coming to believe he caused the situation. In other words"—Quentin gave a little chuckle—"as preposterous as this may seem, Tom actually confessed to killing George Temple."

"That's ridiculous!" Ann's voice was high-pitched, almost hysterical as she defended her husband. "He's no more guilty than the rest of us!"

"Exactly," said Quentin quickly. "And we all know that the British authorities, including Scotland Yard, conducted a thorough inquiry following George Temple's untimely and tragic death and concluded it was the unfortunate result of an extreme asthma attack."

The van swerved and Quentin grabbed the armrest to avoid being thrown out of his seat. Lucy noticed his teeth gleaming in an embarrassed grimace as he regained his equilibrium. "So I think now the best thing is for us to relax and enjoy the rest of the trip back to London."

There was a general sigh of relief in the bus as everyone settled in for the ride. Lucy, however, wasn't satisfied. She couldn't forget the terrible look on Temple's face as he struggled for breath. The group members' actions at the airport and on the plane seemed normal enough, but if you thought about it another way, those actions seemed part of a carefully choreographed dance of death.

"That's quite a story you've concocted," she said, her voice small but firm in the darkness, "but it doesn't add up. I was at the airport. I was right next to George Temple on the plane. I saw what happened. There was a series of small events that seemed innocent enough by themselves but were actually designed to cause his death, and I think you were all part of it in one way or another."

"But why would we do such a thing?" protested Laura. "What would bring us all together to do such a terrible thing?"

"George Temple was an investment advisor who defrauded his clients," said Lucy. "And from what you've told me yourselves in the course of this trip, I suspect you were all victims of his scheme." Lucy's voice dropped a few notes. "Laura, you told me your mother died because of the poor care she received in a second-rate nursing home. Was that all you could afford because Temple swindled you? Or perhaps your mother?"

"That's terrible," said Rachel, her voice rich with sympathy, "and I can understand that you might very well want revenge. But, Lucy, think a minute. Even if all these people were victimized by George Temple, how did they manage to find each other?"

"Through the kids: Autumn, Will, Jennifer, and Caroline. They're all in this support group Quentin was talking about. They all heard each other's stories and put two and two together and realized their families had all suffered because of George Temple."

"Temple deserved to die." It was Dr. Cope, sounding like the voice of doom. "I have no regrets about what we did. He was every bit as evil as a mass murderer. He toyed with his victims. He ruined them—he caused untold suffering. My son-in-law couldn't face the shame when he learned he'd lost everything, and he killed himself, plunging my daughter into despair. She never recovered—she's dependent on psychotropic drugs. She lives in a fog. George Temple took their lives and deprived my granddaughter of her parents' love and support."

"He got off with a tap on the knuckles," Tom hissed. "Two years was all he got. It took Ann longer than that to recover after the accident, and we lost our baby boy. It wouldn't have happened if we'd had the money to repair the car, to keep it up. We were driving a wreck, didn't have a cent to our names. I was a fool. I trusted him with all our savings. He said it was stupid to put money in the bank when you could do so much better in the stock market. But he never invested it. He just used my money to pay other investors, pretending they were making fabulous returns. It was a classic Ponzi scheme and it all fell apart." He paused, clenching his fists. "I'd do it again. If somebody has to be punished, I'd be honored to plead guilty to killing that weasel."

"You shouldn't take the blame. We were all part of it," said Dr. Cope.

"It started with me," said Tom. "I slipped the toy gun in his pocket so he'd be searched by airport security."

"But I was the one who hung around the airport, pretending to be late, just to upset him," declared Will.

"And I kept fretting to add to the tension," admitted Laura, a note of pride in her voice.

"You did a great job," offered Ann, "but I wrapped him up in a mildewed old scarf to get his asthma going."

"I stole the bottle of allergy medicine out of his carry-on bag." Caroline's voice was confident. Lucy noticed she was sitting alone, apart from her parents.

Jennifer chimed in: "I opened the peanuts, knowing he was allergic, and waved the packet under his nose."

Autumn was rubbing her elbow, sore from her fall. "I knocked his rescue inhaler into his drink. . . ."

"It all went off like clockwork," said Dr. Cope, congratulating the group.

Lucy stared from one to the other, hardly believing what she was hearing. They'd conspired to kill a man. They'd acted in cold blood without a shred of compassion, and they seemed proud of what they'd done. She'd been right next to Temple. She'd seen him struggling for breath and was convinced that nobody, no matter what they'd done, should have to suffer like that. She believed in her heart that his killers must be punished.

Dr. Cope was speaking slowly and clearly; he might have been instructing a patient on how to take his medicine. "When they called for a doctor, I used a spent EpiPen, guaranteeing Temple's death. My crime was the worst—I violated my Hippocratic oath. By withholding the epinephrine, I caused his death." He straightened his back, rising a bit in his seat. "I'm the one who should be punished." He turned to Lucy. "Tomorrow, I'll go with you to Scotland Yard and turn myself in."

"But you didn't go to Scotland Yard. What changed your mind?" asked Sue.

Lucy and her three friends were seated in a window table at the Wolseley, a posh Piccadilly restaurant, waiting for the server to deliver their afternoon tea. It was the last day of the trip; they would be flying home first thing the next day.

Lucy glanced around at the sleek art deco dining room, then looked down at the black and silver place mat, the heavy pieces of silverware. She picked up the silky starched linen napkin and spread it on her lap, smoothing it while she gathered her thoughts.

"It was their stories. What happened to the Smiths was terrible—their baby son died because they couldn't afford to get the brakes fixed on their car. And Laura's mother suffered horribly in that nursing home—she actually died from bedsores!"

"Too dreadful," murmured Sue. "And Jennifer's father committed suicide. Families never recover from a thing like that. There's always the feeling that you could have done something to prevent it."

"But the worst was Autumn," said Pam. "Her family became homeless. The bank foreclosed on their house, and they lived in their car for a while, but when her father began drinking, that became impossible for them. Her mother went to a homeless shelter with Autumn, thinking it would be safer, but she was raped there."

"Autumn, too," said Lucy, soothing herself by stroking a spoon that felt pleasantly solid in her hand. "And then her mother got hooked on drugs, and Autumn went into foster care." She put the spoon down as a small parade of waiters approached. "What a nightmare!"

Conversation stopped as the first waiter presented a silver cake stand laden with sandwiches, scones, and cakes and placed it in the center of the table with a flour-

ish. "The scones are cranberry today," he announced.
"The sandwiches are egg and cress on tomato bread,
salmon on wholemeal bread, jambon on cheese bread,
and chicken salad on white bread."

They listened attentively as he pointed out the tiny
triangles that were so artfully arranged. Lucy was starving and her mouth was watering.

"Also, we have an assortment of cakes: mini éclairs,
gateau au chocolat, tartes des fruits, and lemon cup-
cakes. Enjoy!"

"I'm sure we will," said Rachel, somewhat dazed.

"Earl Grey for you, madam?" Another waiter was at
Lucy's elbow, filling her cup with fragrant, steaming tea
and then leaving the silver pot on the table for her. The
others, in turn, received their Lapsang souchong,
Assam, and Darjeeling. Then the servers vanished and
they were confronted with the problem of where to
start.

"I say we go for the cakes first," said Sue. "Why fill up
on the other stuff?"

Rachel adopted her nanny face. "We can't begin with
cake—the sandwiches are the most nourishing."

"Let's compromise and start with the scones," suggested Pam. "Just look at that Devonshire cream."

It took some time to properly assemble the scones
and cream, as well as the strawberry jam, on their
plates, and Lucy became thoughtful. "These are really
good," she said, biting into the warm, buttery, slightly
crisp scone that was a perfect foil for the luscious top-
pings.

"I know," said Sue. "These are amazingly delicious—
so delicious, in fact, that I'm going to pretend they
don't have any calories at all."

"Me too!" declared Pam.

They sat in silence, savoring their treat, until Sue raised her finger, indicating a thought had occurred to her. "Have you heard from Elizabeth, Lucy? I just wondered because, frankly, I could use something a little stronger than tea, and they do have champagne." Her face brightened at the prospect, then adopted a more serious expression. "But if you're strapped, we can certainly stick to the tea."

Lucy shifted her head, mentally changing gears. "You won't believe this. The dean actually thanked her for showing her how important the school's traditions are to the students. She nominated her for the school spirit award."

Pam was grinning. "Maybe it's just me, but school spirit and Elizabeth don't seem like terms I would use in the same sentence."

Lucy shrugged and raised her hand, signaling the waiter. "We'd like champagne all 'round, please."

The waiter nodded, serious in his penguin suit. "Excellent choice, madam."

Chapter Twenty-one

On the flight home, Lucy and her friends were seated separately, scattered throughout the cabin. Lucy, now a seasoned flyer, was flipping through the flight magazine while other passengers were still boarding. It looked to be another crowded flight, and the overhead compartments were filling up fast. Lucy, who was seated once again on the aisle, had to duck when somebody's bag tumbled out and landed in her lap.

"I'm so sorry," said an older gentleman, retrieving his briefcase.

"No damage done," said Lucy, glancing at him and receiving a shock. For a moment, she thought he was George Temple, come back from the grave.

There was a click as the overhead compartment was closed, and he took the seat directly opposite her, on the other side of the aisle. Déjà vu all over again, she thought, stealing another look. The man didn't really look like George, she realized, although he did have gray hair and was wearing a similar jacket.

"I know I'm showing my age but I miss the days when flying was an adventure," he said, smiling at her. "My goodness, they used to treat us like royalty, and the stewardesses were all young and beautiful."

"I guess we were all younger," said Lucy, smiling back. "This is my first overseas trip."

"Did you have a good time?" he asked.

Lucy thought a moment. "It wasn't what I expected," she said finally.

"Well," he replied, opening the packet containing earphones, "I hope we have a pleasant flight."

"Me too," said Lucy, turning back to her magazine.

Takeoff went smoothly and Lucy tried to interest herself in a movie, but her thoughts kept returning to George Temple. She understood that he'd done a terrible thing; she could still hear Tom Smith declaring, "Temple wasn't any better than a serial killer. What's the difference? Bobby died because of George, because of what he did. He never apologized; he never admitted he'd done anything wrong. He thought, right up until the moment he died, that he was better than everybody else. My only regret is that I didn't get to tell him why he was dying, that he was being punished for what he did to us."

Lucy understood his anger, at least she thought she did, but she wasn't at all sure that it was okay for people to take the law into their own hands. Temple was tried; he served jail time. Maybe it wasn't the justice system's shining moment, but in the years she'd covered various trials as a reporter, she'd learned that judges' decisions rarely satisfied everybody. In fact, one lawyer told her that a good decision was one that didn't make either party completely happy.

She squinted at the little screen. Matt Damon sure wasn't happy, and neither was Leonardo DiCaprio, and that Mark Wahlberg guy had a really foul mouth. She

decided to try the BBC news instead, but there were
floods in China and violence in Africa and the world
seemed to be in a dreadful state. Hearing the tinkle of
the drinks cart, she smiled, thinking that Sue would be
pleased. Be honest, she chided herself. She was looking
forward to that white wine, too.

She was finishing up her lunch, tucking the empty
wrappers into a plastic cup that had held spring water,
when a thought struck her. The meal had many compo-
nents: a plastic plate and cutlery, a salad, a foil packet
containing salad dressing, a paper napkin, some sort of
pasta with sauce, all of which came from different sup-
pliers. But, she thought in an aha moment, somebody
had put it all together. Somebody in the British Airways
corporation had chosen these products and arranged
for them to be assembled and distributed to passengers.

Nothing got done without an organizer, she thought.
Not a bake sale, not a school play, and not a murder.
The tour group hadn't all woken up one morning and
decided to murder George Temple; somebody had to
put the idea into their heads. Somebody had organized
the killing and assigned the parts; somebody had convinced the others to share the blame.

"May I take your tray?" asked the stewardess.

Lucy handed it over, and then opened her book, but
she wasn't reading. She was thinking that she knew exactly who had orchestrated Temple's death . . . but
could she prove it?

Her suspicions grew even stronger two months later,
when she was covering the commencement ceremony
at Winchester College. President Chapman announced
that Professor Crighton was now emeritus and that Pro-

fessor Quentin Rae would henceforward occupy the English Literature chair. She sat there, jaw dropping, as Quentin stepped forward to receive his stole, to enthusiastic applause. The applause, she realized, had less to do with Quentin himself than the high spirits of the crowd, who had gathered to congratulate and support their kids. The applause from the section where the faculty was seated was merely polite, but it was difficult to know if that was simply because they had attended so many commencement ceremonies that they were bored or if they believed Quentin unworthy of the honor.

Her mind was in a whirl, but she had to concentrate on getting down President Chapman's speech, all about the impressive work Professor Rea had done through the years, the way he'd reached out to students, especially those having trouble adjusting to college life, and something about the new priorities in which teaching was taking precedence over publishing. Lucy had no idea if this was actually a trend in higher education or a defense against criticism that Quentin hadn't published much.

When all the speeches had been delivered and the diplomas awarded, after the graduates had tossed their caps into the air and were gathered with family members for the traditional photos, she fell into step beside Fred Rumford. Rumford was a history professor, and she'd occasionally interviewed him in the past, most recently when a scuba diver discovered an eighteenth-century shipwreck off the coast.

"Are you looking forward to summer vacation?" she asked.

"Not me," he replied, shaking his head. He'd taken off his black robe and was carrying it over his arm. He'd forgotten his cap, however. It was a rather large beret and gave him a clownish look. "Summer school starts next week. There's no rest for the wicked."

"Too bad." She smiled. "Though I don't imagine it's actually a grueling schedule."

"No." He laughed, pulling off the cap. "Shame on me. It's just one class, but it meets daily for six weeks."

"Then you're free?"

"Yup. I'm heading for Greece, spending August cruising the Greek islands on my friend's schooner." He gave the cap a twirl on his finger.

Lucy pictured sparkling blue water, rocky shores, and dazzling white houses and was sick with envy. "Sounds divine," she said.

He shrugged. "I'm crew. My friend hires the boat out to paying customers. I expect I'll have to do a lot of kowtowing."

Lucy laughed. "That's life." She paused. "Listen, what's up with Quentin Rea? I didn't know he was being considered for a chair."

Rumford grimaced. "It's all about the money. These are tough times—the board of directors can't afford top talent. I heard they were going to give the chair to George Temple, on the cheap. He, at least, has published a few things that were well received. But when he died, they held their noses and voted for Rea."

"I thought he plays kind of fast and loose with the female students. . . ."

"I'm pretty sure Chapman read him the riot act, told him she expected him to behave in a professional manner." He grinned wickedly. "Besides, he is getting older. I think even his tremendous libido may be weakening. And face it, he isn't as attractive as he used to be."

"But I thought that professors were virtually untouchable."

Rumford shook his head. "The world is changing, Lucy. I wouldn't be surprised if she made him sign some sort of contract, with stiff penalties for misconduct."

"Would he sign something like that?"

"In a minute. He was always ambitious, always wanted to be a professor, and I'm sure he realized this was his last chance." Rumford nodded. "Remember, he didn't have a chance in hell of getting the job until Temple died."

"That's what I thought," said Lucy as they came to a fork in the pathway. One way led to the cafeteria, where a reception was in full swing; the other led to the parking lot. "I guess you're expected at the party."

"Punch and cookies," he said. "Used to be we could count on Quentin to spike the punch but now . . ." He trailed off, raising a skeptical eyebrow.

Lucy laughed. "If I don't see you before you leave, have a great time in Greece."

"You, too, Lucy. Have a good summer."

Lucy continued on toward the parking lot, mulling over what Rumford had told her. He'd confirmed her suspicion that Quentin had a strong motive for getting Temple out of the way, a motive that had nothing to do with righting old wrongs or getting revenge. And he could have learned about Temple's past from one of the students he was so friendly with.

Lucy stopped in her tracks, in the middle of the concrete path, and turned around. It was a slim chance—most of the undergraduates had left already—but maybe she could find one of the kids from the tour. Freshmen, she knew, were assigned housing in two dorms, ugly brick boxes that had originally been built to accommodate returning GIs after World War II. One was called Patton and the other Eisenhower.

Patton was the closest. The doors were normally locked and could only be opened by using a special ID card, but practicality had trumped security as students struggled to move out their possessions. Or maybe it was just end-of-term partying; the plain steel door was propped open with a beer keg.

Lucy shook her head at this evidence of underage drinking and entered a dim hallway paved with gray vinyl tiles and lined with doors. She wandered along, peeking from time to time into the abandoned rooms with their stripped beds and open dresser drawers. Here and there, a poster still hung on the painted concrete block walls. She climbed the stairs to the second and third floors, but nobody was there. All the rooms were empty, which puzzled her, because Fred had told her a summer school session was planned. Surely some of the freshmen would be staying on to make up a course or perhaps pick up some extra credits. The answer was in a notice posted on a bulletin board: Patton would be closed for renovations; summer students would have to move to Eisenhower.

Crossing the quad, Lucy found a different atmosphere in the other dorm. The door was also propped open, this time with a lacrosse stick, and most of the rooms were empty, but here and there she found signs of occupation, although the dorm seemed temporarily deserted. It was a nice May day, after all, and those who weren't attending the ceremony were probably out enjoying the weather.

Many of the students had put signs with their names on the doors, and she looked for Caroline, Jennifer, Will, or Autumn but didn't find them. She was about to give up when she heard voices and went to investigate. Maybe she could ask them, whoever they were, if any of the kids from the tour were still on campus.

But as she drew closer, she realized the voices were engaged in an argument.

"Let me go," growled a male voice. "They expect me at the reception."

"No!" The voice was female, young. "Not until you promise."

"You're being ridiculous." The male was losing patience.

"No, I'm not. You said you loved me."

Lucy stopped. Maybe this wasn't the time to strike up a conversation with these two. She had turned around and was heading back to the stairs when she heard something that made her reconsider.

"Autumn, of course I love you."

It was Quentin, she realized. Quentin and Autumn.

"Then why won't you marry me?"

There was a long pause. Lucy found she was holding her breath, waiting for the answer.

"I haven't said I won't marry you."

Lucy's eyebrows went up.

"It's just that marriage is a big step. We should take our time."

"I don't have time. I'm pregnant."

Lucy's jaw dropped.

"It's almost three months. We have to make a decision soon if I'm going to get an abortion."

"I'm aware of that and I'll take care of you, I promise. And the child. But that's not a reason to get married. Not anymore. There's no stigma about being a single mother anymore. . . ."

"Look. I don't want to have the baby unless you're going to marry me."

"How come you weren't on the Pill? Pretty irresponsible if you ask me."

"Right. Like I should poison my body with that stuff. How come you didn't get a vasectomy?"

"Look, I have to get to that reception. We'll talk later."

"NO!" Autumn's voice was a hysterical cry.

"Calm down." Quentin was firm. "I have to go now. We'll talk about this later. We've got plenty of time to discuss this rationally, but this is not the time. I have to make an appearance at the reception."

"Okay, I'll go, too."

"No, you won't." Quentin's voice was threatening and Lucy felt uneasy. "Meet me at my apartment. In an hour."

"No. I'm going to go to the reception and make a big announcement."

Lucy heard a sharp slap, the sound of a hand meeting a cheek, and heard a shriek. She darted into the nearest room and hid behind the door as angry footsteps pounded down the hall. When she heard Quentin start down the stairs, she returned to the hallway, where she heard sobs.

Looking out the window at the end of the hall, she saw Quentin hurrying across the quad, his black gown flapping behind him. She stood watching for a minute, then came to a decision. She could still hear Autumn sobbing as she walked back to the door decorated with nothing but the original computer card the college used to assign rooms. The door was ajar, so she gave a perfunctory knock and pushed it open.

Autumn was sitting on the edge of the bed, grabbing

tissues by the fistful and wiping her eyes. "Wha-what are you doing here?" she demanded, eyes flashing.

"I was looking for you, actually." Lucy noticed Autumn had a new tattoo, a Gothic-style Q on her arm.

"Well, you found me." Autumn blew her nose. "How much did you hear?"

"Just about everything," said Lucy. She seated herself on the single bed next to the girl. "I know it doesn't seem like it right now, but this isn't the end of the world. Whatever you decide, there's help. You'll get through this."

Autumn pounded her fist on her knee. "It's all his fault. If it wasn't for him, I wouldn't be in this mess."

"You have a point." Lucy gave Autumn a quick hug. "But trust me, that kind of thinking is not productive." She paused. "The most you're going to get out of him is money for an abortion."

"I don't want an abortion. I just said that. And I don't want to be a single mom. My mom was a single mom and I know what that's like. And I'm sure not giving up my kid for adoption. I've been a foster kid and it's no fun." She pressed her lips together. "Nope, I'm gonna make him marry me."

Lucy felt her stomach tighten. The girl was playing with fire and didn't know it. "Even if you can blackmail him into marrying you, what sort of start would that be? What kind of marriage would you have?"

Autumn gave her a sweet smile, and Lucy caught a glimpse of the sweet, vulnerable kid underneath the tattoos and piercings and fierce hair. "He said he loved me, and I love him. Love will see us through."

"You threatened to expose him." Lucy was dead serious. "He's a dangerous man. Look how he planned

Temple's murder. He used all of you. He exploited your hurt and desire for revenge for his own advancement."

Autumn's eyes were wide. "How do you know about that?"

Lucy sighed. "It's obvious. He wanted Temple out of the way so he'd get Crighton's job." She slumped, as if a huge weight were pressing on her. "And it's also obvious that he isn't going to marry you."

Autumn's temper flared. "You're just jealous. He told me you two had a fling, years ago."

Lucy felt as if she'd been slapped. "I almost made the biggest mistake of my life, but I was smart enough to stop before I went too far." Lucy's voice was low, her tone serious. She'd been a reporter long enough to know that young women were very vulnerable. A summer rarely passed without some poor girl's body turning up swollen in a pond, or decomposed and ravaged by animals in the woods. Sometimes they just disappeared entirely. "You better think this over very carefully. He's a dangerous man, and there's a tried-and-true remedy for girls who cause trouble: They get killed."

Autumn snorted. "Now you're really being ridiculous. He loves me. You'll see. He just needs some time to calm down and think it over." She smiled a ravishing, confident smile. "I'm going to wear black for the wedding."

"Good thinking," said Lucy, standing up and smoothing out her pants. "Because it will also work for your funeral."

Chapter Twenty-two

"**D**on't forget your boots." Lucy held up a pair of duck boots she'd found in the back of Elizabeth's closet.

Her oldest daughter rolled her eyes. "I won't need them."

"They have rain in Florida."

"I'm not going to wear those, not ever again."

Lucy put the boots back neatly in the corner. "We'll save them for when you come home to visit."

She knew she was going out on a limb here; she was pretty sure Elizabeth was a lot more interested in getting away from home than coming back for visits. After graduating magna cum laude from Chamberlain College, she'd spent a discontented summer working as a chambermaid at the Queen Victoria Inn and looking for a real job. She'd sent out hundreds of résumés to all parts of the country except New England—an omission that had not gone unnoticed by her mother. Now, after a grueling series of interviews, she'd been hired by the Cavendish Hotel chain and was headed for a training session at their flagship hotel in Palm Beach. They were packing a box of clothes to send ahead so she would only need a carry-on for the flight.

"Yeah," said Elizabeth, pulling a bulky sweater out of the huge duffel bag she was packing with clothes, "that's a good idea. I'll leave the warm clothes here."

"Better take a few things. They have cold snaps, you know. They sometimes have to light fires in the groves so the oranges don't freeze on the trees."

Elizabeth looked at her as if she were crazy. "Where do you get these ideas?"

"The news. I've seen it on the TV news." Lucy's cell phone was playing her song, and she pulled it out of her pocket. "Lots of times," she said, flipping it open and seeing her boss, Ted's, number.

"What's up?" she asked.

Ted's voice was apologetic. "I'm sorry to do this to you, but I've got this wedding, Pam's niece. I'm actually in Connecticut."

"No problem. I was just helping Elizabeth pack, but I'm pretty sure she thinks I'm getting in the way."

Elizabeth shook her head but it was a weak protest.

"State police called. They found a body and they're having a press conference. They need help identifying it. Just get the basics—we'll run one of those gray-scale photos with a big question mark. *Who was she?* Heaven knows we don't have much else this week—talk about the dog days of August."

"There's a hurricane off the coast," said Lucy. "They say we might get it."

Ted perked up. "By Wednesday?"

Wednesday was deadline day. "Next weekend, maybe."

"Damn. We'll just have to go with the body. The press conference is two p.m. at the barracks in Shiloh."

* * *

At two o'clock Lucy was seated, along with a handful of reporters and camera crews from the Boston and Portland TV stations, in a basement room used for press conferences. A podium had been set up, backed with an American flag and the Maine state flag, and they billowed gently in the breeze created by a standing fan in the corner. Upstairs was air-conditioned, but thrifty Maine planners had reasoned the basement would be naturally cool. It wasn't. Lucy lifted her shirt off her sweaty shoulders and fanned herself with her reporter's notebook.

"They always turn up in August," said the guy next to her, a stringer for the *Boston Globe*. "I guess they start to smell in the heat. I heard a dog found this one."

Lucy nodded. "You're way ahead of me. Where'd they find it? It's a woman, right?"

"This is unofficial, but I heard some women talking at the gas station. They said it's a girl. She was stuffed in a plastic bag and dumped in the Metinnicut River. The bag snagged on some rocks or logs or something, and when the water level went down, like it does in summer—"

"I get the picture," said Lucy.

There was a small commotion as a group of officials were heard coming down the stairs and entering the room. Lucy recognized Strom Kipfer, the Shiloh police chief; Detective Horowitz from the state police, dressed as usual in a rumpled gray suit; and the county DA, Phil Aucoin. Aucoin took the podium while the others arranged themselves behind him in a row.

"Thanks for coming," he said, fingering a folded piece of paper. "First let me introduce everybody." He worked his way down the row, spelling names and giving each person's title. When he finished, he sighed and began reading a prepared statement.

"Early yesterday morning, a woman walking her dog along the bed of the Metinnicut River, which is quite low this year, discovered a large construction-grade plastic bag snagged on a log. The dog pawed the bag, ripping it and revealing a human foot. The woman called nine-one-one and local police responded, determining that the bag contained the body of a woman. Because of the method of disposal, they assumed the woman was the victim of a murder.

"The body was removed by the medical examiner at nine thirty-three a.m. and subsequently examined. There was some decomposition but the cool water temperature and the plastic bag protected the body, and he was able to determine that she was killed by a single blow to the head. She was about twenty years of age, five feet six inches tall, one hundred fifteen pounds, and in good health apart from the fact that she needed dental care. She had short dark hair and numerous piercings."

Lucy's head snapped up. *Oh, no,* she thought.

"She was dressed in black leggings, a short skirt, and a black T-shirt."

Lucy was scribbling it all down. *Let it be somebody else.*

"The victim was approximately ten weeks pregnant."

Lucy's stomach tied itself into a knot and she felt sick.

"Decomposition was too far advanced to allow for a photograph of the face, but we were able to photograph a tattoo on the woman's body, and we're going to distribute that today and ask that you publish it, bearing in mind that some news outlets may have individual

policies that prohibit the publication of such poten-
tially offensive material."

Lucy was holding her breath when the officer
handed her a color photo. She exhaled slowly, then
forced herself to look. The tattoo was a single letter in
Gothic script: a *Q*.

The DA asked for questions but Lucy wasn't listening. She was picturing Autumn, remembering how
she'd smiled, imagining herself in a black wedding
dress. She'd never got to wear it; in fact, it seemed she
had died in the same outfit she was wearing that day in
June when they'd talked in the dorm. The day Lucy had
warned her that Quentin was a dangerous man. Probably the day she died.

The conference was over. The officials were shaking
hands here and there, making small talk with the reporters who were packing up to leave. Lucy was sitting
there, her notebook in her lap, her pen in one hand
and the photo in the other.

"Is everything all right?" It was her sometime friend
Detective Horowitz. Their jobs tended to make them
adversaries; as a reporter, she usually wanted more information than he wanted to share. But they were also
both aware that they needed each other and had developed a respectful collegiality. As always, he looked tired,
and today he seemed unusually concerned.

"Can I talk to you privately?" she asked.

"Sure."

Lucy got up, dropping the notebook on the floor
and wavering unsteadily on her feet. He took her elbow,
leading her to a side door that opened into a storage
area. She was still clutching the photo in one hand and
the pen in the other. "I know who this is," she said, tears

springing to her eyes. She sobbed. "And I know who killed her."

Two weeks later, Lucy was surprised when Detective Horowitz called her at the office. She'd just sat down, fresh from the airport where she'd waved a brave good-bye to Elizabeth. Truth was, she felt rather down. Elizabeth had never been an easy child, but this summer they'd somehow avoided conflicts, at least most of the time. Lucy had really enjoyed having her eldest daughter home, and she knew she was going to miss her.

Horowitz got right to the point. "Everything you told me checked out," he said.

"So you've arrested him?" asked Lucy. It would be a relief to know Quentin was off the street and behind bars, unable to strike again.

"No."

Lucy couldn't believe it. "Why not?"

"That's why I'm calling you. I need your help."

"I think I've done enough—I gave you the whole case on a platter."

"I know. I've questioned him several times and I'm convinced he did it."

"So what's the problem?"

"It's all circumstantial. He denies everything. Well, he admits he had an affair with the girl but insists he didn't kill her. Which is smart because he knows we can do a DNA test. But even if the kid is his, it's not proof that he killed her."

"But there must be other evidence. Blood? Hair? Fibers?"

"Most likely, but we haven't been able to get a search warrant. The judge turned us down flat—he's a big be-

iever in academic freedom. He says it would 'set a terrible precedent if police were allowed to invade college
campuses like storm troopers and upset the peaceful
and systematic pursuit of knowledge.' I'm quoting
here."

"That's unbelievable."

"Yeah." There was a long pause. "That's why the DA
asked me to get in touch with you." Another pause.
"Well, actually, it was my idea. Your name came up in
the course of the investigation as being someone he'd
had a relationship with."

Lucy was quick to defend herself. "That's not true. I
took a course from him, years ago, and I spent some
time with him on the trip to England, but I wouldn't say
we had a relationship. We were friendly, and that's really
an exaggeration."

Horowitz's voice was conciliatory. "Look, I'm not
making judgments or anything. I'm just asking for some
help—and it would make a good story for your paper."

The man was a devil. Lucy knew when she was beat.
If she said no, he'd just call Ted. "What do you want me
to do?"

"Wear a wire."

The female trooper who helped Lucy with the wire
apparatus was enthusiastic. "These things have really
been improved," she said, displaying a compact plastic
case. "They used to be so bulky, but you can just tuck
this baby into your bra. He won't suspect a thing. It's
even got GPS, but I don't think we'll need that today."
They were in the ladies' room outside the coffee-house
Winchester College had recently added to the student
union building. "Professor Rea teaches an eight a.m.

class on Mondays, Wednesdays, and Fridays, and he always comes here afterward for coffee. You can pretend you're here on a story and strike up a conversation."

"And somehow, in the course of chatting about whether he likes mocha or hazelnut better I'm supposed to get him to confess he's a murderer? How am I supposed to do that?"

She shrugged. "You'll think of something. Horowitz says if anybody can, it's you. He says you're really . . ." She stopped suddenly, her neck reddening.

"Go on. I can take it. What did he say?"

She smiled in apology. "He said you can be a real pain in the butt, that he'd confess just to get rid of you." She suddenly turned her attention to the earpiece she was wearing. "He's here. It's showtime. And remember," she added, giving Lucy a shove toward the door, "you've got plenty of backup. You're perfectly safe."

Lucy's heart was racing when she stepped out of the ladies' room and crossed the cozy space with orange walls and a distressed wood floor, past the scattered tables and comfy armchairs, to get in line at the counter behind Quentin. She didn't say anything and pretended to be going over some notes in her notebook while he ordered. When he turned, coffee in hand, she looked up.

"Hi!" she exclaimed with a big smile.

"Well, hi yourself. What brings you here?"

"Work." She turned to the kid at the counter, who was probably a student. "I'll have a small cappuccino."

"That'll be three-fifty," said the kid.

Lucy reached for her wallet but Quentin was quicker. "Let me treat."

Lucy gave him her best, what she hoped was an absolutely ravishing, smile. "Thanks."

There was a bit of an awkward pause while they waited for the kid to make the cappuccino. The machine was hissing and sputtering; the air was filled with the delicious scent of coffee. "If only it tasted as good as it smells," mused Lucy. She made her eyes big. "By the way, congratulations. I hear you're a professor now."

"Yeah," he said with a crooked smile as the kid passed over a cup topped with milky white froth. Lucy took it and followed him to a corner table flanked with French-style leather armchairs. They sat and Lucy's eyes met his as she took a sip of her cappuccino, making sure plenty of froth stuck to her lip. As she expected, he leaned forward and wiped it away with a finger, which he licked, his eyes never leaving hers. She smiled, a Mona Lisa smile this time. Things were going well—but she felt like throwing up.

"So what's the big story?" he asked.

"Oh, the body," she said as coolly as she could.

Quentin seemed to flinch but quickly recovered. He leaned forward, stroking her hand with his finger. "What body? I haven't heard anything—"

"It's an old story. They found the body of this girl in the river. It was in the news about two weeks ago. *Mystery girl?* You didn't see it?"

Quentin was all innocence. "No."

"Dumped in the river in a plastic bag, no identification. Lady walking her dog discovered it."

"I'm glad I don't have a dog," said Quentin, attempting a joke.

"Yeah." Lucy laughed. "It's dangerous—they're always finding the most unspeakable stuff. My dog came home with half a dead rabbit the other day. So gross."

"So, why did you come here?" Quentin couldn't resist asking. "Do they think this girl was a student here?"

Lucy took another sip of cappuccino and licked her lip, slowly. "You know Ted. He's always looking for an angle. He sent me over to ask if any students were missing."

Quentin leaned back, a study in casual ease. "And was anybody missing?"

"Actually, yes. Somebody was. Or is."

"Really?"

Lucy knew she had to drag this out; she had to play with him and make him tense if she was ever going to get anything out of him. "You know her, and so do I."

Quentin narrowed his eyes. "I think you're playing with me."

"Me? Don't be silly." She licked her lips again and raised her eyes flirtatiously. "Autumn Mackie. Remember? From the London trip?"

"Sure." He crossed his legs. "To tell the truth, that doesn't surprise me. She wasn't college material. She probably realized it and dropped out."

"The registrar said she didn't file a withdrawal or anything."

"Her type never do. They just go on their merry way." He paused. "She probably got mixed up with the wrong sort of guy."

"I'm a little surprised at your attitude. I thought you two had something going on during the trip."

"She may have had a bit of a crush on me," said Quentin in a disapproving tone. "These girls today. They're very forward. I'm afraid I had to discourage her."

"You know, the more I think about it, the more it seems that the girl in the river fits Autumn's description." Lucy looked down at the table. "I hope it isn't her. I hope you're right, that she went on her merry way somewhere."

"I'm sure that's the case." Quentin's eyes were drifting toward the door, and Lucy sensed he was thinking of leaving. She had to do something, fast.

"The girl in the river was pregnant," she said.

Quentin clucked his tongue. "Oh, my."

"Perhaps you could offer to take a look at the body? You would know if it's Autumn."

"Why me? Why not you?"

Lucy fixed her eyes on his. "Because the dead girl has a tattoo of a *Q*, not an *L*."

Quentin shrugged. "Okay, I admit it. I knew about the girl. The cops even interviewed me. I guess they did a computer search for everybody in the area whose name begins with *Q*—which is admittedly a rather small number. But I couldn't help them. I didn't recognize the girl—and I don't know how she got in the river."

Lucy pushed the cup and saucer away. "It is Autumn—they identified her from her dental records."

She was watching Quentin closely, looking for some reaction. "That is terrible," he said. "How awful for her family."

"She didn't have any family, thanks to George Temple, and you know it."

He glanced at his watch. "You know, I think I ought to be going. It was great seeing you, Lucy."

Lucy felt crushed, watching him leave. She was a complete failure. She hadn't got anything out of him. She sat there at the table, replaying the whole conversation in her mind and wondering what she could have said that would have made a difference, when Horowitz materialized and took the other chair.

"I'm sorry," she said.

"It was a long shot." Horowitz sighed. "He's smart—too smart for us. Don't feel bad. You did your best."

"Yeah." Lucy pushed her chair back. "Well, I've got a deadline." She was on her feet and out the door, eager to forget the whole thing. It left a bad taste in her mouth. She didn't like it that a young girl was dead. She thought Quentin was appalling, disgusting, lower than low. She wanted him to pay for what he'd done, but she didn't like being a snitch either.

She blinked, stepping out into the bright September sun, and made her way toward the parking lot. It was hot, a real scorcher. The asphalt had been soaking up heat for weeks, and the air above it was wavery, making her feel disoriented. She'd parked in the shade, thank heavens. The car was tucked beneath a large old maple that was just beginning to turn color, anticipating fall. The leaves were part green, part yellow, she noticed, clicking the button on the key that unlocked the door. She stepped into the shade, feeling the cooler temperature as she reached for the car door, and that's when something tightened around her neck, yanking her backward.

She didn't even get a chance to yell for help, managing only a startled cry, before she was overpowered. She had no air. She struggled, kicked, and tried to grab her assailant's hair, his ear, gouge his eyes with her keys, but she was at a disadvantage. He was behind her and she knew her blows were weak. She was beginning to lose consciousness; black was blocking out the dazzling sunshine, and in one last, desperate effort, she grabbed below his belt, squeezing as hard as she could.

Then, suddenly, the pressure on her neck eased and she was thrown forward, onto her hands and knees.

"Stop! Police!" The voice was female, clear and sharp. "Raise your hands!"

Lucy pushed herself up and saw Detective Horowitz and a couple of uniformed cops thudding across the parking lot, guns drawn. The female state trooper was also holding a gun, legs spread apart, and she had Quentin firmly in her sights.

He was doubled over, clutching himself.

"You have the right to remain silent . . ." she began reciting the Miranda warning as Horowitz applied the cuffs.

"Are you all right?" One of the troopers was helping Lucy to her feet.

"I'm okay," said Lucy, her hand at her neck. "How did you . . . ?"

"The wire. You were still wearing the wire."

Lucy's head was clearing. "GPS," she said, glaring at Horowitz. "GPS! You used me! You knew he'd try to kill me! That was the plan all along."

"Don't be ridiculous. That would be strictly against agency policy," said Horowitz, sounding rather insincere. "Besides, you were never in any danger. We had you covered the entire time." He glanced at the professor. "Anyway, he's in a lot worse shape than you."

"Somehow that's not making me feel all warm and fuzzy," said Lucy.

"Think positively," said Horowitz as a cruiser pulled up. The handcuffed professor was pushed inside, still crouching in pain. "You've got a hell of a story. Ted's gonna love it."

Lucy saw red. "Ted was in on this?"

Horowitz consulted his watch. "You've got just over an hour before deadline."

He was right, realized Lucy, hurrying to get behind

the wheel. She was stiff and sore, her throat was ragged, and her hands were trembling as she started the car. But she had one hell of a story. Maybe Ted would even hold the paper for an hour. She found her phone and called him, popping two aspirin as she navigated the parking lot. "Hey, Ted," she began, when he interrupted.

"Lucy! Are you all right? I've been so worried. . . ."

"Yeah, yeah, yeah. Now listen. Start typing. 'This morning, state police arrested . . .' "

Epilogue

It was about a month later when Lucy received a call from DA Phil Aucoin.

"I need to clear up a few things," he said. "Can you come in today around three?"

Lucy understood that while the time of the conversation might be negotiable, there was no way she was going to get out of the meeting. She knew she would have to testify about the attack, and Aucoin would want to make sure he knew what she was going to say; he wouldn't want any surprises in the courtroom. She wasn't eager to relive the fear she'd felt when that necktie had tightened around her throat but figured she might as well get it over with as soon as possible. "Sure," she said.

Aucoin's office was in the county complex in Gilead, a small boxy brick building dwarfed by the massive jail, with its razor-wire fence, and the stately nineteenth-century courthouse built of gleaming white granite. He didn't look up from his cluttered desk when she entered, so she took the one available chair and looked around. Every surface in the small room, including the floor, was covered with stacks of paper. The one window had a fine view of the Civil War memorial that stood on the green lawn in front of the courthouse, but she couldn't see it because of the pile of thick manila folders that threatened to slip off the sill any minute.

"Just a mo'," he muttered, reaching for the phone. He listened a few minutes, then spoke. "Best I can do is six months served and two years probation," he said.

Lucy could hear the outraged protest coming from the other end of the line.

Aucoin shook his head and rolled his eyes. "Your client assaulted an eighty-two-year-old woman who was on her way to a nursing home to visit her one-hundred-and-one-year-old mother, just like she does every Sunday after church. You wanna go to court with that and take your chances with a jury?"

The sound effects continued, and Aucoin rolled his eyes again. "I'm well aware that your client ended up with a concussion, but believe me, juries love that stuff. Little old ladies who fight back—trust me, we've got an aging population. Most of the jurors are going to be on the far side of forty, and they don't like young punks."

The outraged squawks ceased, Aucoin nodded a few times, said, "Okay," and ended the call. He looked at Lucy. "One down," he said, making a notation on the folder, closing the file and reaching for another, much thicker one. "Quentin Rea wants a deal," he said, locking eyes with her. "He's alleging that the members of a Winchester College tour to England last spring conspired to kill the tour leader, a professor named George Temple. He says you can corroborate the whole story."

Lucy's first reaction was outrage. What a worm! But the more she thought about it, the more typical it seemed. If Quentin Rea was going down, he wasn't going down alone. Biting her lip, attempting to control her emotions, she studied Aucoin's face: the deep grooves that ran from his nose to his mouth, the bags under his eyes, the wiry hair that refused to be tamed and shot up from his forehead in an unruly, oversized pompadour. He was a man who knew only too well that people were capable of doing terrible things to each other; nothing surprised him anymore.

"What exactly is he saying?" asked Lucy.

Aucoin began reading from five or six pages that were clipped together. "He says he was approached in his office last December by a student named Caroline Smith who was in a special support group for freshmen who were having trouble adjusting to college life. She'd figured out that three other students, and herself, had all come from families that had been defrauded by George Temple in the 1990s. These students were the late Autumn Mackie, who Rea is presently under indictment for killing; William Barfield; and Jennifer Fain. Apparently they'd all recounted their tales of woe during the group discussions, and Caroline recognized certain elements that led her to conclude they'd all been wronged by this George Temple, who was now an instructor at the college. She was able to confirm this in subsequent private discussions."

Lucy listened, thinking this might well be true. Caroline's parents, Tom and Ann Smith, had probably talked about Temple a lot through the years, making it quite clear to their surviving child that he was the source of all their troubles. Tom, she knew, had nursed his anger toward Temple. Of the four, Caroline probably was the one who was most aware of Temple's crime. And if she had initiated the plot, she might well have felt guilty enough to try to kill herself by jumping off the Brighton Pier.

Aucoin continued. "George Temple was convicted of

fraud, served time, got hired by Winchester thanks to some social connections. Stayed clean."

Lucy nodded. "I understand he was quite a success at the college. Popular with students and faculty. He was even being considered for a tenure position."

Aucoin made a note. "Not according to our boy, Quentin. He says Temple was unqualified, called him an 'academic bottom-feeder.' But even so, he says he was shocked when this Caroline said she and the others wanted his help in getting back at Temple. He says he absolutely refused to get involved in any way."

"That would be the proper thing to do," said Lucy, who was willing to bet that Rea had chosen to do the exact opposite. He would never pass up an opportunity to get rid of his rival, especially when someone else was willing to do the dirty work.

"However, Rea says he was troubled that the four might go ahead without him and kept an eye on the situation," continued Aucoin.

That was clever of him, thought Lucy. It gave him a reason for knowing about the plot without admitting any responsibility for Temple's murder.

"He claims the four kids and their families got together at a tailgate party at the Polar Bowl on New Year's Day and worked out a plan to kill Temple."

"Over the bratwurst?" asked Lucy.

Aucoin smiled, enjoying her little joke. "He didn't say. I guess he wasn't keeping that close an eye on things. He claims he just happened to see them in the parking lot."

Right, thought Lucy. Like Rea hadn't organized the meeting himself, probably cooked the bratwurst and mulled the cider and sent out the invitations. "Temple died on the plane," she said. "I was sitting across the aisle from him. It was an allergy attack."

"That's what Rea says. The kids knew he had severe allergies, and one of the parents, a Dr. Cope, figured out how they could set off an attack."

"Grandparent," corrected Lucy. "Dr. Cope is Jennifer's grandfather."

Aucoin made another notation, then resumed his narrative. "To make a long story short, they all signed up for Temple's trip to England, took turns waving around mildewed scarves and peanut trail mix, and when he started wheezing, this doctor rushed forward with a fake EpiPen and finished him off."

"That would be a violation of his Hippocratic oath," said Lucy. "I happen to know that Dr. Cope took that very seriously. We talked about it in St. Paul's. He told me he wished he could have saved Temple." She pressed her lips together, remembering the rest of the story, how Dr. Cope had later told her his son-in-law had committed suicide when he learned Temple had impoverished him and that his grief-stricken daughter had turned to drugs for consolation, leaving him to raise Jennifer. She thought of the Smith family, who trusted Temple to invest all their money and when he'd ruined them, lost their precious baby boy in a car accident. An accident they believed could have been avoided if they'd been able to afford new brakes. She remembered sitting in Bath Abbey and listening to Laura Barfield tell how her mother had suffered in that dreadful nursing home, because it was the best she could afford after Temple had lost all her money. She thought of Laura's all-enveloping guilt that she wore like one of those suffocating black chadors Muslim women wrapped themselves in. And then there was Autumn, who'd survived the loss of her home and her parents and years in foster care only to be murdered by Quentin Rea when she posed a threat to his professorship. She came to a decision. She was certainly not going to cause these people any more grief. But she didn't want to lie to Aucoin either. She was going to have to be very careful about what she said.

"It seems to me," she said slowly, "that if anybody wanted Temple dead, it was Quentin Rea. He had the most to gain. Temple was going to get the professorship that Quentin wanted, that he'd worked for his entire life."

Aucoin narrowed his eyes. "Do you think Rea was behind this plot to kill Temple?"

Lucy shrugged, hopefully indicating she didn't have the faintest idea. "I know a little bit about asthma allergies—my oldest daughter is allergic. The hardest thing about being allergic is the unpredictability. Elizabeth knows what her triggers are, but sometimes she forgets and uses a feather pillow, something like that. She might have an attack, but she might not. It all depends on whether she's been taking her medicine, how old the feather pillow is, a whole bunch of factors."

"So you're saying it would be pretty hard to kill someone by triggering an allergic attack?"

"I think it would be close to impossible," said Lucy. She decided to mention something she'd been suspecting, even though it was little more than a wild guess. "You know Rea is an English professor, right? I wouldn't be at all surprised if he has an unpublished manuscript or two in a drawer."

Aucoin's eyes widened. "Actually, we found two. *Death in Florence: An Elizabeth Barrett Browning Mystery* and *Murder on Flight 214: An Homage to Agatha Christie*. Also about twenty rejection slips."

Lucy resisted the impulse to let out a long sigh of relief. "Well, there you have it," she said. "He couldn't sell his little story to a publisher but figured he'd see if you'd buy it and cut him a deal for a reduced sentence."

"I think you're right," said Aucoin, leaning back in his chair. "I'm glad we had this little talk. Some of what he said had the ring of truth. . . ."

"The best lies always do," said Lucy.

Aucoin nodded. "But even if he was telling the truth, I'd never get a jury to believe it."

"The media would love it," said Lucy, putting the final nail in Rea's coffin. "I can see the headlines now: "The Big Sneeze: Allergy Trial Goes to Jury."

Aucoin looked like a man who'd driven to the edge of a cliff and braked just in time, saving himself from a fall down a deadly precipice. He snapped the file shut and pounded it with a rubber stamp. "No deals. We go to trial on what we've got. The murder of Autumn Mackie and the attempted murder of Lucy Stone. I expect we'll put him away for life."

Lucy stood up and smiled. "See you in court."

Between a cutthroat dessert contest and her daughter's new job at the fanciest chocolate shop Tinker's Cove has ever seen, Lucy Stone is on a steady diet of tempting treats! But with a killer on the loose, and Valentine's Day around the corner, there may be nothing sweeter than revenge . . .

It's frigid in snow-covered Tinker's Cove, and Lucy is fighting the winter blues—and her widening waistline. No one in their right mind would vacation in Maine this time of year, but to boost the economy, the town is launching a travel promotion for Valentine's Day. As a reporter for the *Pennysaver*, Lucy is assigned a puff piece on upscale Chanticleer's Chocolates, and its deliciously handsome owner, Trey Meacham. But when a local fisherman drowns suspiciously, Lucy's certain her investigative skills could be put to better use . . .

Everyone is shocked when Fern's Famous Fudge loses its status as "Best Candy on the Coast" to Chanticleer's pricey newfangled confections. And Lucy soon discovers there's another tantalizing tart behind the counter. Sultry store manager Tamzin Graves is only too eager to serve her male clientele—who find her as mouthwatering as her beef-jerky-spiked truffles. Leaving a throng of jealous women in her wake, it's almost no surprise when Tamzin is the next to turn up dead, her body covered in chocolate . . .

Could a bitter ex-wife be behind the crimes? Or a candy shop competitor? There's no sugar-coating the truth, and as Lucy closes in on the culprit, she may find herself locked in the clutches of a half-baked killer . . .

Please turn the page for an exciting sneak peek of Leslie Meier's next Lucy Stone mystery CHOCOLATE COVERED MURDER Now on sale at bookstores everywhere!

Chapter One

If the cold didn't kill her, the slippery ice on the side-walk surely would, thought Lucy Stone as she stepped out of the overheated town hall basement meeting room into a frigid Monday afternoon. January was al-ways cold in the little coastal town of Tinker's Cove, Maine, and this year was a record-breaker. The elec-tronic sign on the bank across the street informed her it was four forty-five and nine, no, eight degrees. The tem-perature was falling fast and was predicted to sink below zero during the night.

Lucy hurried across the frozen parking lot as fast as she dared, mindful that a patch of ice could send her flying. Reaching the car, she made sure the heater was on high, and waited a few minutes for the engine to warm up. While she waited, she thought about the meeting she had just attended and how she would write it up for the local paper, the Tinker's Cove *Pennysaver*.

The topic under discussion was improving toilet fa-cilities at the town beach and quite a crowd had turned out for the meeting. In her experience as a reporter, only dog hearings excited more interest than waste-water issues and this meeting had been no exception.

Of course, people had been complaining about the inadequate facilities for some time; a group of concerned citizens had even entered a float in the Fourth of July parade as a protest. The parade theme had been "From Sea to Shining Sea" and the float depicted the town beach strewn with sewage. The ensuing controversy had prompted the selectmen to address the issue, but there was little agreement on the solution. The budget-minded had favored continuing the present Porta-Potties, the cheapest option. Installing earth closets, the eco-friendly option, had brought out the tree-huggers; the business community, which depended on tourist dollars, had lobbied for conventional toilets, which would require digging a well and putting in an expensive septic system.

This was going to be fun to write up, she thought, as she shifted into drive and proceeded cautiously across the icy parking lot and onto the road. In addition to the cold, they had recently had a big snowfall, so the road was lined with high banks of plowed snow. It was hard to see around the piles of snow, so Lucy inched out into the road, hoping nothing was coming.

As she drove along Main Street, past the police station and clustered stores, past the Community Church with its tall steeple, she thought of possible opening sentences. She'd driven this route so often that her mind was wandering and she was halfway through her story when she cleared town and the landscape opened with harvested cornfields on both sides of the road. The winter sunset was fabulous, the sky a blazing red that took her breath away. She couldn't take her eyes off the gorgeous color that filled the sky and was barely paying attention to the road when a large buck leaped over a snowdrift, landing right in front of her. She slammed on the brakes and skidded, hanging onto the steering wheel for dear life and praying she wouldn't hit the animal, when the car fishtailed and slammed into the snowbank on the opposite side of the road.

Heart pounding, she caught a glimpse of brown rump and white tail bounding unhurt across the field, and sent up a little prayer of thanks. Then she shifted into reverse, intending to back out onto the road. Pressing the accelerator, she heard the dismaying hum of spinning tires. Climbing out of the car, she found the front end deeply imbedded in the snow and the rear tires sunk up to the hubcaps in soft slush and realized she wasn't going to get out without help.

The sun was now falling below the horizon, the sky was a deep purple, and the road was deserted. She got back in the car and reached for her cell phone, remembering she hadn't charged it lately. Indeed, when she flipped it open, the screen blinked BATTERY LOW and immediately went dark. She was only a bit more than a mile from home, but in this frigid weather she didn't dare risk walking. Her best option was to stay with the car and keep the engine running. Unfortunately, she'd been running close to empty for a day or two, too busy to stop and fill the tank.

It was just a matter of time, she told herself, before her husband, Bill, would wonder why she wasn't home and would come out looking for her. Or not. He might figure she was working late, covering an evening meeting, in which case they'd probably find her frozen body the next morning.

Perhaps she should write a note, letting her family know how much she loved them. Then again, she thought, perhaps not. What sort of family didn't come out and look for a missing member, especially on a night when the temperature was predicted to go below zero? She thought of Bill, who habitually watched the five o'clock news, and her teenage daughters Sara and Zoe, probably texting their friends, all in the comfort of their cozy home on Red Top Road. Didn't they miss her? Weren't they worried? They'd be sorry, wouldn't they, when she was on the news tomorrow night. *Local woman freezes to death. Family in shock. "I should have known something was wrong," says grieving husband.*

A tap at the window startled her and she turned to see a smiling, bearded face she recognized as belonging to Max Fraser. She lowered the window.

"Looks like you could use a tow," he said.

"It was a deer," she said. "He jumped in the road and I swerved to avoid him."

"Doesn't look like the car's damaged," he said. "You were lucky."

"I'm lucky you came along," said Lucy. "I don't have much gas and my cell phone is dead."

"I'll have you out of here in no time," he said, signaling that she should close the window.

Max was as good as his word. In a matter of minutes, he had fastened a tow line from his huge pickup to her car. She felt a bump and heard a sudden groaning noise and all of a sudden her car popped out of the snowdrift. Max looked it over for damage and listened to make sure the engine was running okay, and when she offered to pay him for his trouble, he looked offended.

"Folks gotta help folks," he said. "Someday maybe you can help me, or pass it on. Help somebody else."

"I will," promised Lucy. "I certainly will."

* * *

Next morning, Lucy was writing her account of the meeting when Corney Clarke popped into the *Pennysaver* office, like a glowing ember leaping out of a crackling fire and onto the hearth. Her cheeks were red with the cold, her ski parka was bright orange, and her stamping feet sprayed bits of snow in all directions. "This is big, really big," she exclaimed, pulling off her shearling gloves.

Phyllis, the receptionist, peered over her harlequin reading glasses and cast a baleful glance at the melting puddle of snow. She drew her purple sweater across her ample bust and shivered. "Mind shutting the door? There's an awful draft."

"Oh, sorry," said Corney, pushing the door shut with difficulty and setting the old-fashioned wooden blinds rattling. "It's just I'm so excited about my big news." She paused, making sure she had the attention of Ted Stillings, the weekly paper's publisher, editor, and chief reporter.

"I'm listening," said Ted, leaning back in his swivel chair and propping his feet on the half-open file drawer of the sturdy oak roll-top desk he inherited from his grandfather, a legendary New England journalist. Like practically every man in town, he was dressed in a plaid shirt topped with a thick sweater, flannel-lined khaki pants, and duck boots.

Lucy typed the final period and turned around to face Corney. "This better be good," she said. Corney, an interior designer who wrote a monthly lifestyle column for *Maine House and Cottage* magazine, was always pitching stories, looking for free publicity.

"Oh, it is," said Corney. She took a deep breath and paused dramatically, then spoke. "Chanticleer Chocolate was voted 'Best Candy on the Coast.'"

It landed like a bombshell, and for a moment there was stunned silence in the newspaper office.

"You mean . . . ?" began Phyllis.

"What about . . . ?" murmured Ted.

"Talk about an upset!" exclaimed Lucy.

"That's right." Corney gave a self-satisfied nod. "It's the first time since the magazine began the Best of Maine poll that Fern's Famous Fudge hasn't won."

"Fern's Famous is an institution," said Phyllis.

Lucy nodded, thinking of the quaint little shop with the red-and-white striped awning that had stood on Main Street in Tinker's Cove since, well, forever. The business was started by Fern Macdougal, who needed a source of income after her husband was killed in the Korean War. She started selling her homemade fudge through local shops, eventually buying her own place as the little business took off in the nineteen fifties when tourists began flocking to the Maine coast. Fern's Famous, with its big copper kettle and marble counters, was a must-see and nobody passed through town without picking up one of the red-and-white striped boxes of fudge or salt water taffy. Nowadays, Fern was in her nineties, but she still kept a sharp eye on the business, which was run by her daughter Flora Riggs, who had added a catering service to the company, and her granddaughter Dora Fraser, Max's ex-wife.

"Now, Ted," said Corney, turning to the reason for her visit. "You have to admit this is a big story. And, it just happens to tie in very nicely with the Chamber of Commerce's *Love Is Best on the Coast* February travel promotion." Corney, as they all knew only too well, was chairman of the Chamber's publicity committee.

"Whoa," said Ted, raising his hand. "February travel

promotion? Are you crazy? This is Maine. I don't know if you've noticed, but there's two feet of snow on the ground, the temperature is fifteen degrees, and the forecast is for, surprise, more snow."

"Sleet," said Lucy. "We're supposed to have a warm spell. Global warming."

"Either way, snow or sleet," said Ted, "it's not exactly picnic weather."

"Maine is beautiful every time of year," said Corney, "but winter is my favorite time. The snow is so beautiful . . ."

"It's treacherous," said Lucy. "I barely made it home alive last night. If Max Fraser hadn't come along, I'd be headline news this morning. I got stuck in a snowdrift when a buck jumped in front of my car, out by those cornfields."

"There's a lot of deer out there," said Phyllis. "They eat the corn the harvester missed."

"You've got to be careful in the snow," said Corney, "but the town does an excellent job with the plowing. And you have to admit, on a day like today, when the sun makes the snow sparkle and the air is crisp, it's just a little bit of heaven here in Tinker's Cove."

Corney had a point, thought Lucy, thinking of her antique farmhouse on Red Top Road and how pretty it looked covered with snow, especially at night when the windows glowed with lamplight. Of course, the snow made it impossible to keep the house clean inside. Her daughters, Sara and Zoe, were constantly tracking in snow and mud, as did her husband, Bill. Even the dog added to the mess, rolling in the snow and shaking it off as soon as she came through the door. The kitchen floor was littered with boots and shoes; the coat rack was loaded with jackets and scarves and ski pants. Hats and mittens and gloves were spread on the old-fashioned radiators to dry.

It wasn't just the constant sweeping and tidying that got her down in winter, it was the way the house seemed to shrink in the bleak months after Christmas. The walls seemed to move in and the furniture grew larger. Every surface became cluttered with projects and busywork: the fishing reel Bill was repairing, the scarf Sara was knitting for the high school Good Neighbor Club, Zoe's rock display for eighth-grade science.

Going out for a meal or a movie, even a shopping trip, was the obvious cure for cabin fever, but it wasn't easy. It took a lot of determination to get anywhere. First you had to layer on all those clothes, then you had to shovel your way to the car, which might or might not start. Once you were on the road, you had to be constantly vigilant, watching for slick spots and creeping slowly through intersections made blind by enormous piles of snow, and you had to remember to start braking well in advance of every stop sign. Once you reached your destination, you had to hunt for a plowed parking spot and then you had to watch your step when you got out of the car because the sidewalks, even when shoveled, soon became slick with ice.

None of that seemed to bother Corney, who was listing the advantages of winter. "Sleigh rides in the snowy woods," she said, prompting a snort from Phyllis.

"Endless shoveling," complained Ted. "Heart attacks—did you see the obits last week? Three old guys, in one week."

Corney ignored him. "We have all these romantic B&Bs with canopy beds and fireplaces. . . ."

"Fireplaces are awful messy. Wood chips, twigs, even

leaves, and then there's the ashes. Filthy," said Phyllis. "And that stuff jams up the vacuum."

"Hot toddies and cocoa with tiny marshmallows," said Corney, as if she were raising the stakes in a poker game.

"The stink of wet wool," countered Lucy.

"Tree branches coated in ice, sparkling in the sun," said Corney, laying down a few more chips.

"Broken bones from falls on the icy sidewalks," said Ted. "The waiting time at the emergency room last week was three hours."

"We need to let the world know that Maine doesn't shut down in winter," declared Corney, ready to show her hand.

"It doesn't?" Lucy was skeptical.

"We have so much to offer," insisted Corney.

"Cabin fever. She's been cooped up too long and now she's hallucinating," said Ted.

"I'm sure that's it," said Lucy, laughing.

"Have your fun," said Corney, slipping off her fur-trimmed hood and giving her short, frosted blond hair a shake. "Let's face it: the economy sucks. Businesses are going bankrupt, people are losing their jobs, even their houses. Things are bad."

It was true, thought Lucy. Bill, a restoration carpenter, hadn't had a big job in over a year. He was making do, barely, with window replacements and repairs. Her oldest, her son, Toby, who was married and the father of little Patrick, now almost three, had become disillusioned with his prospects as a lobsterman and had taken out student loans to finish up the business degree he had abandoned. Even her oldest daughter, Elizabeth, who had landed a dream job with the Cavendish

Hotel chain after graduating from college, was worried about looming layoffs.

"We have to do whatever we can to attract customers and get things rolling again," said Corney, "and that's what the *Love Is Best on the Coast* Valentine's Day promotion is designed to do." She smiled, as if explaining basic arithmetic to first graders. "Who cares if it's cold outside? That's better for business. The tourists will have nothing to do except shop and eat and drink. They'll have to spend money."

Ted was scratching his chin. "So what do you want? I can't write about Fern's Famous losing, they're one of my biggest advertisers."

"They didn't lose," said Corney, who always saw the glass as half full. "They came in second, just a hair behind Chanticleer. We have the two best candy shops in Maine right here in Tinker's Cove!"

"I suppose Lucy could do something with that," speculated Ted. "She can be pretty tactful, when she tries."

Lucy gave Ted a look. "Thanks for the vote of confidence."

"I know Lucy will do a great job." Corney turned her big blue eyes on Lucy. "You're going to love Trey Meacham. He's a fascinating guy, and a real visionary. Chanticleer Chocolate typifies the kind of success an enterprising entrepreneur can have in Maine. We're becoming a lot more sophisticated, it's not about whirligigs and fudge anymore. We have top-notch craftsmen and artists making beautiful things—oil paintings and handwoven shawls and burl bowls. And the local food movement is the next big thing: fudge and lobster rolls are great, but there are small breweries, artisanal bakeries, and farmers' markets with hydroponically grown vegetables, free-range chickens, grass-fed beef, all raised locally. That's the market that Trey has captured. His chocolates are very sophisticated, very unusual."

Phyllis raised one of the thin penciled lines that served as eyebrows. "I like fudge myself. With walnuts."

"I have absolutely nothing against fudge, especially Fern's Famous Fudge. This is a win-win situation. Two terrific candy shops. The old and the new. Something for everyone." Corney paused. "And believe me, Lucy, you're going to love Trey."

"I'm married," said Lucy. "I have four kids. I'm a grandma." She paused. "A young grandma."

"You're not blind, are you?"

Lucy laughed. "Not yet."

"Well, Trey is very easy on the eyes, and he's got an interesting story. He left a successful business career, got disillusioned with corporate life, and decided to break out on his own. It's been a little more than a year and he's already got several shops in prime spots on the coast. He's a marketing genius. In fact, the Valentine's Day promotion was his idea. He says all the merchants in town need to work together to attract business. Competition is out; cooperation is in. A rising tide raises all ships."

"Okay, you win," said Ted, holding his hands up in surrender. "I'm thinking we can maybe do a special advertising promo, a double page, maybe even an entire special section, if there's enough interest."

"Now you're talking," said Corney. "The Chamber's going to have colorful cupid flags for participating businesses, radio spots; we're hoping for some TV coverage. I've got an appointment at NECN with the producer of *This Week in New England.*"

"Sounds good," said Ted. "Keep us posted."

"You know I will," said Corney, flashing a grin. With a

wave, she was gone, leaving the door ajar, swinging in the wind.

Phyllis heaved herself to her feet with a big sigh and went around the reception counter, shaking her head as she struggled to shut the door. "You've got to get this door fixed, Ted, before I catch my death of cold."

"I know a terrific carpenter," said Lucy.

"Cash flow's a problem," said Ted. "Can we work out a barter deal?"

Lucy was intrigued; Bill had a lot of time on his hands these days. "What do you have in mind?"

"I have an old guitar. . . ."

"Absolutely not."

Ted was making a mental inventory of his possessions. "A typewriter?"

"Donate it to a museum," said Lucy, laughing.

"A frozen turkey? We didn't eat it at Christmas."

Lucy was tempted. "It's a start."

"I'm pretty sure Pam's got all the fixings: stuffing, cranberry sauce, canned yams."

"Throw in a bag of frozen shrimp and you've got a deal," said Lucy.

"You're a tough woman, Lucy."

"I've got hungry kids at home."

"How soon can we do this?" asked Phyllis, as a gust of wind rattled the door in its frame.

"I'll call him right now," said Lucy, reaching for the phone.

"Might as well set something up with the chocolate guy, too," reminded Ted. "What's his name? Meeker?"

"Meacham, Trey Meacham," said Lucy, as she started dialing.

A sudden burst of static from the police scanner on Ted's desk caught her attention and she paused, finger in the air, waiting for it to clear. The dispatcher's voice finally came through, ordering all rescue personnel to Blueberry Pond where a fisherman had fallen through the ice.

Lucy looked at Ted. "Are you going or should I?"

"You." He paused. "I'd go but I've got a phone interview with the governor's wife in half an hour."

"Really?" asked Lucy.

"Yeah. She's calling for a renewed effort in the war on drugs."

"Stop the presses," said Lucy, sarcastically, as she began pulling on her snow pants, boots, scarf, jacket, hat, and gloves. She checked her bag and made sure she had her camera and notebook, also her car keys.

"You better hurry," said Ted. "You'll miss the dramatic rescue."

"Yeah, well, I don't want to be a frostbite victim," said Lucy, stepping out and making sure the door caught behind her.

A frigid blast of wind snapped her scarf against her face and she pulled her hood up over her hat, blinking back tears as she struggled across the sidewalk to her car. Inside, the air was still and cold, and she checked to make sure the heater was set on high as she started the engine. While the engine warmed up, she blew her nose and wiped her eyes, then dug a tube of lip balm out of her bag and smeared it on her lips. She flipped on her signal and cautiously pulled out into the snow-covered road.

The sun was bright and sparkling snow squalls filled the air as she drove down Main Street and out onto Route 1. There was little traffic, except for a police cruiser and an ambulance that passed her, lights flashing and sirens blaring. She followed them, eventually reaching the unpaved road leading to the pond, where a cluster of vehicles were scattered in the clearing that served as a parking area. She recognized Max's huge pickup among them, with his snowmobile in the back.

She turned the engine off, regretting the immediate loss of heat, and climbed out of the car, into the icy blast blowing off the pond. She clutched her hood tight around her head and hurried down the path that had been trodden into the snow by booted feet. Ice fishing was a popular pastime this time of year, and several fishermen had even built shacks on the pond. Lucy had never quite understood the attraction of hanging out on treacherous ice waiting for a trap to spring, indicating a bite on the line, but then she didn't understand why people played golf, either.

Reaching the pond, she hesitated. She didn't like walking on ice; she didn't trust it. But there was quite a group standing about a hundred feet from the shore, so it seemed safe enough. The temperature had been well below freezing since Christmas, she reminded herself, imagining the ice must be several feet thick. They used to cut huge chunks of ice from this pond, in the days before refrigeration. She'd seen photographs at the historical society of the ice cutters, with their horses and sledges loaded with enormous blocks of ice that were packed in straw and stored in ice houses until needed in summer.

The ice was slippery underfoot and she walked carefully, leaning forward and making sure to keep her hands free for balance, resisting the urge to stuff them in her pockets. Approaching the group, she spotted her friend, Officer Barney Culpepper, and quickened her pace. That was a mistake, as she ended up sliding into him and would have fallen if he hadn't grabbed her by the arm.

"Whoa, Lucy. Take it easy."

Barney was dressed for the weather in an oversized, official blue snowsuit, his graying buzz cut concealed by a fur-lined hat that had flaps covering his ears. His eyes were watering, and his jowly cheeks were bright red, as was his nose.

"What's going on?" she asked.

"Somebody went through the ice."

"How can that be? It must be a couple of feet thick," she said, looking around at the little cluster of wooden fishing shacks.

"Dunno." Barney shrugged and wiped his eyes with a gloved hand. "Mebbe he made the hole too big, mebbe there's currents that make the ice thin in spots. I dunno. Seems like a terrible way to go."

There was a sudden surge of activity and Lucy pulled out her camera, thinking it wasn't going to be easy to get a photo in this weather, and with the crowd of rescuers and fishermen blocking her view. Then the crowd broke apart to make way for a stretcher and Lucy got a clear shot.

She yanked off her glove, stuffing it under her arm, and raised the camera to her eyes, automatically snapping several pictures of the blanketed victim. Then, when she'd lowered her camera, a stiff gust of wind lifted the blanket, revealing the drowned man's bearded face. Horrified, she recognized Max Fraser. Moving woodenly, she followed as the stretcher was carried to the waiting ambulance and was trundled inside. The doors were slammed shut and the ambulance took off, slowly, down the snowy track. There was no need to hurry.

Blinking back tears, Lucy turned to Barney. "Did you see what I saw?" she asked.